M000112445

THE
QUARTER
BOYS

Copyright © 2010 Blue Spike Publishing

All rights reserved. No part of this book may be reproduced in whole or in part without written permission from the publisher, except by reviewers who may quote brief excerpts in connection with a review in a newspaper, magazine, or electronic publication; nor may any part of this book be reproduced, stored in a retrieval system, or transmitted in any form or by any means electronic, mechanical, photocopying, or other, without written permission of the publisher.

This novel is a work of fiction. Names, characters, places, and incidents are either the product of the author's imagination or are used fictitiously. Any resemblance to actual persons, living or dead, is entirely coincidental.

Library of Congress Control Number: 2009911172

Book Surge ISBN: 1-4392-6363-9

www.bluespikepublishing.com

Printed in the United States of America

To Brian

Acknowledgments

Beyond what I'd picked up during two trips to New Orleans, I really had no knowledge about the history, culture, or neighborhoods of the city prior to writing this novel. I'm indebted to the following resources for information: Fodor's New Orleans 2005 guide book (Copyright © 2005 Fodors LLC), www.wikipedia.com, www.faubourgmarigny.org, and www.nola.com.

My love of writing started early and was fostered through the years by some truly dedicated and generous teachers, many of whom are no longer with us. In particular, I'd like to acknowledge Jane Huisman, Mary Nichols, Ellen Dale, Annette Busey, and Tamas Aczel. Also, my thanks to Ed Makuta for being a mentor and for pushing me to delve deeper into character in my writing.

I am indebted to my family for their love and encouragement: my maternal grandparents, Peter and Eva Bellini, who patiently listened to my endless stories when I was a child (because the key to nurturing a future writer, after all, is a captive and appreciative early audience); my great grandfather, Augusto Govoni, who provided a creative role model; my stepgrandmother, Phyllis Rogers, who inspired me with her generosity of spirit; my aunt, Marilyn Fall, and cousin, Lisa Bellini, who read the manuscript and made me believe there might be an audience; my parents (biological and step) for supporting my aspirations while keeping me grounded; and my sister Debbie for always encouraging my creativity and thinking the stuff I did was good.

Special thanks to Callie Crossley, my first reader. Without your candor, constructive criticism, and insights into tone and character, this book would not have been the same. It was a hard thing to turn my "baby" over to someone else, wondering what their reaction would be, but your honesty and belief in my talent helped me stick with it.

Thanks to my proofreaders and friends Toby Hollander and Vion DeCew for your keen eyes and support.

My deepest gratitude to my best friend, Bob Mitchell. You were with me on the trip to New Orleans that planted the seed for this story, you encouraged me to write it (for many years), you reminded me that a story set in New Orleans ought to have some black main characters (even though I didn't take your advice and write a character for Denzel to play), and you continued to push me to publish. Thanks also for your invaluable proofreading and editing. Mostly, though, thank you for your friendship and support for the past two-plus decades.

And finally, thanks to Brian Hughes. Though you weren't in my life when I actually wrote this, you've been my biggest fan since. Thanks for making me believe that this book was worthwhile, and for encouraging me to do something with it when I was just too lazy.

Author's Notes

So why would a guy who's lived almost his entire life in the Boston area decide to write a novel set in New Orleans? Well, for one thing, because I love New Orleans. I love the people, I love the pace of life, I love the food and architecture, I love the history. I even sort of like the oppressive heat and humidity during the summer months. New Orleans is a very special city. It has a character unlike any other place I've ever been, and if I were to live any place else, it would be New Orleans. The second reason is that other authors, chiefly Dennis Lehane and Robert Parker, have already done a peerless job of creating mysteries set in the Boston area. What else could I say about the local culture and sociology that they haven't?

The idea for this novel came to me in 1997 as I waited in the New Orleans airport. During my vacation I'd met a guy named Joel who'd recently moved to New Orleans from Mississippi. As I sat in the airport, tired and perhaps a tad hung over, I started to wonder what would happen to Joel in his new home. For whatever reason, the idea of him getting pulled into the dark underbelly of the city and ending up in the path of a serial killer popped into my head. What can I say? I was feeling a little melancholy at the time. Fortunately, aside from the move, none of the events depicted in the life of the fictional Joel happened to the real Joel.

One of the interesting things that happened when I began sharing drafts of the book with friends is that two of them remarked on a similarity between my character of Lady Chanel and the "character" of the Lady Chablis in John Berendt's "Midnight in the Garden of Good and Evil." It was something that hadn't even occurred to me so I was surprised, but since Mr. Berendt sold millions of copies of his book, I figure I should probably address it.

The simple truth is that Lady Chanel isn't based on the Lady Chablis. I have to admit that I'm one of the few people who didn't read Mr. Berendt's acclaimed novel, and the movie version hadn't come out yet when I first conceived of Lady Chanel. The actual inspirations for Lady Chanel were Samuel L. Jackson and "Priscilla, Queen of the Desert."

As I sat on the plane sketching out my first ideas, I immediately jumped ahead and started thinking about the movie version (because I always think in cinematic terms and have a very rich fantasy life). At that point, I was somewhat obsessed with the fact that Samuel L. Jackson had never won an Oscar®, so I decided to create a character that would finally win him his golden statuette. I wanted to come up with something so different from anything else he'd ever done that it would be automatic Oscar® bait, and that's when I remembered Terence Stamp's understated, dignified Bernadette in "Priscilla, Queen of the Desert." I decided that Samuel L Jackson could do something similar, so I created Lady Chanel. So if anyone knows Mr. Jackson and wants to pass a copy of this book along to him, it would be much appreciated.

As for the character's name, I chose "Chanel" because it's a name that has been synonymous with style, sophistication, and elegance for decades. And I added "Lady" because that worked better with "Chanel" that "Miss" or "Madame." So that's the story with that.

Another interesting thing I learned when I shared my manuscript is that none of my friends or relatives took French in high school (or perhaps they just think I don't know how to spell). Invariably when discussing the characters, they would refer to Michel Doucette as "Michael." It's actually Michel, pronounced mi-SHELL, just like the woman's name. I decide to give him the French version of Michael to reflect the strong French influence in New Orleans. His last name is doo-SETT. And Stan Lecher's last name is pronounced le-SHAY, not like he's a dirty old man. Okay, so maybe setting a novel in New Orleans wasn't such a smart idea after all.

When I got home from my trip I promptly put my notes in a drawer. Over the next seven years I'd occasionally take them out and maybe add a few new ideas, but it wasn't until May 2004 (the year in which the story is set) that I finally sat down to write the first draft. And then it was another six years before I published. As a result, some of the references are dated. In April 2009 I took my first trip back to New Orleans in five years and discovered that the Mississippi River Bottom (MRB) is apparently no longer a gay bar, and that Parade hasn't had foam parties in many years. Oh well. I apologize to the people of New Orleans for any anachronisms resulting from my procrastination.

I hope you enjoy the book.

D.L.

OTHER BOOKS FROM DAVID LENNON

Echoes

Second Chance

Blue's Bayou

Reckoning
(Available April 2012)

Fierce
(Available April 2013)

THE

THE
QUARTER
BOYS

A Novel

DAVID LENNON

Chapter 1

Father Kenneth Brennan lay face down on the bed of his hotel room. He was naked, his wrists and ankles bound to the scarred wooden posts of the bed.

Now this is a vacation, he thought.

"How does that feel, baby?" a soft voice purred near his right ear.

"That feels great," Brennan replied in his best husky, porn-star voice. "You're so fucking hot."

He didn't really want to talk to the stranger. He just wanted to lose himself in the pleasure he was feeling. He felt he deserved a bit of fun. After all, he kept himself in check fifty weeks of the year back home in Minnesota. He kept his hands off the altar boys, stayed away from the few known cruising spots in the small town, and took only an occasional trip into the twin cities to experience the night life. He felt his annual two-week pilgrimages to the gay meccas of the world were a just reward for his otherwise saintly behavior.

He'd played his way through San Francisco, Key West, Provincetown, New York, West Hollywood, Amsterdam, Prague, Rio and Paris many times during his thirty years as a priest. This was his first trip to New Orleans, though, and so far his first night in the French Quarter was exceeding all of his expectations.

When the knife plunged into his upper back the first time, Brennan thought the stranger had punched him. He lifted his head and tried to cry out in protest but no sound came out.

1

Instead he felt his chest constrict painfully and a warm trickle ran out of the corner of his mouth. Even in the dim light he could see a dark stain begin to grow on the pale pillowcase.

He felt another punch to his back, lower this time and close to his spine. For a moment he felt nothing, then a searing pain convulsed his body. He gasped and felt a bubble of hot wetness draw inward from his lips and burst. It tasted salty and metallic. He began to claw frantically at the sheets, trying to pull himself out from under the stranger but there was no strength in his arms. His fingers only managed to bunch the white cotton into the palms of his hands.

He felt the stranger punching down into his back again, and then again.

"How does that feel, baby?" he heard the voice whisper again.

The sound seemed to be coming from inside his head. His only reply was a wet, strangled gasp.

He began to feel himself floating up from the bed. The pain was beginning to fade and he was aware only of the connection between his own body and the stranger. He felt the stranger pushing into him more rapidly now and could hear quickening breathing all around him. He was dimly aware of the stranger's arm reaching around his neck. Suddenly everything stopped for a moment. Then he heard a loud gasp and felt the stranger's body shuddering against him as the stranger's arm moved quickly back across his throat.

Then it was silent. He felt no pain. He felt nothing. Where was the stranger? Had he dreamt it? He was very tired. He wanted to sleep. He felt a profound weariness sucking him downward. Then nothing.

The stranger stepped from the bed, picked up the long, red silk dress that lay on a chair by the door, and dressed silently in the dark.

Chapter 2

Joel Faulkner stepped from the bus onto the crowded sidewalk. Even being a native southerner he was struck by the force of the New Orleans' humidity. It had a tangible quality. He could feel it pressing in on him, slowing his movements as though he were underwater.

Maybe I should have moved here after the summer, he thought wryly. That would have given me a whole five months to get ready for this.

He surveyed the crowd at the terminal, carefully studying each face as he looked for Chance. Although he and Chance had known one another since kindergarten, he knew that Chance had probably changed his hair color at least three times since they'd last seen one another six months earlier. Satisfied that Chance wasn't there yet, he settled himself on top of his battered, blue linoleum trunk and lit a Camel Light.

He was used to people running late here. Exact time didn't seem to have much relevance to people in the Quarter—or exact change, or exactly what you ordered, or exact anything. Close enough was good enough and that's what he liked about it. No one seemed to sweat the small details.

That was one of the reasons he'd finally decided to move to New Orleans. Back home in Natchez with his maternal grandparents, Pappy and Mammau Gaulthier, everything had to be exact: wake up exactly at 6, eat breakfast exactly at 6:30, always dress and act exactly proper, be exactly heterosexual. He loved his grandparents with all his heart but he knew that he

3

couldn't stay there. The pressure was just too great and he'd felt like he was playing a role as the perfect grandson. For twenty two years he'd been pretending to be exactly what they expected.

In New Orleans he'd be free to be exactly who he was...whoever that might be. So far all he knew was that the real Joel liked boys and he smoked...at least he had since he'd picked up the Camels at a diner outside Baton Rouge. And he supposed that he was sort of handsome, at least according to Mammau and Chance. Lady Chanel—the "Queen Mother of Bourbon Street"—had even told him he was pretty on his last visit.

"Don't be trying to put too much muscle on them bones," she'd told him, "or you'll be ruining what God gave you."

Joel had never met a drag queen before and Lady Chanel hadn't been at all what he'd expected. She had the natural dignity and quiet grace of a true Southern lady. She'd immediately taken him under her wing and told him everything he needed to stay clear of trouble: which areas to avoid, which men were problems, and to never leave his drink unattended on the bar when he went to use the bathroom. Knowing that Lady Chanel was going to be there made his decision to move easier. He loved Chance and knew Chance loved him, but Chance was more than a little mercurial. He felt that with Lady Chanel there he'd have some semblance of a real family and someone to look out for him.

Chance had moved to the Quarter just after he'd turned seventeen, five years earlier. His family had been "river people" for many generations. At one point they'd been traders and fairly well-to-do, but succeeding generations had shown a profound proclivity for alcohol and bad business decisions, and now whatever fortune they'd once had was gone. His grandfather had been a violent drunk, and Chance's father had followed in his footsteps. Chance's mother had finally tired of the beatings and left one night when Chance was seven years old. His father had taken out his anger about her leaving on Chance for the next ten years.

Chance and his father had lived alone in a house by the river. Joel had seen it only once, but his memory of it was still vivid. One day when they were in the fourth grade, Chance hadn't shown up at school so Joel had ridden his bike the three miles out of town to see if he was sick. At that point in his life Joel had had only a vague understanding that Chance's life was different from his own. He didn't know about things like poverty and abuse and alcoholism. He knew only that Chance didn't talk much about his home and that when he asked his grandparents questions about the LeDucs their responses were hushed and non-committal.

The house sat nestled in the corner of a field, in the shade of a cluster of majestic elms. The rutted dirt road leading to the house looked like a curved reddish scar cutting through the tall green grass. From across the field the house still suggested its former grandness. It was a pale gray two-story Colonial with a low porch that wrapped the first floor and a small fenced yard in front. As he pedaled closer, however, Joel could see the signs of decades of neglect. What had seemed to be shadows along the roofline and sides of the building were scraps of torn tar paper that had been tacked over the clapboard. Occasional patches of faded white paint hinted at the former color. The screens of the porch were torn in the upper corners and bulged outward, rippling softly in the breeze.

He'd leaned his bike against what remained of the low picket fence and walked through the barren yard to the porch. He could still remember the sickly sweet smell, like overripened fruit, that overwhelmed him as he'd stepped through the battered screen door. Cases of empty beer and scotch bottles were haphazardly stacked at the right end of the porch and he'd wondered if the smell came from them. As he'd stepped closer to the door and the open windows leading into the house, however, the smell had grown stronger and his stomach had begun to churn, both from the smell and fear. He didn't want to go into the house. He didn't want to know what made the smell or what had happened to Chance. He didn't want to see Mr. LeDuc with his swollen angry eyes.

He'd stood there for minutes, his small fist poised inches from the scarred and peeling green door, breathing quickly through his mouth as he felt the sweat trickle down his back. Then he'd turned away, almost running back to his bike, and begun pedaling quickly back up the road.

As he passed the corpses of three rusted cars that peaked out of the tall fall grass, he'd looked back over his shoulder. For a moment he was sure he'd seen Chance's face in a window on the second floor. Then it was gone. There was something in the look on Chance's face that made him feel profoundly sad and embarrassed. He'd decided then not to mention his visit to the house and Chance had never brought it up, though he'd been uncharacteristically quiet for the next few days. Remembering the house now through the eyes of an adult, Joel recognized the feeling of a slow, lingering death that emanated from it.

Chance and his father didn't have any close neighbors, and what few lived nearby kept their distances, so Chance had learned early to look after himself. When he was fifteen he'd dropped out of school and started working for Pappy and Mammau, doing odd jobs around the house. He never told his father and knew there wasn't much chance of his father ever finding out since he rarely made his way to town unless he was headed to a bar.

Joel's grandparents didn't really need Chance's help since Joel could do the work himself, but Pappy knew that Chance was in a bad situation and felt it was the Christian thing to do. He didn't approve of Chance dropping out of school, but he was a pragmatist and hoped that with a little help and guidance Chance might be able to escape becoming like his father. By then Joel had understood exactly what that meant. Pappy gave Chance books to read between his chores and spent hours talking with him about the importance of taking responsibility for his own life. On several occasions Pappy had told Joel that he knew that Chance was a soul in torment but that he had a good heart and that with support and guidance he could become a fine man.

But Joel knew Chance better than Pappy did. He believed that Chance had a good heart, but he also knew that Chance was a skilled reader of people and a natural chameleon, capable of being whoever he knew someone wanted him to be...and whoever would work to his best advantage. Chance made a great show of absorbing all the lessons Pappy taught him, but he was always just biding his time until he could leave Natchez. At night he would tell Joel about his dreams of moving to New Orleans and becoming a bright light of the city's famed nightlife. Someday he wanted to open a nightclub and have all the important and fabulous people come to him.

Joel felt a little guilty that Pappy was being duped, but he also knew that Chance had to get out of Natchez or risk being killed by his father. So for two years Joel had played along while Chance saved every dime he made, and finally, when he'd saved enough for bus fare and what he imagined he'd need to live for a month, Chance was gone. A week later a postcard arrived thanking Pappy and Mammau for all their help and apologizing for not saying goodbye. The card didn't say where Chance was, but the postmark read "NOLA."

Pappy was unusually subdued for several weeks after that. He didn't mention Chance, but Joel knew that the old man's heart was in pain: he felt betrayed and foolish for believing that he could change Chance. After a while, though, Pappy had begun to ask Joel occasionally if he'd heard any word from Chance, and when the phone calls began six months later Pappy seemed genuinely pleased to hear that Chance was doing well in New Orleans. For all his sermonizing and strict ways, Pappy had a genuinely large and open heart, Joel knew.

A year later Joel had made his first trip to visit Chance in New Orleans. He suspected that in that large and open heart his grandfather knew it was only a matter of time before Joel would want to move on as well. Maybe Pappy believed that with the strong values he'd instilled in Joel and those he'd tried to impart to Chance it would all work out fine in the end. Joel had never talked with his grandparents about his sexuality or Chance's—it just wasn't something one talked about—but maybe they suspected that as well and knew he'd be better off in a place that was more accepting of differences in people. Whatever the case, three years later when he'd told them he wanted to move to New Orleans they'd given him their blessing and five hundred dollars.

A sudden kiss and tongue running up the back of his neck brought Joel back to the present. He turned to find Chance standing behind him, a wide grin on his face.

"Been waiting long, girl?" Chance asked with an exaggerated drawl.

He stood with his hands on his hips, his body twisted in what seemed to be intended as a seductive posture. His straight black hair was longer now, reaching almost to his shoulders on the sides and in back. His light blue eyes peered out through wispy bangs. He was dressed in a tight black tank top that clung to his narrow torso, long baggy green shorts and flip flops. The shorts were slung low on his bony hips and three inches of tanned stomach peeked out. Joel caught a glint of something shiny nestled in the thin line of hair running below Chance's navel.

"So aren't you going to tell me how fabulous I look?" Chance asked loudly, throwing his arms out dramatically and taking a runway turn.

Joel laughed.

"Yes, you do look fabulous, madame," he said, bowing slightly.

"That's mademoiselle, bitch! You don't see any diamond on these fingers do you?" Chance asked archly, wiggling the fingers of his left hand in the air and shaking his head from side to side.

Then he broke into a large smile and threw his arms around Joel, hugging him tightly.

"Give mama some sugar," he said into Joel's neck.

They stood embracing for a few moments until they heard the blare of a car horn and a soft, throaty voice called out.

"Am I going to have to get you girls a hotel room?"

Joel turned to see Lady Chanel in the driver's seat of a turquoise and white Bel Air convertible parked by the curb. It was immaculate, the sun glinting brightly off the polished chrome bumpers. Lady Chanel was dressed in a sleeveless sundress of bright pastel flowers, cinched at the waist by a wide white belt. Her platinum hair was held in place by a thin silk scarf that perfectly matched the turquoise of the car, and she stared at them in mock annoyance over large pink tortoise-shell sunglasses that rested on the tip of her broad nose. Around her neck was a strand of small white pearls that stood out in sharp contrast against her dark chocolate skin. Joel knew that this was a conservative look, toned down several notches from her usual nighttime attire. He also knew that even toned down, Lady Chanel was attracting a lot of attention from the rest of the crowd gathered in front of the bus station.

He and Chance grabbed the handles at each end of his trunk and walked to the car.

"You all can put that in the back seat," Lady Chanel drawled, "and Chance, you can sit your narrow ass back there as well. Joel is going to sit up front with his Auntie Chanel. And be careful you don't scratch the paint."

As Joel climbed into the car Lady Chanel leaned her lanky body across the front seat and kissed him on both cheeks.

"Welcome to your new home, baby," she said warmly as she put the car in gear and smoothly pulled away from the curb, heading for the French Quarter.

Chapter 3

Detective Michel Doucette sat at the bar in Cafe Lafitte in Exile, his third Jack Daniels resting comfortably in his right hand. It was 4 pm and he'd been sitting there for a little over an hour. He'd told himself he'd come in for a quick one to escape the afternoon heat, but somehow the time had continued to pass and one drink had turned into three. It happened that way sometimes on these lazy summer days when nothing much was going on in the city.

It had been happening more frequently since May when his mother had died. He'd found that hours and even days could go by without feeling as though he'd taken an active part in them. He'd continued the usual routines he'd always had, seen the usual people and had the usual conversations, but he'd often felt as though it were all part of a dream. Only his thoughts seemed real, and he didn't want to be alone with his those for very long. Passing the hours in a cool, dark bar seemed like a good way to escape both the heat and his thoughts.

Although he'd grown up in the Faubourg Marigny, just outside the French Quarter, Michel's experience with the local gay bars had been limited. He'd been to a few in other cities on his infrequent vacations, but had largely stayed clear of the bars in the Quarter. He knew that in many ways New Orleans was a small town, and it wasn't uncommon to run into an acquaintance and have them mention that they'd seen him in a restaurant or walking down the street. So he'd chosen to be discreet, for both professional and personal reasons. He'd inhabited a largely straight world, and his relationships with men had been short-lived and clandestine, usually ending before the sun came up. The only gay bars in the Quarter he'd visited on a handful of occasions were the Good Friends and MRB, which were quieter and located off the main thoroughfares.

Since his mother's death, however, his visits had become more regular and he'd even ventured into the larger clubs like the Bourbon Pub and Oz. His impression of these clubs had always been negative, based on what he'd observed while walking down Bourbon Street. He'd imagined an atmosphere of conformity and forced participation, with everyone eager to fit a prescribed image of what a gay man should be: how he should dress, where he should live, how he should act. While his low expectations had been met by some of the younger guys, among most of the patrons he'd discovered a tremendous diversity and sense of individuality that appealed to him.

He'd always been somewhat of a loner. Not that he was cold or disdainful of others, but he had always been most comfortable by himself or in small groups where he knew everyone. He'd found that the bars allowed him to be both alone and a part of something larger at the same time, and that helped ease the loneliness he'd begun to feel. Before he'd always had his work to give him an identity and a sense of purpose, but after his mother's death he'd started to long for something more, for a greater sense of connection. That sudden longing was unfamiliar and frightening, and at first he'd stayed to himself, observing from the periphery. Over time, however, he'd begun to meet a few men—not friends, but acquaintances— and while he was still reticent to share the details of his life with them, he found their company comforting.

As summer tightened its grip on the city he'd begun stopping by Lafitte's regularly during the day. He felt as though he'd stumbled into a subculture he'd never known existed. At any hour of the day at least a half dozen men could be found sitting at the bar. Some worked nights and came in the early morning for a drink before heading off to sleep. Others seemed to have no jobs at all. There was even the occasional tourist— rare during the summer—who came in to scope out the scene before it got too crowded.

The day patrons were unguarded and friendly. They greeted one another by name and settled into small groups to drink and chat away the hours. Not that he was interested in joining in their conversations, but he appreciated the fact that he was welcomed without question.

As he reached for his cigarettes on the stained and worn wooden bar, Michel felt his cell phone begin to vibrate against his left hip. He pushed himself reluctantly off his stool and walked toward an open side door that fronted Bourbon Street. It was much brighter there and he had to shade his eyes for a moment.

"Doucette" he said wearily into the phone.

"Michel, are you sober?"

It was his partner, Alexandra "Sassy" Jones.

"Sober enough. Why, what's up, Sas?"

"We've got a murder at the Creole House," Sassy replied. "The housekeeper found one of the guests dead in his room about fifteen minutes ago."

"Okay, I'm a few blocks away. I'll be right over." Michel said.

"You sure you're up to this right now?" Sassy asked.

Michel could hear the genuine concern in her voice and for a moment he started to choke up. Sometimes Sassy acted more like a mother than a partner. At times it pissed him off, but now it touched him. He brought a hand to his eyes and pushed gently for a moment while he took a few deep breaths.

"Yeah, I'm fine." he said finally. "I'll be there in a few minutes."

He walked back to the bar and laid down a $20 bill, deciding not to finish his drink. He nodded to the bartender as he lifted his suit jacket from the stool and headed to the door.

"Heat coming up from the pavement and banging from the walls of houses with enough force to kill a man," he thought as he stepped into the bright afternoon sun. It was a phrase from *Giovanni's Room* by James Baldwin that came to him often during the summer months. But unlike the Brooklyn heat in the book, Michel imagined the heat of New Orleans as being more sinuous and insidious. It didn't bang. It seeped its way into the pores, thickening the blood and slowly draining the energy from the body.

He checked his reflection in the window and straightened his tie. He looked like a black and white photo of himself in another ten years. The paleness of his skin contrasted sharply with his black hair and the dark Vs formed by the shadows under his cheekbones. Even the color of his eyes and lips seemed to be oddly muted. When did this happen?, he wondered as he popped a stick of Doublemint into his mouth.

He turned right onto Bourbon Street and began walking quickly toward St. Ann Street.

*****

The narrow street in front of the Creole House was cordoned off on both sides of the building by yellow tape. Several police cruisers were parked inside the tape, their lights still flashing. Police officers along the tape kept watch over a small but excited crowd. As he made his way up the sidewalk, Michel noticed several reporters and photographers in the crowd. That was quick, he thought. Must be a slow news day. As he approached the cordoned off area he flashed his badge and ducked under the tape.

"Second floor, detective," said the nearest officer. "Room 202."

Michel exchanged greetings with several of the officers in front of the white stucco building as he made his way to the door. Inside it was dark and cooler, but the air was electric with tension and activity. Sergeant Al Ribodeau was standing with a small group by the front desk. When he saw Michel he nodded and walked over.

"Hey, Michel. How's it going?"

"Okay, Al," Michel responded evenly." So what do we have?"

"A priest from Minnesota. Name of Kenneth Brennan. 55-year-old white male. Down here on vacation apparently. A houseboy found him 20 minutes ago when he went to make up the room. Several stab wounds in his back and his throat was cut."

"When did it happen?"

"Coroner just got here but looks like sometime between 1 and 4 a.m."

"Anybody see him come in with anyone?"

"We're questioning everyone, but the kid who worked last night isn't answering his phone. He's due back here at 6. So far nothing."

"Okay. Sassy upstairs?"

"Yup. Up the stairs, take a left. You can't miss the crowd."

"Thanks, Al," Michel said, tapping Ribodeau on the shoulder.

As he made his way up the stairs, Michel noticed the quiet. Even with a crowd in the lobby the building was nearly silent. It's the way these old buildings were made, he thought. Solid. There could be a hurricane outside and you'd never know it unless you opened a window. When everything else is gone you'll still have the French Quarter, cockroaches and Cher. It was a twist on an old joke but it made him laugh a little as he pictured Cher sitting in the Bourbon Pub sharing cocktails with a bunch of giant roaches.

"What's so funny?"

Sassy stood at the top of the stairs waiting for him. Though not tall, she was an imposing figure, with sturdy legs, wide hips and large breasts: the body of a beautiful African woman she always told him. Though she weighed close to 200 lbs., there was nothing fleshy or slack about her. She was just solid. Michel could never think of a better way to describe her. As always she looked impeccable: close cropped hair with just a few hints of silver beginning to creep through the black, tailored aubergine slacks and jacket, a bright tangerine silk shirt. The only jewelry she wore was a thin gold watch and a pair of gold hoop earrings ringed with multi-colored glass beads. Sassy had a knack for seamlessly blending the aspects of her personality when she dressed, managing to look both professional and bold.

Anyone meeting Sassy for the first time would have been struck by the irony of her name, which conjured images of a loud, boisterous, fast-talking woman. The reality was a composed, assured woman who understood that an economy of words increased the impact of each. Sassy was an affectionate nickname bestowed by her mother's mother on her shy, bookish granddaughter when she was six. The name had stuck and Sassy had eventually grown into it somewhat, developing a sly, caustic wit she could unleash to withering effect. Still, there was nothing frivolous about her.

"Nothing," Michel replied, shaking his head. "Just something to do with Cher, too much alcohol and too little sleep."

"You queens and your Cher," Sassy said quietly, shaking her head and giving him a playful smile.

Sassy was always careful to keep her comments about Michel's sexuality private. Both of them knew that he risked becoming marginalized and having his career stalled if it became openly known within the department. Michel gave a dainty wave of his hand and smiled sweetly at her as he passed by and started down the hall.

"So what does it look like? Robbery? A crime of passion? A really elaborate suicide?"

"None of the above," Sassy replied. "Looks like someone

just wanted to kill the fuck out of this guy."

"The fuck? Where would that be located exactly?"

"In this case, his ass. It looks like he was literally getting fucked when he got sliced and diced."

"Do you kiss your mother with that mouth?" Michel asked with mock offense.

"Only on her cootchie," Sassy shot back with a satisfied smirk as they entered Room 202.

*****

The room was typical of most guest house rooms in the Quarter: what the decorators on television would call "shabby chic." The walls were covered by faded maroon wallpaper with a flocked gold fleur de lis pattern. The curtains and bedspread all had thick bands of ruby, sapphire, emerald and cream, with a gold fringe along the bottom. Years of carelessly carried luggage had rubbed the edges of the mismatched Mahogany furniture a pale brown. It looked as though someone had tried to recreate one of the grand salons of old New Orleans using pieces found at a yard sale.

The body lay on the bed, its livid nude limbs still tied to the posts. The torso was thickly coated by dried blood which had run in rivulets onto the sheets, leaving small merlot-colored stains along the sides of the body. The pillows and sheets under the neck were nearly black. Stan Lecher, chief investigator for the Orleans Parish Coroner's Office, was making his way methodically around the body while a photographer shot pictures from various angles. As Michel and Sassy entered the room, Lecher looked up momentarily and acknowledged them with a small nod.

Michel and Sassy had worked with Lecher enough to know not to ask him questions. They knew he would begin to give them details when he was ready so they stood silently and waited while he conducted his examination. Michel looked around the room. He noted a pair of white linen pants and a cornflower blue cashmere sweater folded neatly on top of the low dresser by the door. Next to the clothes lay a gold Cartier wrist watch and black leather wallet. On the floor directly below the clothes were two black leather sandals, perfectly aligned side-by-side.

Okay, so the guy was a neat freak and had expensive taste, Michel thought, as he began to automatically compile a list of observations and questions: the watch wasn't taken so it couldn't be robbery; if he had expensive tastes why didn't he stay at someplace like the Saint Louis Hotel?; probably wanted someplace more discreet where he could bring guys back without drawing attention; where did he go last night?; has he been here before?; does he know anybody in town?; was he into anything kinky...besides getting tied up?

"Looks like the Father got tied up willingly, but I don't think it's something usual for him," Lecher began suddenly.

He looked up momentarily to make sure that Michel and Sassy were paying attention then quickly resumed his examination. His delivery was matter-of-fact, almost stream-of-conscious, as he made his way quickly around the body and began pointing out details.

"The towels used to tie him are rough. If he'd been tied against his will there'd be more abrasions on the skin. There's very little damage. Even when he was being stabbed it looks like he didn't put up much of a struggle."

"Could he have been drugged?" Sassy asked.

"If he was it wasn't until he was already on the bed," Lecher replied. "He's gotta weigh a good 250. Would take someone awfully strong to maneuver him around. Plus those clothes you noticed on the dresser, assuming that's what he was wearing last night, looks like he took the time to fold them carefully. Of course we'll check those for hair fibers in case the killer liked a tidy crime scene."

Michel smiled slightly, appreciating Lecher's combination

of efficiency and caustic humor. How did Lecher know he'd seen the clothes? he wondered. Lecher would have made one hell of a detective, he thought.

"But it doesn't look like the good Father made this a regular habit because there's no scar tissue on his wrists or ankles," Lecher continued. "It doesn't look like he's a stranger to anal penetration, however. There's evidence of repeated minor trauma to the sphincter and he's got a pretty good set of hemorrhoids. Of course maybe he just didn't get enough fiber in his diet.

"There was definitely trauma last night and I'd say the guy we're looking for is pretty well endowed. That should make for an interesting line-up, eh?"

Lecher looked up at Michel and Sassy and for a split second Michel thought he caught a pointed look in Lecher's eyes.

"Was he killed before or after?" Sassy asked quickly.

"During or after." Lecher replied.

"How can you be sure?" Michel asked

"If he'd already been dead there'd be less trauma. You want me to show you?" Lecher asked with a hint of annoyance as he began to reach toward the body.

"No, that's okay," Michel and Sassy replied in unison.

"The murder weapon was definitely a knife. I'll have to measure the depth but based on the surface dimensions of the wounds it looks like it was a good size. Probably a hunting knife. Very sharp. The edges of the cuts are clean. He was stabbed 4 times in the back and his throat was cut, left to right. Severed the carotid artery on the left side and continued to the larynx. The killer was a rightie or ambidextrous. That's all I can tell you until I get him back to the lab and do a thorough exam."

Lecher straightened up and removed his rubber gloves, neatly folding them and tucking them into a small plastic pouch that he placed into an evidence bag.

"Any trace evidence?" Sassy asked.

"Nothing I could see but we'll vacuum the scene and the body and I'll run a scan for bodily fluids."

"You think the killer shot his wad?" Michel asked.

"It's the killing that gets these guys off, right?" Lecher replied, shrugging his shoulders. "But it's probably in a condom in a dumpster someplace by now."

Along with ten thousand others, Michel thought, frowning. He could feel a hangover beginning to haunt the edges of his brain as he and Sassy made their way out of the building.

Chapter 4

My first night as an official New Orleanian, Joel thought as he rubbed the towel across his wet chest.

After Lady Chanel had dropped them at their apartment on Governor Nicholls, he and Chance had spent the afternoon walking around the Quarter, picking up groceries and sharing the latest gossip in their lives. Although Joel had been in the Quarter only a few times before, it had felt entirely familiar being there with Chance. It had felt like home.

They'd stopped at the Good Friends Bar around 4 pm and were standing on the wrought iron balcony that wrapped the corner of the building when the wail of distant sirens pierced the lazy stillness. The sound grew steadily louder and a minute later three police cars had raced down St. Ann with their lights flashing, the blare of the sirens so shrill that Joel and Chance had covered their ears. The cars stopped abruptly halfway up the block, in front of the Creole House, and it had been suddenly quiet again. Two uniformed officers had run inside the Creole House while four others began to stretch yellow tape across the width of the street.

Joel and Chance could see the patrons on the first floor filtering out into the street below and more people walking up St. Ann from the Bourbon Pub. They'd grabbed their plastic "go cups" and walked downstairs and out into the street to join the crowd, taking up positions against a pink stucco building on the left side of the street, close to the yellow tape. They'd smoked and sipped their beers as they listened to the crowd excitedly speculating on what had happened, and Chance had gone back into the bar twice to get them more beer. After an hour a metal gurney with what looked like a large black garment bag stuffed with pumpkins had been wheeled out to an ambulance that had arrived a few minutes before. After the ambulance left they'd walked the four blocks up Dauphine Street to their apartment.

As soon as they got home Chance went to his room to take a "disco nap" and Joel had unpacked and cleaned his room. As excited as Chance had been that Joel was moving in with him, he hadn't bothered to clean the room since his last roommate had left two months earlier. The window sills were still littered with empty beer cans filled with cigarette butts and candy wrappers, and the floor and furniture were coated with a fine brown dust.

An hour later, as Joel was wrapping the cord around the vacuum, Chance had appeared in his bedroom doorway wearing only black thong underwear and asked if Joel needed any help. Joel suspected that Chance had waited until he heard the vacuum safely turned off before making the offer and reached out to pinch one of Chance's nipples in mock annoyance. Chance jumped back with a small cry and then pushed past Joel, flopping onto his stomach on the freshly made bed.

"Hungry?" he asked, lifting his ass slightly off the bed.

Though they'd fooled around occasionally in the past, Joel had decided that he didn't want to confuse the boundaries of their relationship now that they would be living together.

"Ew, don't you get that skanky old thing on my clean sheets," he said. "Who knows where it's been?"

Although his tone was joking, he meant the rebuke seriously and hoped that Chance would understand without them having to talk about it. Joel thought that he saw a glimpse of genuine hurt in Chance's eyes, but then Chance had smiled at him.

"Fine, be that way," he'd said, rolling onto his back and wriggling against the sheets as though wiping himself. Then he jumped off the bed and grabbed Joel's arm, pulling him into the living room.

"Let's have a cocktail."

They sat in the living room drinking Dixie beer and smoking until it began to get dark. Then they heated up the fried chicken they'd bought at the market that afternoon and sat on opposite ends of the couch eating, loudly licking the salty grease from their fingers as they finished. After another cigarette Chance stood up and called first dibs on the shower.

"I figured we could start at the Bourbon and then head down to Lafitte's, then Oz around midnight. Maybe we can hook up with a party after that," he said arching his eyebrows, a salacious grin on his face.

"Cool," Joel deadpanned, looking at an invisible watch on his wrist. "So if you're gonna shower, I can probably nap for the next two hours."

"Fuck you, bitch," Chance had replied dryly. "When you look this fab it only takes a few minutes to get ready. It's gonna take you at least an hour to wash the bumpkin off you, however."

"Cute," said Joel, scrunching his face into a sarcastic smile. "By the way, do you ever wear actual pants at home? This whole place is going to smell like ass."

"Only if we're lucky," Chance had said with a big smile.

As he turned to go into the bathroom he'd bent slightly at the waist and pushed his ass out toward Joel. Joel gave it a sharp swat with the back of his right hand and Chance had run laughing into the bathroom.

*****

An hour later they left the apartment. The night air was warm and heavy, and no stars were visible through the dense humidity enveloping the city. They had both dressed in baggy Abercrombie & Fitch khaki shorts and black flip flops. Chance wore a tight, white, ribbed tank top emblazoned with a red Diesel logo across the chest. He'd adorned both wrists with dozens of tiny bracelets made of colored string. Joel wore a plain, red, cotton tank top that hung loosely over his narrow chest and waist. They walked the five blocks to the Bourbon Pub, stopping at a corner convenience store along the way to pick up more cigarettes.

As they entered the pub through one of the French doors along St. Ann, Joel heard Lady Chanel's voice above the crowd.

"Over here children."

Lady Chanel sat at a tall round table along the Bourbon Street side of the bar, surrounded by a small group. She was dressed in a strapless gold sequined sheath that was slit to the right thigh. Her shoulder-length platinum hair was swept up and held in place by a small triangular tiara of faux diamonds and she wore a five-strand choker of matching stones around her swan-like neck. Her slender hands and forearms were covered by gold silk gloves that reached just below her elbows, and both wrists were wrapped by narrow bands of faux diamonds. Gold powder thickly dusted her upper eyelids, transitioning to white as it reached her thin arched eyebrows. She waved to them and they began pushing their way toward her. Although he knew she had to be in her late fifties or older, Joel admired the glimpse he caught of her shapely right leg through the crowd.

As they got closer Joel recognized the others around Lady Chanel. To the far right was Taylor. Joel's first impression of Taylor when they'd met had been of an overgrown child. Though he was over six feet tall, Taylor's shoulders and chest had the delicacy of a child, the bones clearly visible through his milky skin. His round head seemed to balance precariously on his thin neck, and his features, too, seemed childlike. He had small, pouting lips and a rounded nose with a spattering of pale freckles across the bridge and on his cheeks. His large blue eyes were rimmed by long dark lashes. A bowl of straight, white-blond hair formed a tilted halo around his head, running from just below the crown in the back across the tops of his pink ears to a point halfway down his nose. He had the habit of swinging his head elaborately to the right every few minutes in order to see.

On Lady Chanel's left was Louis. Louis was smaller and far more exotic looking than Taylor. His eyes were large and pale green, contrasting strikingly with his caramel-toned skin. He had full lips and wide cheekbones, with a fine, delicate jawline. His body was small but tightly muscled and smooth. Whereas Taylor was cute, Joel thought that Louis was almost beautiful. Joel had met them both on his previous visits and knew that both had grown up in rural Louisiana and had moved to the Quarter when they'd graduated high school a few years ago.

On a stool to the far left, slightly apart from the others, sat Miss Zelda. No one seemed to know how or when Zelda and Chanel had met, but they'd been a part of the Quarter's social scene together for as long as anyone could remember. Looking at the two sitting across the table from one another, Joel had the impression of mismatched bookends.

They appeared to be about the same age and equally uncreased by time, but where Chanel was tall and slender, Zelda was short and almost brutish. She had a thick body and limbs and coarse, heavy features. Her skin was darker than Chanel's, appearing almost blue black in the dim bar lights. She was dressed in a long-sleeved lavender dress that covered her knees, and low-heeled matching pumps. Her reddish brown hair was cut in a page boy style that curled under at the ends, and she wore a small lavender pill box hat. Joel thought she looked as if she'd wandered into the bar by accident on her way to a Baptist prayer meeting. He noticed that her face was puffier than the last time he'd seen her and she looked tired. Her gaze seemed remote and unfocused. He wondered if she was drunk.

He'd always felt ambivalent toward Zelda. While she'd never been less than polite to him, she was usually surly to Chance and the others. Even with the bitchy interplay he'd come to expect within the group, her remarks seemed more pointed and cruel. He also felt a certain amount of pity for her. She lacked the natural charm and charisma of Lady Chanel and he imagined that it was difficult for her living in Chanel's shadow. At times he noticed that she seemed lost in thought, staring blankly off into the distance, and he wondered what she was thinking about.

"Give auntie a kiss," Chanel said as they walked up, leaning forward and extending a cheek to each of them.

Joel and Chance exchanged elaborate hugs and kisses with Taylor and Louis, then nodded to Zelda who remained motionless on her stool, seemingly disinterested in their arrival.

"In honor of Joel moving to our fey city, the cocktails are on me, so tell them it's on the Lady's tab," Chanel said, shooing Joel and Chance toward the bar with both hands.

When they returned to the table she raised her Cosmopolitan.

"To the newest member of our family," she said.

They all touched their glasses together except for Zelda, who merely lifted her glass and smiled sourly. Joel thanked Chanel and kissed her again on the cheek.

"Now why don't you boys go upstairs and dance with the other pretty young things," Chanel said. "There's no need for you to be babysitting us. We'll be here when you get tired."

The four boys smiled and headed off in a single-file line through the crowd toward the stairs leading to Parade, the upstairs bar and dance club. As they crossed the room, Chance suddenly reached back and grabbed Joel's right hand for a moment, pressing something into the palm. Then he let go. Joel looked down and saw a small white tablet nestled into his palm.

"What is it?" he asked, leaning forward and yelling into Chance's ear.

Half turning, Chance held three fingers out sideways in the shape of an E. He smiled at Joel, raising his eyebrows devilishly. Joel gave him an uncomprehending look and shrugged his shoulders. He'd smoked weed back home but had never experimented with any pills. Chance stopped and leaned back into Joel, cupping his hand over Joel's left ear.

"Don't worry, it's just Ecstasy. It won't fuck you up. It'll just make you feel really good."

He gave Joel a kiss on the cheek and then pulled back, extending his tongue quickly to show a matching white tablet resting near the tip. Then he smiled and began moving toward the stairs again.

Joel paused for a moment, then lifted his hand discreetly and flicked his tongue out as he looked around warily to see if anyone was watching him. Oh well, he thought as he swallowed the tablet, new life, new experiences.

*****

The main room of Parade was packed. Small groups of excited boys flitted about in all directions as if on a mission, chatting loudly as they went.

"Oh shit," Chance exclaimed as they pushed toward the dance floor. "I forgot tonight was a Foam Party."

Joel looked toward the dance floor. The perimeter had been surrounded by a five-foot-high black wall and soap foam cascaded down from the ceiling onto the dance floor. Two dozen shirtless boys danced and writhed against one another in the white foam that reached to their chests.

"Fuck Lafitte's and Oz. We're staying here," Chance declared, a big smile spreading across his face.

A line of boys in various states of undress snaked around the corner to a clothes check. As they joined the end of the line, Taylor, Louis and Chance began peeling off their tank tops.

"We don't take everything off, do we?" Joel asked nervously.

"No, country boy," Chance replied. "Keep your panties and your shoes on...just like everybody else."

He gestured elaborately toward the front of the line where a muscular redhead in sneakers and a navy Speedo was placing his clothes on a counter and gave Joel a look that asked "could you be more stupid?"

Joel glowered at Chance but began to slowly undress.

"Damn, if I'd known it was a Foam Party I would have worn something else," Chance said as he stepped out of his shorts to reveal a white thong. "I'm going to be showing my ass to the whole room."

"Not like everyone hasn't already seen it," said Louis.

"Or fucked it," added Taylor.

"Y'all are just jealous bitches." replied Chance haughtily.

"Damn girl, you wearing your grandpa's drawers?" Louis suddenly exclaimed, looking at Joel with exaggerated revulsion.

With his khaki shorts around his ankles, Joel looked down at his red and white check boxers and shrugged. Taylor and Chance turned to look and began laughing.

"What? Excuse me for having a little modesty," Joel said curtly, lifting one foot out of his shorts and feigning indignity.

"Ain't gonna be all that modest once they get wet and start clinging to your hang," Louis replied, causing Joel to blush for a moment.

After checking their clothes they moved to the narrow entrance to the dance floor where a staff member used a small piece of plywood to push the foam back onto the floor. They stepped over a low barrier and pushed their way toward a far corner of the floor as the music began to shift and the first notes of Deborah Cox's "Absolutely Not" started to blare from the speakers. Taylor and Louis screamed shrilly in unison, throwing their arms over their heads and swinging their barely-existent hips from side to side as they rushed into the corner.

The four boys began to dance. Chance stepped behind Joel and embraced him, sliding his hands over Joel's chest and stomach in time with the music. Joel could feel a tingling on the surface of his skin. It felt electric. He reached back and ran his hands up the back of Chance's thighs to his buttocks. Chance's skin was slick and velvety from the foam. Joel thought that he'd never felt anything so soft in his life. He closed his eyes and concentrated on the sensations across the palms of his hands and on his chest and stomach. Although he was slightly aroused, it wasn't a distinctly sexual feeling. It was somehow more sensual. He felt hands running up the front of his thighs and leaned back into Chance, rubbing his back slowly side to side against Chance's chest. He wanted to touch and be touched by everyone around him. He'd never felt so good.

*****

They danced for almost an hour, their bodies glistening with foam and sweat. Finally Chance yelled over the music that they should get another drink and they pushed their way through the pulsating bodies to the edge of the dance floor and headed to the bar. Each ordered a Sex on the Beach. Louis, who had collected money from the others as they undressed, paid for the drinks with a sodden $20 bill that he pulled out of the front of his black jockey shorts. They stood for a moment surveying the crowd while they sipped their drinks through the tiny stirring straws. Taylor suggested they go out on the balcony.

Even in the heat Joel felt a slight chill over his damp body as they stepped into the night air. They each "borrowed" cigarettes and stood along the wrought iron rail sipping their drinks and trying not to dampen their cigarettes with their wet fingers. Nearby a group carried on a hushed but urgent conversation.

"I heard he had a heart attack."

"No, he was killed."

"What? Where'd you hear that?"

"My friend Jason works there. He said the cops questioned

everyone. The guy was chopped up into little pieces. They even think whoever killed him ate some of him."

"Get out!"

"I'm serious."

"You guys talking about the guy at Creole House?" Chance broke into their conversation.

The group eyed him suspiciously for a moment.

"Yeah."

"We saw them take the body out this afternoon." Chance said.

This seemed to warm the group to him.

"Was there a lot of blood?" one of them asked excitedly, looking at Chance with large, expectant eyes.

"He was in a body bag," Chance replied casually. "We couldn't see anything. So the guy was murdered?"

"Yeah, he was all cut up," the other replied, seemingly disappointed that Chance knew less than he did.

As Chance, Taylor and Louis merged with the other group, Joel looked around the balcony. He realized that the same conversation was taking place all around him. Small groups huddled together sharing the details and rumors they'd picked up throughout the afternoon. The murder at the Creole House had become the topic du jour.

As he looked farther up the balcony he noticed one figure by himself, leaning on the railing and smoking. The man turned his head toward Joel and Joel caught his breath. The man was beautiful. He had an angular face with sharp cheekbones and a strong jaw, and a thin straight nose over full lips. Most striking of all, however, were his eyes. They were dark and expressive, and framed by thick lashes. They seemed to convey everything that the man was feeling at once.

Joel thought there was almost something pretty about the man, yet he seemed entirely masculine at the same time. Although he was dressed in a loose t-shirt and jeans, Joel could tell his body was lean and muscular. He looked older than the rest of the crowd—perhaps in his early thirties—but he didn't seem to feel out of place. He was composed, pensive. For just a few seconds the man's eyes locked on Joel's and Joel was sure he saw a hint of a smile pass the man's lips. Flustered, Joel quickly looked away. When he looked back a minute later the man was gone.

"I'm going to take a walk," Joel said suddenly, interrupting the conversation next to him.

"Wait, we'll go with you," Chance said.

Joel wanted to look for the man by himself, but his friends were already extricating themselves from the other group.

"Where to?" asked Chance.

"I just figured we could walk around and maybe go back downstairs to see Lady Chanel and Zelda."

"Okay, let's go." Chance replied.

He began to head toward the nearest door but Joel stopped him.

"Why don't we walk around the balcony and see what's here first?" Joel asked, trying to sound casual.

"Okay, freak. Whatever you say," Chance replied, rolling his eyes.

Joel waited until Taylor and Louis began walking, then he and Chance followed. Joel hung back a step so that when they were forced into a single line to pass through the crowds he was the last in line. They turned the corner onto the section of the balcony fronting Bourbon Street. A large group had commandeered the end of the balcony in front of them. The man was standing in the shadows by the door to the left of the group. Joel couldn't tell if the man was looking at him. He felt nervous and vulnerable.

"Okay, this bites," Taylor exclaimed loudly. "Let's go back inside."

He headed toward the door, followed by Louis and Chance. Again Joel hung back for a second. He waited until Taylor and Louis were already inside and Chance was in the doorway, then took a step forward. He could see the man's face clearly now. The man was looking directly at him and smiling. Joel felt his heart jump and paused for a moment. He felt both embarrassed and excited. He muttered hello and tried to smile.

Suddenly a hand closed on his left wrist and he was yanked awkwardly through the door.

"Ewwww, he's old!" Chance said, standing in front of Joel and staring at him with an expression of disgust.

"Who?" asked Louis.

"The geezer standing by the door," Chance shot back.

"Oh, I saw him. I thought he was kind of hot," Taylor said.

"Oh pul-lease," Chance replied. "He was so not hot. You all must be on drugs."

Taylor, Louis and Chance began giggling uncontrollably. Joel just stared at them. He wanted to go back outside, but after being unceremoniously ripped through the door he felt humiliated. He stood there a moment feeling foolish and helpless, then suddenly started in the direction of the stairs.

The others laughed even harder, doubling over and spilling their drinks on the floor. When Joel was halfway across the room Chance finally started after him. The others followed. Joel could hear Chance calling his name but he kept going. He was angry now and he didn't want to talk to them. He hurried down the stairs and pushed his way through the crowd to where Lady Chanel and Zelda still sat on their perches. Even in his anger, Joel couldn't help but notice that Zelda looked like a trained bear in a dress.

"What's the matter?" Chanel asked when he reached them.

She could see faint tears in Joel's eyes and reached out to touch his cheek.

"Nothing. It's no big deal."

"Come on, you can tell the Lady," Chanel said as the others reached them.

Joel took a few steps toward Zelda, leaving Chance, Taylor and Louis directly in front of Lady Chanel. She sat up straighter

31

on her stool and glared at them.

"What have you done to Joel?" she asked, narrowing her eyes at them.

"Nothing," Chance said defensively. "I just saved him from talking to some old geezer."

As soon as the words were out of his mouth, Chance realized he'd made a mistake and he lowered his eyes.

"I see," Chanel said quietly. "And what is it that gives you the right exactly to determine who Joel can be attracted to?"

Her voice was controlled but the anger was unmistakable. Taylor and Louis took a half step back from Chance but Lady Chanel caught their movement and froze them with a quick shift of her eyes. She leaned forward into Chance's face.

"Maybe you haven't realized it yet," she said, "but one of these days—if you are very, very lucky—you're going to be one of those 'geezers.' And when and if that happens, I hope that you will be treated with a little more respect by the tweaked out twinkies running around you than you are showing yourself. I know it feels like you are ruling this world right now, but you are not. And you need to learn to treat everybody with dignity and respect, regardless of how they look, what they do, how much money they have, or how old they are. I'm very disappointed that you haven't learned that yet."

"I'm sorry," Chance said quietly, still looking at the floor.

Taylor and Louis made faint sounds of apology beside him. Joel turned to face them. They looked like grade schoolers being reprimanded by the principal and it almost made him laugh.

"I hope you are," Lady Chanel continued, "but for now I think you three need to leave. If Joel wants to stay and talk to his gentleman, then that's his business."

Suddenly Joel sensed Zelda moving behind him and felt a large hand on his shoulder. Zelda's raspy voice spoke close to his ear.

"Besides, shouldn't you be working by now, Coco?"

Chance looked as though he'd been slapped. He glanced quickly at Joel, panic seeming to register on his face, then settled his eyes on Zelda. Joel was confused but he could see that Chance was furious. He was breathing hard and the muscles on his face twitched. Joel knew that Chance had inherited his father's temper but he'd never seen him so angry. He suspected that if Lady Chanel weren't there, Chance would try to choke Zelda.

Chance stood silently for a minute, his fury palpable. Then he seemed to get it under control. Still staring at Zelda he simply said, "You fucking cunt," then turned quickly and headed for the stairs, presumably to retrieve his clothes. Taylor and Louis stood in obvious shock for a moment, then finally managed to say goodbye and follow.

Joel turned to face Lady Chanel and Zelda. Zelda settled back on her stool, a satisfied smile on her face.

"What the fuck happened?" Joel asked with bewilderment, slightly embarrassed that he'd sworn in front of Lady Chanel.

Zelda continued to smile, looking like the bear who'd eaten the canary.

"Nothing to trouble yourself about," Chanel said quickly. "Miss Zelda just took an extra dose of evil pills today."

She shot Zelda an angry glance.

"But what pissed Chance off so much? I've never seen him like that."

"That's just old business between Zelda and Chance," Lady Chanel said dismissively. "We all have to love each other but we don't all have to like one another. Sometimes Zelda can be a bit judgmental."

"About what?"

"You need to ask Chance about that, Joel. It's not my business to tell you."

Joel realized that Chanel wasn't going to tell him anything. He suspected that if Zelda were alone she would have been only too happy to tell him everything, but for now that wasn't going to happen.

"If I were you, I'd put the whole thing out of my head right now and go find that gentleman you fancied so much." Chanel said.

Joel considered it for a minute. A part of him felt he should go find his friends, but he was still angry at them. And a larger part of him wanted to meet the beautiful man. Finally he decided it couldn't hurt to just see if the man was still upstairs. He gave Lady Chanel a kiss on the cheek, then decided to kiss Zelda as well. He wasn't sure why, but he felt as though Zelda had somehow been trying to protect him.

"Thank you," he said as he kissed her left cheek.

"Nothing at all," she replied, giving him a genuinely warm smile and lightly touching his arm.

Joel sensed that she was somewhat surprised and touched by his gesture.

"We're going to head back to the home soon so we probably won't see you again tonight," Chanel said. "You have yourself a good time...but remember to play safe."

Joel was slightly embarrassed by the implications of her words but said good night and headed back toward the stairs to Parade. He hoped that Chance and the others had left by now because it was time to find his beautiful man.

Chapter 5

Joel was dimly aware of noise somewhere in the distance and the smell of bacon frying. He wondered if his grandmother was making breakfast. He rolled over and slowly opened his eyes.

Okay, I'm not in Natchez anymore, he thought as he saw the unfamiliar ceiling above him. He turned his head to one side and then the other, taking in the room around him. The walls were painted a pale yellow with stark black and white photos in ornate black frames spaced evenly throughout the room. The headboard behind him was dark cherry in a Mission style. He sat up slowly. He could feel a dull throbbing now in his head and his mouth was dry and sticky.

He continued to look around the room. The polished oak floor was covered in the center by a braided oval rug with bands of bright red, green, yellow, blue and white. There were two dressers that matched the style of the headboard. The higher one was slightly to his right against the wall in front of him. The top was covered by what looked like family photos in simple silver frames. The lower dresser was to his left. The top was clear except for a wallet, keys, watch and a vase with freshly cut flowers. Joel could make out lilacs, gerber daisies and lavender. A door that seemed to lead to a hallway was open directly in front of him. A patchwork quilt rested against the footboard of the bed. The patches were in paler tones of the colors of the rug. The room was immaculately clean but inviting, with little touches of bright color throughout.

He lifted the pale green sheet that draped his body. Yup, naked, he thought, shaking his head slowly. So where the fuck am I and whose house is this?

He heard soft footsteps approaching the door and considered dropping back down and pretending he was still asleep. Then suddenly the beautiful man was in the doorway, wearing only pale blue boxer shorts and carrying a large yellow ceramic mug.

"Oh good, you're awake," the man said.

"Yeah," Joel replied, sounding not too sure that was true.

"I thought you might want some coffee," the man said walking to the side of the bed.

Joel stared at the man's body as he approached. Damn, he's beautiful all over, he thought. The man had long muscular legs and a tight, well-muscled torso like a middleweight boxer. His upper chest and legs were covered with fine black hair and a line of hair ran from his navel to the top of his boxer shorts.

Joel took the cup unsteadily and said thank you. He wanted to keep looking at the man's body but he had more immediate needs.

"Do you have a bathroom?"

"Yeah, right through that door," the man said pointing to a closed door along the left wall. "I put a towel out in case you want to shower before breakfast. Are you in a hurry to get going?"

"Um, no," Joel replied feeling stupid.

"Okay, well when you're ready the kitchen is down the hall to the left."

"Thanks," Joel said.

He needed to pee badly but waited until the man left the room before getting out of bed. He knew the man must have already seen him naked but he was still embarrassed.

After emptying his bladder Joel stepped into the shower. As the warm water hit his skin a thick foam began to form. Startled for a moment, he suddenly remembered the Foam

36

Party the night before. Great, I probably left soap scum all over the guy's bed, he thought.

He showered and dried himself quickly, then brushed his teeth using his index finger and toothpaste he found on the counter. Finally he helped himself to some Tylenol from the medicine cabinet over the sink. His hangover wasn't too bad yet, but he was still feeling a bit drunk and suspected it was going to get worse.

He walked back into the bedroom wrapped in a towel. On the edge of the bed his clothes lay neatly folded. He picked up his tank top and brought it to his nose. It was warm and had the slightly flowery scent of fabric softener. That's a first, he thought. He dropped the towel and slipped on his boxer shorts. He was about to put on his shorts and shirt but decided against it. If boxers were good enough for the beautiful man they were good enough for him. He was feeling a little bold and adventurous as he headed toward the kitchen, wet towel and coffee cup in hand.

Like the bedroom, the kitchen was airy and inviting. The cabinets and crown moldings were bright white and ornately detailed. A wide horizontal stripe of warm red ran along the center and right walls between the cabinets and countertops. The ceiling was high and made of pressed tin which had been painted white, and the floors were checkered by large black and white tiles. The stainless steel appliances and dark slate countertops were spotless and free of clutter.

The beautiful man was leaning against the counter next to the stove, sipping from a mug that matched the one in Joel's hand. He was intently reading a neatly folded newspaper.

"Hey," Joel said sheepishly.

The man looked up and smiled.

"I brought my dirty towel in," Joel said offering it up and averting his eyes.

"You can just throw it on the floor of the laundry room behind you," the man replied, indicating an open door behind

Joel. "I've got some more laundry to do anyway."

"Yeah, sorry about that," Joel said, shrugging his shoulders apologetically. "I didn't mean to get your sheets all crusty."

"Crusty?" the man asked, pursing his lips comically. "I don't remember doing anything to get my sheets crusty."

"I meant from the Foam Party. It was all over my skin. You should have seen me in the shower."

Joel stopped, suddenly embarrassed when the man arched his eyebrows playfully as if to say, "should I have?" He paused for a moment trying to regain his composure, then gave the man a curious look.

"So then we didn't do anything last night?" he asked.

The man laughed warmly.

"You don't remember?"

"Well, I remember seeing you at Parade and wanting to meet you, but I don't remember much after that. I had a few drinks and I was on Ecstasy, which was probably a mistake."

"I don't think you should tell me that," the man said frowning slightly. "Remember, I'm a cop."

Joel stared at him in disbelief.

"You serious? Fuck..."

"Don't worry, I'm not on duty, but I'd rather not know about it."

"Okay," Joel said, wishing he could crawl into a hole and die.

"So do you remember actually meeting me?"

"No, I'm really sorry," Joel replied.

He winced slightly and tried to smile.

"I remember my friends and I had a big fight because they made me look like a total ass in front of you, and then after they left I went back upstairs to look for you. But I was really nervous and I remember getting two shots of Jagermeister. Then it's all kind of fuzzy. Pretty romantic, huh?"

The man laughed.

"Not very, I suppose."

He walked over to Joel and extended his hand.

"My name is Michel."

"Joel," Joel replied, shaking his hand.

"Yes, I remember your name," Michel said with a playful smirk. "We met on the balcony around 1:30. You were pretty drunk...but charming. And we chatted for a while. And you kept trying to kiss me. Then you dragged me to the dance floor and convinced me to check my clothes and dance with you. So you're not the only one who got my bed all crusty. I finally managed to get you out of there around three but you wouldn't tell me where you lived because you said your roommate was an asshole, so I brought you back here."

"Which is...?" Joel asked embarrassedly.

"Frenchman Street...in the Marigny."

Joel nodded, trying to piece the night back together in his mind.

"And we didn't do anything?"

"Well, we kissed for a while, but then you passed out and I wasn't going to take advantage of you like that."

"So how did I get naked?"

"Well, I didn't say I didn't take a peek," Michel replied, grinning broadly. "Actually, as I recall, I had a hard time keeping your underwear on you. They went missing for awhile when we were dancing and I had to fish them off the floor before we could leave. And the last time you were in my bathroom you came out without them. I found them stuffed behind the toilet this morning."

"I'm so embarrassed" Joel said, covering his face with his hands. "I'm really sorry. I was a total fucking nightmare for you."

"Not at all," Michel said, taking a few steps forward and pulling Joel's hands away from his face. "It was cute. You were cute. And I had a lot of fun. For the first time in a long time."

He leaned forward and gave Joel a soft kiss.

"So how about some breakfast?"

*****

They ate side by side on stools at the counter, Joel's right leg entwined with Michel's left. His hangover had never materialized and he felt good. Michel had prepared scrambled eggs with cheddar cheese, biscuits and bacon. As they ate Joel talked about his grandparents and his decision to move to New Orleans. Michel listened without saying much about his own life.

"What was the deal with the body at the Creole House yesterday?" Joel asked suddenly. "Everyone was talking about it last night. Some guys said the body was all chopped up and the killer ate some of it."

Michel smiled and shook his head.

"I'm sure people are saying worse than that. We don't know what happened yet. One of the guests was stabbed and killed. We're still waiting for a report from the coroner's office to see if they found any clues."

He didn't want to upset Joel with the details of the murder.

"That's creepy," Joel said, giving a slight shudder.

Michel leaned over and kissed him on the cheek, resting his left hand on Joel's thigh.

"Don't worry, I'll protect you," he said.

After breakfast they shared a cigarette, then Joel helped load the dishwasher and clean the kitchen. In the back of his mind he could hear Mammau's voice telling him how important it was to be a considerate guest.

While Michel showered, Joel flopped onto the bed. He couldn't remember the last time he'd had so much fun with a guy. He really liked Michel. He was also starting to get excited. When he heard the shower turn off he rolled onto his back, positioning one arm behind his head and spreading his knees apart so that Michel could see up the legs of his boxers.

Michel walked into the room wrapped in a towel. When he

saw Joel he stopped. Joel was beautiful. His soft brown hair was swept casually across his pale blue eyes and he had a small seductive smile on his lips. His pale body was stretched out, the skin smooth and unblemished. The only hair on his body was a light covering on his legs and a thick patch in his exposed armpit. Michel could feel himself swelling against the towel.

"So you want to come back to bed?" Joel asked, patting the sheet next to him.

Michel faltered for a moment. He wanted nothing more than to jump into bed with Joel and cover his body with kisses, but something told him he should wait. He didn't want to rush and risk ruining things before they got started.

"I can't," he said finally. "I want to, but it's already 11 and I was due at the station an hour ago."

Joel frowned slightly.

"That's okay. I understand. I forgot some people actually have jobs they have to go to."

Michel walked over to the side of the bed and sat down.

"I'm sorry," he said, leaning down to kiss Joel.

They kissed for what seemed like an hour, their tongues rolling over one another and their lips pressed tightly together. Finally Joel pulled back and smiled up at Michel.

"We better stop that or you're not getting out of here."

"Yeah, I know," Michel said, reaching down to adjust the front of his towel. "Maybe it would be better if you got dressed in the living room while I get dressed in here. I don't think this would be a good time to be naked in the same room with you."

Joel flicked his tongue out between his teeth and smiled.

"Okay coward," he said, lightly pinching one of Michel's nipples. "But next time you're mine."

Then he slid across the bed, grabbed his shorts and tank top and left the room.

Michel sat on the bed for a minute composing himself. He knew it was silly to feel so much for Joel so quickly, but he didn't want the feeling to go away. He hadn't felt so alive in

41

months. He felt like a 7th grader with a first crush. At the same time he felt uneasy. He thought about Joel's friends and wondered what Joel was expecting from him. All right, he told himself, you need to pull yourself together and get to work.

*****

Ten minutes later they left Michel's apartment. Although it was only a short walk, Michel offered to give Joel a ride home and Joel accepted gladly, wanting to extend his time with Michel as much as possible. They were both quiet on the drive, each lost in his own thoughts. As they pulled up in front of Joel's apartment, Michel killed the engine and turned to face Joel. Joel noticed the worried look on Michel's face and waited for him to speak.

"This is kind of awkward," Michel finally managed, "but you aren't really expecting anything, are you?"

"You mean like do I expect to get together again? I guess not if you don't want to."

Joel felt a sharp pang of hurt and turned his face toward the passenger window.

"No," Michel said quickly. "I mean, I'd love to get together again. I had a great time. But I just didn't know if you were serious about...getting paid."

Joel looked back at Michel with an expression of both disbelief and offense.

"What? I'm not some fucking prostitute," he said sharply.

"No, I didn't think so," Michel stammered, "...but I wasn't sure....because of what you said last night."

Joel's expression went blank.

"You really don't remember last night, do you?" Michel asked.

The car suddenly felt very small and hot to him.

"What are you talking about?" Joel asked with a hint of annoyance.

Michel loosened his tie and ran his right hand over the lower half of his face, wiping away the sweat that had formed on his upper lip.

"I asked you if you were a hustler and you told me you were. You said it would cost me $100 for the night."

"What?" Joel asked incredulously. "Why the fuck would you ask me if I was a hustler?"

He felt anger pulsing his temples.

"Because of your friends," Michel replied defensively.

His mouth was dry and tasted coppery.

"Coco, Desiree and the other one," he finished.

Joel remembered the night before when Zelda had called Chance "Coco" and the way Chance had reacted. He felt a sudden apprehension.

"Who the fuck are Coco and Desiree?" he asked cautiously.

"The guys you were with," Michel answered weakly.

"Chance, Taylor and Louis?"

"Yeah," Michel replied, nodding.

"What about them?" Joel asked.

He could feel tension building in his stomach.

"Well, they're trannie hustlers, right?"

Joel felt dizzy and gripped the armrest with his right hand.

"What do you mean, trannie hustlers?" he asked thickly.

"Chicks with dicks," Michel replied carefully, trying to maintain his composure.

The conversation was going far worse than he'd anticipated.

"I know what a transvestite is, but what do you mean they're trannie hustlers?" Joel asked, measuring each syllable as if talking to a child.

"I mean," Michel replied in the same measured tone, "that your friends have sex for money dressed as women. You didn't know?"

Joel shook his head.

"No, I didn't know," he said quietly. "Are you serious?"

Even as he asked the question he knew the answer. He could

feel his stomach tightening and took a deep breath against the nausea.

"Yeah," Michel replied.

He reached across the car and touched the side of Joel's face.

"I'm sorry. I thought... Do you want to go get a cup of coffee and talk about it?"

Joel sat staring at his feet for a moment. He felt angry and hurt, though he wasn't sure by who. Finally he shook his head.

"No, I better get going," he said flatly.

He opened the door and stepped out of the car. His legs felt shaky. Michel hesitated, unsure what to do, then Joel turned to him.

"Nice meeting you," Joel said without feeling. "I guess I'll be seeing you around."

Joel closed the car door and walked into the apartment building. Michel sat in his car, his eyes closed and his hands locked on the steering wheel. What the fuck did I do? he thought. He wanted to go after Joel but didn't know the number of Joel's apartment, and he wasn't sure it would do any good anyway. The damage was done. Reluctantly he started the car and pulled away.

Chapter 6

Joel stood outside the door to the apartment, absently worrying the small brass key in the fingers of his right hand. After Michel had left he'd walked back out to the sidewalk and vomited into the planter by the entrance. He'd been standing in the darkened hallway for the five minutes since. His stomach still ached and the sour taste lingered in his mouth. He felt drained and wanted to sleep, but he pictured Chance waiting for him on the other side of the door and he didn't want to see him yet. His emotions were too raw and his thoughts too confused and angry. He felt that both Chance and Michel had somehow betrayed him.

He wasn't angry at Chance so much for keeping the truth from him. Chance had always lied when it served his purposes and Joel had long ago accepted that as part of their friendship. He knew that Chance hadn't intentionally hurt him. But he felt somehow tainted by what Chance was doing. He remembered how he'd felt in the car when Michel asked him if he expected to be paid. Logically he knew it had nothing to do with who he really was, but for just a moment he saw himself through Michel's eyes and he felt sick and dirty. It had changed everything.

The morning had been perfect. He could feel himself falling in love. Michel was beautiful and kind and smart. He was thoughtful. But now that all felt like a million years ago. Michel had thought he was a hustler, or at least considered the possibility. Whatever else Michel had felt, that had been in the back of his mind the whole time. It had colored the way Michel had looked at him and knowing that made everything that had happened seem false.

It felt as though a darkness was eating its way into his life, changing it. He wanted to be clean, unsullied. He wanted to be worthy of love.

He put the key in his pocket and walked out of the building, turning right toward the river.

Chapter 7

Michel pulled into the parking garage below the station. He knew that normally he'd catch holy hell for being so late, but everyone had been giving him a wide berth the last few months. Although he knew the grace period wouldn't last forever, he was grateful for it now. He turned off the engine and lit a cigarette.

He felt guilty. It was that simple: guilty that he'd thought Joel might be a hustler, guilty that he'd hurt Joel. He felt his throat tighten involuntarily as he remembered the look in Joel's eyes and the anger and pain in Joel's voice. He'd grown accustomed to anger and pain in his work and had learned to detach himself from the suffering of the families of victims, but this was different. This time he'd inflicted the pain himself. His eyes burned and he closed them for a moment.

There was something else, too. More than guilt, he felt a sense of loss. His behavior last night and this morning had been uncharacteristic and he'd found it both unnerving and exhilarating. He didn't hold hands with men on balconies. He didn't bring them home and let them spend the night and make them breakfast in the morning. He didn't care about them. With Joel he'd been able to relax. He'd allowed himself to live in the moment in a way he hadn't experienced before.

He knew he wasn't a romantic. He was a pragmatist, always studying the situation, searching for the logic. The only place he'd ever allowed passion and intuition to come into play had been in his work. He was comfortable with them there. He'd learned to rely on them and was willing to let them lead him down trails that seemingly had no logical end, confident that eventually they would make sense. That willingness had served him well professionally. At thirty-one he was the youngest detective in the department.

His personal life, however, had always been different. There he'd always been cautious. Maybe overly so. He'd never allowed himself to even entertain the idea of a relationship. He didn't see the sense in pursuing something that was likely to fail. He liked to maintain a comfortable emotional balance, never soaring too high or dipping too low. He liked to be in control of his feelings, and the idea of love seemed threatening: all-consuming, capable of taking over his life and distorting his judgment.

But Joel had awakened a desire in him to experience more. He knew that part of it had to do with Joel directly, and part of it had to do with the possibilities Joel allowed him to see in himself. He admired Joel. Joel was thoughtful and intelligent and grounded, but he also had an openness and willingness to experience life that Michel wanted for himself. On some level he supposed he was jealous. He wanted to be Joel, or possess him in hopes of sharing Joel's optimism and willingness to take risks. Thinking about the years he had spent shielding himself from taking chances, locked into his comfortable existence, made him sad. He regretted the opportunities he may have missed.

Joel made him feel hopeful. He knew it was narcissistic, but he liked the image of himself that he saw reflected in Joel's eyes. For the past few months he'd been unfamiliar to himself. It had been like watching the world through the eyes of a stranger: someone who sleepwalked through each day. In Joel's eyes he could see himself as he had been. More, he saw the possibilities of who he could become. He saw the possibilities of embracing life. He wondered what it would be like to commit himself completely to somebody else and open himself up to love.

He thought back to the previous night. At first he'd thought that Joel was just a cute kid and he'd been flattered by the attention. He usually felt below the radar of the younger guys in the clubs, but Joel had pursued him. As he'd stood on the balcony Joel had suddenly appeared beside him, smiling shyly.

Their conversation had been awkward and halting in the beginning. Michel was cautious. He'd seen Joel's friends before and had heard rumors that they were hustlers. In the back of his mind he wondered whether Joel might think he was a potential trick. It made him nervous to think that he might be seen from the street with a hustler and he'd been relieved when Joel dragged him to the dance floor. He'd hesitated only for a minute before stripping to his boxers.

Joel had been flirtatious and silly, gyrating and grinding drunkenly in the chest-high foam. Michel didn't sense any guile and his hesitancy had eased a notch. Then Joel had wrapped his arms around Michel's neck and pulled him close, kissing him softly. Michel had stood awkwardly for a moment, embarrassed and unsure how to react. Slowly he'd moved his hands to Joel's hips and kissed him back. He'd felt smooth skin against his palms and slid his hands lower. Joel was naked. They'd remained that way for ten minutes, swaying to the music, kissing, rubbing their bodies together. Finally Joel had suggested they go back out to the balcony and Michel had found Joel's soggy boxer shorts on the floor and helped him put them back on.

They'd walked outside and found a bench at the quiet end of the balcony along St. Ann. As soon as they sat down Joel had taken Michel's left hand into his right and leaned his head against Michel's shoulder. For a minute they sat in silence, sharing a cigarette. Then Joel had begun to talk. He was more relaxed than he'd been earlier, almost melancholy.

It pained Michel momentarily to realize that Joel had no apparent recollection of their conversation. He remembered every word of it.

"My grandparents would shit if they could see me now,"

Joel said, shaking his head slightly. "Sitting here holding hands with a beautiful man for all the world to see."

"What about your parents?" Michel asked.

"They died when I was six. A car accident."

"I'm sorry."

"It's okay. It was a long time ago," Joel said quickly.

He lit another cigarette and took a long drag on it.

"Do you remember much about them?"

Michel could feel Joel's head shaking against his shoulder.

"No. I just remember my mother hugging me a lot. She was beautiful."

"What are your grandparents like?"

"They're nice," Joel replied, "but I think I disappoint them."

"In what way?"

"I don't think I live up to their expectations. I don't know. Sometimes I think it was more of an obligation for them than a choice having me around. They shouldn't have had to raise another kid."

Joel's tone was matter-of-fact. Michel couldn't hear any hurt or accusation in it.

"I'm sure that's not true," he said. "I'm sure they wanted you there."

Joel shrugged.

"Maybe. But they sure didn't try to stop me when I said I was coming here," he said with a laugh.

Again Michel tried to read the tone of the words.

"Maybe they knew it was best for you," he said reassuringly, squeezing Joel's hand. "Do they know you're gay?"

"God no. They don't even know gay people exist in Natchez."

Joel was silent for a moment.

"That's why I wanted to come here," he said finally. "I wanted to be someplace where I could be myself and be accepted."

"Even here it's not always that easy," Michel replied. "I

think you have to accept yourself first."

He wondered when he would reach that point himself.

"I love them," Joel said, "but I know it would be hard for them to accept me for who I am. I want a family who can. Like Lady Chanel and Chance."

"She's quite a character, Lady Chanel," Michel said.

"Do you know her?" Joel asked.

"No," Michel replied, "but for as long as I can remember she's been around. She lives in the Marigny, not too far from where I grew up. When I was a kid I remember seeing her and thinking she was the most exotic creature I'd ever seen. She fascinated me, but I was always a little bit afraid of her."

"Afraid? Of what?"

"I don't know. I'm not even sure that I knew she was a man until I was a teenager. But I knew there was something different about her. She just seemed so sure of herself, so comfortable being who she was. I think that's what scared me."

Michel stopped, considering the implications of what he'd said.

"She sure is that," Joel said with a small laugh. "What did your folks say about her?"

"My father left before I was born," Michel replied.

To his surprise, he realized that he found it oddly liberating to talk about his personal life with Joel.

"I don't remember my mother ever saying anything about Chanel, but they'd always say hello to one another when we passed her on the street. I guess I had the sense that my mother respected her."

Joel shook his head in amazement.

"I wish I'd had someone like her around when I was growing up. It would have made me feel more normal. Does your mother know you're gay?"

Michel hesitated, feeling suddenly uncomfortable.

"No. I never had the chance to tell her. She passed away a few months ago."

"I'm really sorry," Joel said, lifting his head to kiss Michel on the cheek. "I'm sure she loved you."

Michel could feel tears welling in his eyes. He squeezed Joel's hands more tightly.

"It takes time," Joel said quietly.

Michel tried to imagine the pain Joel had experienced trying to come to terms with the loss of two parents.

"Thank you," he said.

They sat quietly for a few minutes.

"You know, I never even heard the word 'gay' until Chance told it to me when we were thirteen," Joel said finally. "Of course by then we'd already been doing gay stuff together for years."

"You grew up with Chance?" Michel asked with surprise.

"Yeah. I've known him for forever," Joel replied.

Michel smiled to himself, thinking about the relative nature of forever.

"We met in kindergarten and have been best friends ever since," Joel continued. "My grandparents even kind of took him in in high school."

"Why?"

"His mom left when he was little and his dad used to beat him up," Joel replied softly. "His daddy was a drunk. Chance dropped out of school and Pappy gave him a job doing chores around the house and tried to help him out."

"That's rough," Michel said, trying not to sound trite.

"I know," Joel said, "but sometimes I feel like he was lucky."

"Why?"

"Because no matter what he does in life, he's still going to be better than his daddy. There's no pressure."

Michel was silent for a moment. He wondered whether Joel understood the psychological scars Chance would bear for the rest of his life. He also wondered whether Joel considered hustling to be "better" and felt his apprehension return.

"So are you like Chance?" he asked finally, trying to keep

his tone even.

"No," Joel said, shaking his head slowly.

His eyes were closed and his voice had become soft and lilting.

"Chance is wild. He just does whatever pops into his head. And he's smarter about people than me. He knows how to read them. He can turn himself into whatever he thinks you want him to be."

Michel considered what Joel had said before responding.

"So then he does feel the pressure to meet people's expectation."

"No," Joel said with conviction. "He just does it to get what he wants. I don't think he even knows he's doing it half the time. It's just an instinct."

Michel thought about how to proceed for a moment.

"But are you like him in other ways?" he asked more pointedly.

Joel sat up and turned toward Michel. His eyes were slightly unfocused and dreamlike.

"How do you mean?" he asked.

"Well, are you a hustler, too?"

Michel could feel tension across his shoulders and held his breath. Joel stared at him blankly for a moment, then broke into a wide grin and winked.

"You know it, baby" he said, "and it's gonna cost you a hundred bucks to spend the night with me."

He kissed Michel lingeringly, then began to giggle drunkenly to himself.

Michel looked at Joel carefully, trying to gauge the truth of what he'd said. Joel closed his eyes again and began humming tunelessly. He leaned back into Michel's shoulder and wrapped his left hand over Michel's bicep. Michel knew he'd reached a point where he needed to decide whether to trust Joel or not. He looked down the balcony toward the river. Beyond Bourbon Street only a few lights were visible. The city was going to sleep.

He took a deep breath and decided to take the risk. His instincts told him to trust.

They'd sat in silence for a while after. When Michel had looked at his watch it was after 3 am. He'd told Joel he needed to go home and they'd gone inside to claim the rest of their clothes. Outside, Michel had offered to give Joel a ride home, but Joel had said he wanted to go home with Michel. He'd said he didn't want to go home because Chance was an asshole, and he wouldn't tell Michel his address. He'd said that he'd sleep on the street if Michel didn't take him home. Finally Michel had relented.

As they'd walked in the front door of Michel's house, Joel had grabbed Michel and kissed him hard, pushing him against the wall of the narrow hallway. Michel could feel the dampness of Joel's body through his shirt. Michel had broken the kiss and lead Joel to the bedroom. While Joel went into the bathroom Michel had undressed and changed into dry boxer shorts, then went to the kitchen and drank a glass of water. When he got back to the bedroom Joel had been laying face down diagonally across the bed. He was naked and his eyes were closed. Michel could see his back rising and falling slowly.

Michel had walked to the bed and carefully slid his hands under Joel's chest, lifting him slightly, then pulled him toward the left side of the mattress. As he'd settled Joel's head onto the pillow Joel had rolled toward him and put his arms around Michel's neck.

"I want to make love with you," Joel had said.

He'd smiled sweetly as he struggled to keep his eyes open.

"Not now," Michel had said softly, looking into Joel's eyes.

"Not fair," Joel had replied, frowning comically.

"I know, but it will be better after we've gotten some sleep."

Michel had meant what he said, but at the same time he'd known it might be a lie. In the morning his doubts might have returned.

"Promise?"

"Cross my heart," Michel had said, marking a small X on his chest with his right index finger.

"Okay," Joel had said sighing. "But you better or you're in big trouble."

They'd lain together on the bed, Michel's right arm cradling Joel and Joel pressed tightly against Michel's body, his right hand resting over Michel's heart. After a few minutes Michel could hear Joel's breathing slow and thicken. He'd lifted his head and looked down. Joel's eyes were closed and his mouth was slightly open. He looked even younger than he had before and Michel had felt a momentary stab of guilt. He'd reached out with his left hand, careful not to move the rest of his body, and turned off the light. He'd lain awake in the darkness listening to Joel's breathing and feeling Joel's chest rising and falling against his ribs. He'd felt contented. Finally as the sun had begun to rise he'd fallen asleep.

Thinking back on it Michel cursed himself silently. How could he have thought Joel was a hustler? Why had he felt the need to pursue it again this morning? Being with Joel had made him happy, had made him feel alive. He angrily stubbed out his cigarette in the ashtray and opened the door.

*****

The police headquarters for the 8th district was located on the corner of Royal and Conti streets, a few blocks from Jackson Square. The detective division was on the fifth floor.

As he entered the squad room Michel was aware of eyes noting his arrival time. While members of the force liked to describe themselves as a brotherhood, they were also human and keenly aware of anyone receiving special privileges. Fortunately, the room was almost empty. Most of the teams would be on the streets by now doing follow up investigations on active cases. He nodded to the few remaining men and women as he made his way to his desk.

Sassy was already seated at the desk across from his own, studying the contents of a manila folder.

"Coroner's report?" Michel asked.

"Yes, and good morning to you, too. Or should I say afternoon?" Sassy added looking at her watch.

"Yeah, sorry about that," Michel said as he removed his jacket, placing it carefully over the back of his chair. "You want some coffee?"

"No, I'm good. I'm almost ready for happy hour."

Michel realized that for the first time in months the idea of having a cocktail at that hour didn't appeal to him. He walked to the battered coffee maker and poured a cup, adding three sugars to blunt the bitterness he knew to expect. You'd think you'd be able to get a decent cup of coffee, he thought as he walked slowly back to Sassy. I mean this is New Orleans, right?

He sat on the edge of Sassy's desk and waited for her to finish reading the file.

"So was this a good late or a bad late?" she asked without looking up.

"A little of both," Michel replied, "but I don't want to talk about it right now."

"Okay," Sassy said, settling back into her chair and clasping her hands across her stomach. "Suit yourself."

"No, I'm serious," Michel said. "I really don't. Not yet."

This had always been a game between them, part of the rhythm of their relationship. He would act coy about his private life and she would feign disinterest until he relented. Sassy regarded him carefully, gauging whether or not she was supposed to continue. She knew that understanding unspoken communication was a key to a successful partnership. Finally she decided not pursue it further.

"So the report came in about two hours ago," she began.

Michel was grateful she'd decided to let things go for now. He knew she'd eventually come back to it.

"And?"

"And nothing we didn't already know. Fucked, stabbed, sliced, dead."

"In that order?"

"Pretty much, though it looks like the penetration was ongoing." Sassy gave a wry shudder. "I don't even want to know how they know that, but that's what they say."

"What about the knife?"

"Just as Lecher thought," Sassy replied. "A hunting knife, nine-inch curved blade. Nothing special about it. The sort of thing you could buy at any hunting or sporting goods shop. I've already started compiling a list of all the stores likely to sell something like that within a 20-mile radius so we can send out an inquiry, but it's not an expensive knife so it was probably a cash purchase. I doubt we'll find much."

"What about forensics? Any fluids, hair, fibers?" Michel asked.

"Lecher said there was powder residue in the rectum so the killer was wearing a rubber. Lots of hair, fibers and fingerprints, but they could belong to anyone who's been in the room in the last ten years. You know how they clean those places. Lecher said they'll sift through them and see if there's anything unique and try to lift some clear prints."

"Okay. What about interviews?"

Michel felt suddenly guilty, realizing that he'd left Sassy to shoulder all of the responsibility.

"First one's at noon, then every thirty minutes til we're done. Eight guests and five employees."

"Including the night clerk?"

Sassy shook her head.

"He didn't show up last night. The owner said he found a message on his answering machine after we left yesterday. One of the guy's friends calling to say he was too sick to come in. We got his address."

"Let's send a squad car over and see just how sick he is."

"Already on its way," Sassy replied with a small shrug.

Michel reached out and touched her arm. It was an unusual gesture for him and she looked at him quizzically.

"Look, Sas, I know I haven't been pulling my weight. I'm sorry."

"I know," she said, giving him a sad smile.

Michel knew it wasn't pity.

"I just want you to know I appreciate you picking up the slack," he said. "I promise I'm finding my way back. Thank you."

"I've never doubted it," Sassy replied warmly. "Let's grab a bite before we have to start the interviews.

Chapter 8

Joel sat cross-legged on the bank overlooking the Mississippi River. He'd wandered northeast along the shore away from Jackson Square until he found a secluded spot where the embankment had been reinforced with stone. He looked out at the swirling brown water and took a slow drag on his cigarette. He felt surprisingly at peace. The confusion and anger he'd felt an hour before had quieted.

He'd decided to move out of the apartment. He felt both relief and sadness at his decision, but he knew it was the right thing to do. Although he still wanted to be Chance's friend, he didn't want what Chance did to be a part of his life. He would ask Lady Chanel if she had a room to rent or if she knew of anyone looking for a roommate. And if he couldn't find a new place, then he'd go back home for a while. The decision felt comfortable. It made him feel in control.

He still didn't know how he felt about Michel. It hurt to think that Michel had believed he might be a hustler. He didn't know if he could forgive him for that. At least I got a free breakfast, he thought ruefully. Maybe I am a hustler after all. Hustling for bacon and eggs. He let out a small, hard laugh.

He knew logically that he couldn't blame Michel. All Michel really knew about him was that all his friends were hustlers. But it felt like there had been a real connection. He wondered if he'd just imagined it: wishful thinking. If it had been real, wouldn't Michel have known in his heart that he wasn't a hustler?

Joel stubbed out his cigarette and stood, stretching for a moment in the sun. He didn't need to make a decision about Michel right now. He needed to talk to Lady Chanel.

*****

The Faubourg Marigny, abutting the northeast edge of the French Quarter, was the first suburb of New Orleans. Originally settled in 1805 by Creoles and European immigrants on land purchased from Bernard Xavier Phillippe de Marigny de Mandeville, a son of New Orlean's wealthiest family, the area continued to develop throughout the 19th and early 20th centuries as families and businesses moved there, turning the Marigny into a thriving residential, commercial and social district.

Following World War II, however, the Marigny began a steep decline. As government loans for new construction encouraged returning soldiers and their families to migrate farther from the city, the once neat Creole and "shotgun" cottages that lined the narrow streets fell into disrepair and the area became home to indigents and those on government assistance. The crime rate became one of the highest in a city known for its crime.

In the early 1970s the Marigny was "rediscovered" and was named to the National Registry of Historic Places in 1974. The area's renaissance continued slowly into the late 1980s when the federal government started a new loan program designed to encourage revitalization of inner city neighborhoods. Throughout the 1990s, artists, service workers from the Quarter, and a large population of gay men and woman began moving into and restoring the area, starting at the river end of Esplanade Street and gradually spreading north and east.

Lady Chanel's house was located on Dauphine Street near Elysian Field Avenue, in a section not yet fully reached by the economic revitalization. Unlike most of the houses that surrounded it, however, the large Victorian was immaculately maintained, with lush gardens in the front and rear yards.

More than just tolerated, Lady Chanel was venerated by her neighbors and the large homeless contingent who congregated in the nearby park. In part because of her kindness and generosity, and in part because of the unique culture of New Orleans that allows for the embrace of misfits and eccentrics, they respected and accepted her as one of their own. The men in the park kept watch over her house and moved quickly to intimidate any suspicious strangers in the area. Despite the neighborhood's high crime rate, Lady Chanel and her tenants—a man and a woman who had lived in the house since the mid-1970s—were never bothered. Now all in their sixties, they could walk the streets safely at any time of the day or night.

As he walked up Touro Street toward Burgundy, Joel thought that the neighborhood was a fitting place for Lady Chanel. Despite the age and overall air of neglect, there was a warmth and vitality to it. Brilliantly colored flowers cascaded onto the sidewalks from long untended gardens. Brightly painted houses peaked out from behind crumbling brick walls. Both Lady Chanel and the neighborhood had seen better days, he mused, but they were strong and they would go on. He decided not to share his insight with Lady Chanel.

As he approached the house, Joel could hear low voices coming from the shadows of the front porch.

"Well isn't this a pleasant surprise," Lady Chanel's voice called out from the darkness. "Come on up and have something cold to drink."

Joel wondered what a stranger would imagine if he heard Lady Chanel without seeing her. Her phrasing and tone seemed naturally feminine, yet there was a masculine undertone to her voice. It managed to be both soft and forceful at the same time.

When he reached the top step of the porch, Joel could see Lady Chanel and Miss Zelda seated at the far end on high backed rattan chairs. They were dressed almost identically in loose cotton shifts and Espadrille sandals, their hair pulled back under floral scarves. Lady Chanel's shift was pink with large orange flowers. Zelda's was turquoise with white polka dots. On a table in front of them rested a tray with a round glass pitcher of iced tea and four empty glasses.

"I'm sorry, are you expecting company?" Joel asked uncertainly, eyeing the empty glasses.

"You never know when company might show up," Lady Chanel replied, gesturing toward the empty chair closest to her.

"Thank you," Joel said as Lady Chanel leaned forward and poured him a glass of iced tea.

"Hello, Joel. How are you today?" Zelda asked.

She sat back in her chair eyeing him curiously. There was something almost challenging in her tone.

"I'm okay," he replied, taking the iced tea from Lady Chanel. "How are you?"

He quickly downed half of the iced tea.

Zelda replied with a benign smile and Joel shifted in his chair. Zelda always made him feel uncomfortable because he could never quite read the look on her face, and he wondered now if she were somehow mocking him.

"So how was last night?" Lady Chanel asked, tilting her head and regarding him thoughtfully. "Did you meet your dream man?"

Quickly looking away from Zelda, Joel took another sip from his iced tea.

"Yeah," he said.

"And was it love?"

Joel began to recount the details of the previous night (those he could remember) and that morning, pausing occasionally to answer questions or sip his tea. When he was finished, Lady Chanel leaned forward and placed her hand on his arm.

"Don't be too harsh on him, Joel," she said, looking at him kindly. "Michel's been going through a difficult time. He probably didn't tell you but he lost his mama about two months ago."

Joel gave Lady Chanel a surprised look.

"You know him?"

"This is a very small town, my dear. I don't know him, but I know of him. I knew his mama, Miss Verna. She owned the house over on Frenchman where he lives. They were very close and I'm sure he's in a lot of pain. She died very quickly. There wasn't a lot of time for him to prepare for losing her and I think he's still grieving. I don't like to carry tales, but I've heard tell that he's been spending time at Lafitte's."

She didn't elaborate, but Joel understood what she meant. He sat in silence for a minute, thinking about how he'd felt when he lost his own parents. For years he'd felt adrift, cut off from everything familiar. He remembered the hurt and the anger he'd felt at them for leaving him, and the guilt he'd felt for feeling that way. It had taken him years to feel like himself again, and even now he wondered if he ever really did feel as he had before, or if he'd just grown accustomed to feeling different.

"Thank you for telling me that," he said to Lady Chanel. "I won't say anything to him, but it helps to know."

"I knew you'd understand," she replied softly.

Zelda suddenly sat forward in her seat, resting her arms across her knees and looking directly into Joel's eyes. Her whole demeanor had changed. There was nothing cold or mocking in her gaze. She seemed genuinely concerned for him.

"And what about Chance?" she asked. "How are things between you?"

"That's why I came here," Joel replied. "Michel told me about Coco and I've decided that I can't stay there. I want to be his friend, but I don't want to live with him. I was wondering if maybe you'd have a room to rent."

He looked hopefully at Lady Chanel.

"Or maybe you know someone who needs a roommate?"

Lady Chanel laughed softly.

63

"The only way I'm going to have a room to rent is if one of those old coots drops dead, and I have a feeling they're going to be dancing on my grave."

Joel frowned to himself. He'd hoped that Lady Chanel might offer him a room in her own apartment on the top floor of the house.

"I might be able to help you out," Zelda said suddenly. "One of my tenants is behind on the rent and the only reason I haven't kicked his sorry ass out is because I didn't have anyone else to take the room."

Joel knew that Zelda owned a large boarding house somewhere beyond Elysian Fields Avenue. Neither Zelda nor Lady Chanel had ever worked so far as anyone could remember, and it was supposed that they earned all their income renting rooms. Joel had never been to Zelda's house.

Lady Chanel sat forward and turned slightly to face Zelda.

"I don't know if that's such a good idea," she said. "It's awfully far out and Joel doesn't have a car. There aren't any jobs out that way and he's probably going to have to come into the Quarter to work."

"It'll be fine," Zelda replied, slowly shaking her head. "He can take a bus. I'm sure it won't be a problem. He should be with someone who can look after him."

She smiled at Joel. Lady Chanel sat back in her seat, studying Zelda's face carefully.

"Okay," she said finally.

There was nothing unusual in their words, but Joel sensed that an unspoken negotiation had taken place.

Zelda turned back to Joel.

"What do you think?"

"Yeah, I guess so," he said. "How much?"

"Fifty dollars a week, but if you don't have the money right away you can work it off around the house. Lord knows I need help keeping up with the place."

Joel looked at Lady Chanel for reassurance. Her eyes were down as she lit a cigarette.

"Okay," he said.

Chapter 9

Speck Bouchard, the night clerk at the Creole House, was a hard looking thirty years old. Slight and pale, in the dim lights of the bars he could still look almost boyish, but now, under the harsh lights of the holding cell, fifteen years of alcohol and drug abuse were clearly etched in the deep creases around his mouth and the bruised circles under his eyes.

He'd been awakened at 11:45 that morning by loud pounding on his door. Struggling up from the couch where he'd passed out the night before, he'd staggered to the door and thrown it open, yelling "fuck you." Two policemen had been standing to either side of the door. They'd asked his name and informed him he needed to accompany them to the police station for questioning. Nervous, suffering from a hangover, and still feeling the residual effects of a 34-hour crystal meth binge, he'd asked if he could take a shower first and invited them in to wait without thinking. When they'd seen the glass pipe and small packets of white crystals on his coffee table they'd arrested him. He'd been sitting in the holding cell for almost five hours now.

Michel and Sassy had known Speck was in custody, but had opted to complete the other interviews before talking to him, knowing that the longer they waited the more likely he'd be to tell them something if he'd been involved with or knew anything about the murder. Drug withdrawal was a great facilitator for cooperation. Finally at 5:15 pm they had him brought into the interrogation room.

Speck was ghostly white and slick with cold sweat as he sat at a small table in the center of the room. His eyes darted back and forth from the door to the mirror in front of him to his hands. The fluorescent lights made his skin almost translucent. Behind the mirrored glass Sassy watched carefully. She knew it wouldn't take long if he knew anything. It looked like he was using heavily and he'd be anxious to get something to ease his withdrawal pains. He'd know they could make it a very long night for him. According to Speck's rap sheet, he'd spent three six-month stretches in prison—most recently for dealing Ecstasy and GHB, and twice for prostitution in his mid-twenties. He must have looked a lot better back then, Sassy thought. He was still on parole for the last drug conviction.

The door to the room opened and Michel walked in. He and Sassy had decided he'd take the first crack at Speck.

"Hey Speck, I'm Detective Doucette," Michel said. "I brought you some coffee."

Michel's tone was even, almost friendly. He placed the coffee in front of Speck, then took a seat along the side of the table. Rather than taking the seat directly opposite Speck, he and Sassy had decided to try a less adversarial tact.

"Smoke?"

Michel laid the pack on the table halfway between Bouchard and himself. Speck immediately reached for it and managed to dislodge a cigarette with his shaking hands. Michel leaned forward and smoothly guided a lighter to the end of the cigarette. Speck took an unsteady drag and seemed to relax slightly, slouching back against his chair.

"That wasn't my stuff, you know," he said matter-of-factly.

Though his voice was ragged, he had the practiced tone of someone accustomed to trying to save himself.

"Doesn't matter to me," Michel replied nonchalantly, lighting his own cigarette and settling back into his chair. "That's between you and the DA. I wanted to talk to you about the other night at the Creole House."

"What about it?"

"Did you see anything? Hear anything?"

Speck stared at him blankly and shrugged his shoulders exaggeratedly.

"Such as?"

"I don't have any plans for dinner, Speck," Michel said. "In fact, I don't have any plans all night. You want to play, that's fine with me."

Speck sat up straighter.

"Look, Detective Doucette. I'm not trying to fuck with you. I don't know what you mean. I see a lot of things when I'm working. Give me a hint."

Michel studied Speck closely. His confusion seemed genuine.

"One of your guests was murdered the other night. While you were on duty. About 3 am."

"No shit?"

It was more an exclamation than a question. Speck sat back in his chair.

"Fuck. Who was it?"

"Father Kenneth Brennan," Michel replied.

"Oh yeah," Speck said, shaking his head slowly in recognition. "I checked him in around 6:30. Nice enough guy."

"And that was the last time you saw him?"

"No. He went out about an hour later. Asked if there was anyplace good nearby to get a quick dinner. I told him to try the Quarter Scene. He came back a little while later and went back upstairs."

Speck closed his eyes and tilted his head slightly. He seemed to be searching for something in his mind. On the table in front of him his fingers tapped out arrhythmic beats.

"Then he went out again," he said. "Must have been around 10:15 cuz I was watching 'Seinfeld' reruns in the office. He wanted to know what bars to go to. I asked him what he was into and he said he wanted to watch some strippers. I told him about a couple of the places down on Bourbon. Then he asked me if those were girl strippers or guys. I remember he seemed sort of uncomfortable. I told him they were girls, but if he wanted guys he should go to MRB. Then he left. I didn't see him come back."

"But he did."

"If you say so."

"But you didn't see him?"

"Uh uh," Speck said, opening his eyes and shaking his head emphatically.

"Any reason?"

"Maybe I was taking a piss. I don't know. But I didn't see him."

"And you didn't see anyone leaving between three and six?"

Again Speck shook his head. Michel sensed there was something Speck wasn't telling him.

"Speck, maybe it hasn't occurred to you," he began slowly, "but unless you can give us some information that leads us to someone else, you're the best suspect we have right now."

He gave Speck a hard smile.

"Fuck that!" Speck exclaimed, rocking forward suddenly in his chair. "You've got nothing to link me to that guy. You can't charge me just for being there. It's my fucking job. And there were like ten other people staying there that night. Why don't you charge all of them?"

Michel had hoped that Speck was strung out enough that he wouldn't see the logic of the situation. He'd hit a dead end.

Suddenly the door opened and Sassy entered. She walked to the end of the table opposite Speck and leaned forward, placing her hands on the edge.

"Speck, do you know anything about mandatory sentencing in Louisiana?" she asked.

Her tone was flat but her eyes shone darkly as she stared at him.

"You're on parole. If you get convicted of possession it's a mandatory ten years. Frankly Speck, you don't look like you're going to last that long to me.

"The DA doesn't really care about you. You walk or you go to jail, it's all the same. No big deal. But this is a big deal. It's bad for tourism when people get murdered down here, and the Mayor doesn't like that. And when the Mayor is unhappy, the DA is unhappy. So if you want to fuck with our investigation then the DA will be happy to fuck with you. We're not stupid, Speck. We know there's some itty bitty little detail you're leaving out."

She let her words hang in the air as she gazed coolly at Speck. Michel could see Speck calculating how to minimize the damage to himself. Finally Speck let out a loud breath and sat back in his chair.

"I wasn't there," he said quietly, folding his arms across his chest.

"You want to expand on that a bit?" Michel asked.

"I left the Creole about 1 and I didn't get back until 5:30 am, just before my shift ended."

"Where were you?" Sassy asked.

"Guess." Speck replied, eyeing them derisively.

"Getting high?"

"Could be!" Speck replied, tapping the tip of his nose with his index finger, a large mocking grin on his lips.

"Where?" Michel asked.

"At my place. I only left long enough to punch out and I didn't leave again until your pals woke me up this morning."

"Were you alone?" Sassy asked.

"Hell, no. Many of the city's finest citizens were with me."

"I'll bet," Sassy said. "And I'm sure you won't mind giving us some of their names?"

"Absolutely not," Speck replied, tapping out his cigarette and smiling with mock geniality. "As soon as I talk to a lawyer."

Chapter 10

It was after six by the time Joel got back to the apartment. He'd spent the afternoon with Lady Chanel and Miss Zelda. Although she'd seemed subdued for a while after he'd agreed to move into Zelda's house, Chanel had soon returned to her usual self and Joel had begun to feel better about his decision. Whatever had happened between Lady Chanel and Zelda seemed to have been forgotten.

As he opened the door to the apartment he saw Chance sitting on the couch smoking, a bottle of Dixie resting between his thighs.

"Where the fuck have you been?" he asked.

He seemed both angry and concerned.

"I just had to do some thinking."

"All night? Where'd you sleep?"

"At that guy's house."

"The geezer?"

"He's not a geezer," Joel said sharply. "He's a nice guy. His name's Michel. And he's a cop."

Joel said the last word with emphasis, studying Chance's face for a reaction. There was none.

"No shit. So did he use handcuffs on you?" Chance asked with a mischievous smile.

"No. Nothing like that. I just spent the night and then he made me breakfast this morning."

"Cool. You been there since?"

"No, he dropped me off a few hours ago but I wasn't ready to see you yet."

Chance gave Joel a worried look.

"Why not? You still pissed at me about last night?"

"No, not about that," Joel replied. "Actually I'm not pissed at all anymore, but I was this morning."

"About?"

Joel hesitated, carefully considering his words.

"About you and Louis and Taylor. About you guys hustling," he said.

He stared at the floor, afraid to look at Chance.

"I know about Coco and Desiree."

Chance was silent for a moment. He stared at Joel, his mouth slightly open, a combination of fear and embarrassment playing across his face.

"Don't forget Ebony," he said finally.

"Ebony?" Joel asked, suddenly laughing. "Louis?"

Chance nodded his head and gave Joel a sad half smile.

"That's classic," Joel said, shaking his head. "I'll never think of him the same way again."

"And what about me?" Chance asked quietly.

His face was suddenly serious and he studied Joel carefully as Joel considered his answer.

"I don't know," Joel said finally. "It freaked me out pretty badly when I found out."

"That cunt Zelda."

"It wasn't Zelda. Michel told me. He thought I was a hustler, too. Because I'm friends with you."

"I'm sorry," Chance said.

Joel could see a shimmer along Chance's lower eyelids. He moved to the couch and sat down sideways with his feet pressed against Chance's right leg. He leaned forward and swept Chance's hair back with his left hand, then settled the hand against the side of Chance's neck.

"It's not your fault. I just wish you'd told me," he said.

"I was afraid you wouldn't want to be friends anymore."

"Never," Joel said, stroking the side of Chance's neck.

Chance managed a small smile and tilted his head, rubbing his cheek against the back of Joel's hand.

"But I can't stay here," Joel said.

For a moment the words hung between them and time seemed to stop. Then Chance jerked away as though Joel's hand had burned him. He turned his head to face Joel.

"Why not?" he asked, his tone suddenly cold, angry.

"Because I don't want to be around what you're doing."

"You mean you don't want to be around me."

"No, I do want to be around you," Joel said, his voice nearly pleading. "I still want to be friends. But I don't want to be around you hustling and if I live here I won't be able to get away from it."

"Fuck you," Chance said, standing suddenly and taking a few steps away.

He turned back to face Joel, his face contorted with both anger and sadness.

"You have no right to judge me!" he yelled.

"I'm not judging you. You can do whatever you want to do. I'm not asking you to stop. But I have to do what's right for me, too."

Joel started to stand. He wanted to hold Chance, make him understand that he still loved him. Chance took a step toward him, his fists clenched at his sides. Joel eased himself back onto the couch, unwilling to test Chance's anger.

"Good. Get the fuck out of here," Chance said.

His voice was low and menacing.

"We're not friends anymore. You're not the person I thought you were."

For a second Joel felt a spark of rage. He wanted to scream the same words back at Chance. He wanted to hurt him. But he stopped himself. He knew in his heart that it wasn't true: Chance was exactly who he'd always been. This was just a new way of doing whatever was convenient and necessary to survive.

"Fine," he said finally. "I'll be gone the day after tomorrow."

"No," Chance said. "I want you out now. And I wouldn't show my face at the Pub for a while either."

Chance turned before Joel could respond and walked into his bedroom, slamming the door behind him. Joel stared at the door. He understood the implied threat and it stunned him. He'd never expected things to happen the way they had. He'd expected Chance to be hurt, but not angry. He'd honestly believed that they would be able to remain friends.

Maybe it's a mistake to stay here now, he thought. Maybe I should just move back home. He knew that if Chance was against him, Taylor and Louis would be, too. His only friend would be Lady Chanel, and maybe Zelda. He knew they wouldn't turn against him. Lady Chanel wouldn't choose sides and Zelda disliked, maybe even hated, Chance.

Slowly he rose from the couch and walked to his room to pack. For tonight he'd stay in a hotel. He'd make his decision in the morning.

Chapter 11

The Youth Outreach Workshop finished at 4:30 pm and the participants from the Conference of Southern Methodist Ministers began filing out of the Morial Convention Center into the oppressive afternoon heat. As the others began making their way in small groups to the nearby Embassy Suites, the Rev. Caleb Reynolds started briskly north along Convention Boulevard. Preferring a more intimate setting that would allow him to get a feel for the unfamiliar city, he'd found a room at the Royal Inn near Jackson Square. The ground floor room lacked a street view, but it was neat and clean and opened onto a pleasant patio area. It was also less expensive than the upper rooms that overlooked the street.

When he got back to the inn he undressed, set the alarm clock for 6 pm, and took a nap. When he woke, he dressed in the clothes he'd worn earlier, ran a comb through his thinning auburn hair, and went out for a quick dinner at the Clover Grill on Bourbon Street. Returning to his room a little after seven, he called his family in Topeka. He recounted the activities of the day to his wife, then spoke briefly to his three children. After about fifteen minutes, he told his wife he loved her and would call her again tomorrow night. He hung up the phone and took a long shower.

After showering and drying himself in the bathroom, Reynolds walked back into the bedroom. He stood naked in front of the full length mirror on the back of the door and regarded himself, turning sideways and sucking in the slight paunch that had recently begun to develop. Not bad for an old man, he thought. Although he was only 35 years old, he'd begun to feel much older the last few years. As his responsibilities at the church grew and his eldest son entered high school, it felt as though his youth was part of a distant past. He couldn't remember anymore what it had felt like to be young and care-free.

He walked to the dresser and pulled out a pair of faded jeans and a black t-shirt. These were clothes his wife, Sarah, would frown upon at home, feeling that they were inappropriate for a minister. She'd packed them up for the Salvation Army two years ago, but he'd retrieved them from the bag and tucked them into the back of an old filing cabinet of tax receipts in the attic. He knew Sarah was afraid to go in the attic because she thought there were bats and raccoons living up there. This was the first time he'd worn the clothes in over three years. They felt good. He felt sexy and attractive.

A little after 8 pm he turned off the lights and left his room. He walked out of the inn and stood on the corner of Royal and St. Philip. He wanted to get a drink, and maybe find some company.

In the fourteen years they'd been married, he'd cheated on his wife only once, shortly after their seventh anniversary. It had been during a family vacation in Nashville when Sarah was 7-months pregnant with Isaac, their third child. During dinner, Sam, their eldest, had developed one of those mysterious stomach ailments that kids only seem to develop during vacations. When they got back to their room Sarah had insisted that Caleb go back out and enjoy himself while she looked after the children. She'd said that it made no sense for them both to waste the evening. So he'd gone to a nearby bar where a country-western duo was performing and sat in the darkness sipping scotch and enjoying the feeling of being alone.

After a while he'd realized that a woman had taken the stool next to him at the bar. He could see a mass of blond hair out of the corner of his eye. After a while he'd grown bolder and stolen a glance at her. She was looking directly at him. He'd quickly looked away, embarrassed but also intrigued.

"Do you have a light?" she'd asked suddenly.

He'd turned to face the woman. She held a long cigarette in her teeth, looking at him expectantly.

"I'm sorry but I don't smoke," he'd replied nervously.

She'd nodded her head, indicating a bowl of matches that rested on the bar in front of him. He'd pulled out a pack and finally managed to light one with his shaking hands. As he brought the match to her cigarette he could see her more clearly. She was much older than he'd first thought. Her face looked weathered, with small wrinkles lacing the outer edges of her lips. But there was something attractive about her. She had a certainty in her gaze and an unvarnished femininity. There was nothing silly or girlish about her as there often was with Sarah.

"Thank you," she'd said.

Her voice was throaty, almost harsh.

"You're welcome," he'd replied, searching for some way to keep the conversation going.

He wanted this woman. It had been almost two months since he and Sarah had been intimate, and his sexual desire and the liquor were beginning to overcome rational thought.

She'd reached out and touched his arm, resting her hand on his forearm.

"I'm not really thirsty," she'd said. "Why don't you take a walk with me?"

He'd known it wasn't really a question, but he'd struggled to answer her. A combination of lust and guilt flooded his mind. He'd felt her other hand begin to move up his right leg and his heart had begun to race.

"Okay," he'd finally managed.

His voice was barely audible. His mouth was dry and his tongue felt heavy and slow.

They'd walked outside and she'd lead him to a small wood building at the edge of the parking lot. She'd taken his hand and pulled him behind her as she moved through the dense bushes along the side of the building. As they entered a small clearing she'd turned and kissed him—hard, passionately. And he'd responded.

He'd felt as if he were in a dream, watching himself from a distance as he pulled up her skirt and pushed his hands into her panties; as she undid his pants and slid them down, taking him into her hands and her mouth; as he pushed inside her from behind while she leaned against the peeling rear wall of the building. He'd never felt such overwhelming desire, never felt such intense pleasure.

When it was over she'd asked him for fifty dollars. He'd given her the thirty-five dollars in his wallet without complaining. He'd actually apologized, feeling guilty that he hadn't had the full amount. Then he'd walked back to the hotel and showered quietly before slipping into bed beside Sarah. She'd woken up briefly and asked him why he'd showered and he'd told her that he smelled like smoke from the bar he'd gone to and didn't want to sleep beside her smelling like that. She'd given him a small kiss and drifted back to sleep as he lay in the dark reliving the night and wondering why he didn't feel more guilty.

Now he stood outside the Royal Inn and wondered which way would lead him to adventure. Maybe it was time to scratch his second-seven-year itch, he mused. He saw neon lights in the windows of a building a block and a half toward the river on St. Philip. As good a place as any to start, he thought, as he began walking down the block.

The bar was almost empty. A few groups of men were scattered throughout the room chatting. The place seemed friendly enough, so Caleb ordered a scotch and settled in at the bar. It was still early and he hoped that the women would show up before too long.

He was halfway through his first drink when a man moved up to the bar next to him and ordered a Cosmopolitan. The man was tall and angular, with deep brown skin and close cropped silver hair. He was dressed in jeans, a plaid button-down shirt and a loose-fitting blue blazer and looked to be in his late 50s or early 60s. There was something odd about his face, as though the details were missing, but Caleb couldn't figure out exactly why.

"Hello, how are you?" the man asked as he took his drink. His voice was soft, almost feminine.

"Fine, thanks," Caleb replied. "How about you?"

"Wonderful," the man said as he settled onto a stool.

"Kind of slow in here tonight, huh?" Caleb asked, looking around the room.

"It'll pick up," the man said, nodding as he lit a cigarette. "It usually gets busy around ten. I'm Cally, by the way."

Caleb gave a small laugh.

"I'm Caleb," he said, extending his hand. "So is Cally short for something?"

Cally shook Caleb's hand. Caleb noticed that Cally's grip was deceptively strong given his slender frame.

"It's short for Calvin," Cally said in a hushed voice, "but don't tell anyone."

He made an elaborate show of looking around them to make sure no one was listening, then gave Caleb a warm smile.

They continued chatting for a few minutes. Cally asked Caleb where he was from and what had brought him to New Orleans. Caleb was purposely vague, saying only that he was in town for a conference. Cally just nodded and gave Caleb a small smile.

As he finished his drink, Caleb excused himself to the restroom. He planned to leave afterward, but when he walked out Cally was standing nearby with a fresh drink for him. He suggested that they go out to the patio in back and Caleb reluctantly agreed. He was beginning to feel uncomfortable.

The area was nicer than Caleb had expected based on the interior of the bar. There were small, brightly colored paper lanterns strung around the perimeter, and tables and chairs were set among flowering bushes on a flagstone patio. It was surprisingly warm and comfortable. The two men sat down and Caleb raised his drink, offering a casual toast in Cally's direction. Cally smiled and returned the toast, tilting his glass at Caleb. His eyes remained locked on Caleb's.

"May I ask you a personal question?" he asked after a moment.

His tone was more serious than it had been before.

"Yeah, I guess so."

"I noticed that you're wearing a wedding ring. Yet I sense that you're looking for something tonight. Or someone."

Caleb hesitated.

"That's not really a question," he said finally.

"No, I suppose not," Cally replied, sipping his drink and smiling, "but if you were looking for someone, what might that someone look like?"

Caleb stared at Cally for a minute, trying to gauge the reason for the question. Was Cally a pimp? Did he have a wife at home waiting for her husband to bring another man back to their bed? He started to feel anxious and slightly angry.

"Well, I suppose I'd be looking for a hot blond with big tits and a nice pussy," he said pointedly.

Though it was unlike Caleb to use any sort of profanity, he hoped the words might shock Cally and stop him from asking further questions. Instead Cally began chuckling, softly at first and then more deeply.

"That's what I thought," he said, shaking his head and grinning at Caleb. "I'm afraid you won't find that here."

Caleb felt himself turning red. He felt that he was being mocked.

"What are you talking about?" he said, the anger in his voice clear.

"I'm sorry," Cally said quickly, "I'm not laughing at you. But you've come into the wrong place. This is a gay bar."

Caleb was stunned. It had never occurred to him that such a place would exist on a street where anyone could walk in. Then he began to laugh, too. Suddenly he understood why Cally had made him feel so uncomfortable.

"Oh, Lord," he said, "what have I gotten myself into?"

Cally waved a playfully dismissive hand at him.

"Not to worry. Everyone is welcome here," he said, giving Caleb a wry smile. "I just thought you might like to know."

They continued talking. Cally told Caleb about the gay scene in the Quarter, and suggested sites that he should visit during his stay. Caleb felt more relaxed and even enjoyed the thought that he was sitting in a gay bar sharing a drink with a gay man. It made him feel more worldly. When they finished their drinks he bought another round.

He began to chat more easily, telling Cally that he was a minister and about his wife and three children. He watched Cally carefully, looking for some sign of judgment, and when he didn't see any he relaxed even more. He admitted that he'd never met anyone gay before. Cally shook his head and told him that he undoubtedly had but hadn't known it. For a moment Caleb became lost in his thoughts, wondering who back home might be gay.

Eventually he told Cally that he was hoping that he might find some company later that night. Again he saw no judgment in Cally's eyes. It had made him feel good to be so open with his thoughts. He felt that he could trust Cally, and thought that maybe he'd even come back the next night to look for him again.

After he finished his third scotch, Caleb announced it was time to say good night. Cally recommended a few bars down by the river that might be more to his taste and Caleb headed off.

*****

It was almost 2 am when he left the last bar of the night. He was tired and pleasantly drunk. Maybe more than pleasantly drunk, he thought, as he made his way past the small groups who still milled around Jackson Square. Most were younger, dressed in black, their faces powdered stark white. Vampires, he mused, crossing himself sloppily and laughing quietly.

The night hadn't been a total bust, he thought. At least he'd had fun. By the time he'd reached the third bar, Jimmy Buffett's Margaritaville down by the French Market, he'd pretty much given up on finding any company for the night anyway. He just wanted to drink and not be a father or a husband or a minister for one night. Still he wouldn't have turned it down if it fell into his lap.

As he turned left onto St. Philip from Decatur Street he saw the neon lights in the window of MRB. My first gay bar, he thought, and probably my last. As he passed on the opposite side of the street he could see a small crowd inside and wondered if Cally was still there. He smiled as he imagined the laughter he'd get at the Masonic Temple when he told the story. Of course he'd never tell Sarah. She didn't approve of him drinking, except for a glass of wine with dinner on holidays and special occasions.

As he neared the end of the block he noticed a figure standing directly in front of him halfway up the next block. He hesitated for a minute, wondering whether he should cross the street or turn back the way he had come. Then he saw a flare of light as the figure lit a cigarette. It was a woman.

She was dressed in a long red dress and white gloves that reached to her elbows. For a second he wondered if he was imagining it, but as he moved a few steps closer he could see her more clearly. She looked as though she had been at an opera. The distant lights of Bourbon street created a halo in her pale blond hair. There was something familiar about her. Suddenly he thought of the woman in Nashville. He smiled and began walking toward her more quickly.

Chapter 12

Michel stared out the window of the squad room, watching the Quarter come to life in the hazy late morning sun. He'd been sitting there silently for almost an hour. Reviewing case files at her desk, Sassy occasionally looked up to see if he'd moved. After five years she'd learned to read the almost imperceptible signs from her partner. She knew that he was sifting the evidence they'd collected the last two weeks since the killing of Caleb Reynolds, searching for a way to connect it to the killing of Kenneth Brennan. She knew that any slight change in his position could indicate that he'd found some hidden thread that wove the strands of the two investigations together. While they were equally matched intellectually, Sassy had always felt that Michel had a greater instinct for seeing the ways in which seemingly unrelated pieces fit together. Though sometimes farfetched, his ideas had often proven to be correct. So far he hadn't moved.

The two murders were officially being treated as unrelated by the department, though Michel and Sassy had been assigned to both as a precaution. The obvious similarities in the cases— that both victims had been members of the clergy and had been killed with similar knives—seemed abrogated by the circumstances of Caleb Reynolds' murder.

There was no evidence of any sexual relations between Reynolds and his killer. He'd been found fully clothed on the bathroom floor of his room, and examination of his body had found no evidence of anal penetration or recent ejaculation.

There were no traces of foreign saliva on him. Numerous stab wounds to his hands and arms indicated that he had tried to protect himself, and his blood on the back of the bathroom door and door knob suggested he'd tried to lock himself in the room, presumably to escape from the killer.

There was also no evidence to suggest that Reynolds had ever participated in any homosexual activity. Topeka and Kansas State Police had conducted interviews with his family, friends and neighbors, as well as the staff at the two gay bars within a 30-mile radius of his house. Both his home and office computers had been examined to determine if he had visited any gay websites. Nothing had turned up.

An interview with the night clerk at the Royal Inn had been equally unenlightening. She'd been immersed in reading for a summer course she was taking at Tulane and didn't have a clear recollection of seeing Reynolds return to his room. She remembered seeing a man and woman enter the side door of the lobby at approximately 2 am, but couldn't remember what either had looked like. She'd looked up only long enough to determine that the couple didn't seem obviously threatening. She remembered several other people coming into the lobby over the next few hours, but didn't recall seeing anyone leave.

Michel and Sassy were at a standstill on both cases. Speck Bouchard's alibi for the first murder had checked out and he'd been released by the DA on the drug charges. A discreet canvas of the gay bars in the Quarter had revealed that in addition to MRB, Brennan had been seen at Lafitte's and Good Friends the night he was killed, but no one remembered seeing him talking with anyone. Reynolds had receipts in his pocket indicating that he'd been at Margaritaville and had taken sixty dollars out at an ATM at a small bar on Decatur a little after 1 am. There was no forensic evidence linking the two crimes.

As he watched a young couple walking down the street toward Jackson Square, Michel took a deep breath and tried to clear his mind. He knew he needed to step back from the details of the cases and allow the bigger picture to take shape. It was at those moments when he could view things at the greatest distance that the connections became obvious.

He began to think of Joel. He hadn't seen him since the morning he'd dropped him outside his apartment. He'd stopped by the Bourbon Pub and passed the apartment of Gov. Nicholls a few times hoping to run into him. He wondered if Joel was still in the city and if he was okay. It still hurt him to think about that morning, but the pain was getting less acute. Still, he wanted to see Joel again, talk to him. Even if it went no further, he wanted to try to make things right between them.

He stretched and turned on his chair to face Sassy. She was looking at him expectantly. He shrugged and gave her a small apologetic smile.

"What do you say we grab an early lunch?" he asked sheepishly.

Chapter 13

Joel was floating in the space between dreams and waking. He could hear voices, but they kept changing: first the voices of friends from high school, then Lady Chanel and Zelda, then the cooks and busboys he worked with at Peristyle. Finally, with an effort, he opened his eyes. He felt like hell. The walls of the room seemed to be spinning slowly around him. He focused his eyes on the ceiling and spread his arms out to his sides. It seemed to get a little better. I've got to stop drinking, he thought.

Since he'd moved into Zelda's house and started working as a dishwasher at the restaurant two weeks ago, he'd found himself waking up this way more often than not. Every night after the restaurant closed, the kitchen and wait staffs congregated at the bar while the waiters and waitresses counted their tips. After a drink or two they'd move on to another bar and continue drinking for a few hours before heading home. Joel had never known about the secret social rituals of restaurant workers before.

He had been consciously trying to make a good impression on his new co-workers. He hadn't wanted to appear antisocial or unfriendly, but at the same time he hadn't wanted to appear to be a drunk. He'd decided that the best approach was to have a drink at the restaurant and then one more at the next bar before he headed home.

The problem he'd run into came after he left the others. Although he hadn't gone to the Bourbon Pub or any of the other gay bars in the Quarter since his first night, there was always a party at the house when he got home. Like him, all of the boys who lived there worked at night, returning after midnight and sleeping late each morning. Zelda slept in a room on the fourth floor, and after she'd gone to bed the boys would gather in the living room to drink and get high until 4 or 5 in the morning. Joel had fallen right into the habit with them.

The four other boarders at the house were all around Joel's age. Raphael, a tall dark Brazilian, was the oldest at twenty five. The youngest, Peter, was nineteen. Hunter and Jared, blond twins from Idaho, had just turned twenty two. Joel had been amazed at how beautiful they all were when he'd first met them.

The other boys had immediately welcomed Joel into the house and had seemed to make it a point to invite him when they went to lunch or were having parties. Still he felt as though he were an outsider to the group. There seemed to be a bond between them that excluded him. Though Raphael was straight, there was a casual level of physical affection between all four boys that sometimes made Joel wonder whether they were all sleeping together. More than that, though, there was an emotional intimacy they seemed to share. Although he had resolved not to sleep with any them in order to avoid tension in the house, Joel longed to share in their connection.

After five minutes of staring at the ceiling, Joel sat up and pushed himself to the edge of the bed, resting his feet on the floor while he gained his equilibrium. Finally he stood and made his way to the bathroom he shared with the twins on the second floor. Raphael and Peter had bedrooms on the third floor.

As he walked into the bathroom and shut the door, the shower curtain opened and Hunter stepped out. He smiled at Joel and said good morning as he reached for a nearby towel.

"I'm sorry," Joel said, flustered. "I didn't know you were in here. I have to take a piss."

"That's okay," Hunter said casually. "Help yourself."

Joel turned toward the toilet and pulled open the front of his boxers, trying to concentrate as he stared down at the toilet. He could sense Hunter directly behind him, slowly rubbing the towel over his body. Although his bladder was painfully full, Joel could feel himself growing hard. Suddenly he felt Hunter pressing up against his right side.

"Need any help with that?" Hunter asked close to Joel's ear as he leaned forward and gazed down the front of Joel's body.

Joel couldn't speak. He felt his pulse quicken as Hunter pushed harder against him, grinding his crotch against Joel's hip. Joel could feel Hunter's breath against the side of his face and could see his smooth body out of the corner of his eye. Finally he took a sharp breath and turned his head to look at Hunter. The blond's face was only inches from his own. His lips were slightly parted and he stared intently into Joel's eyes. Then he smiled and leaned in, giving Joel a quick kiss. The tension Joel was feeling was suddenly gone and Hunter stepped back, grinning broadly.

"Be careful you don't hurt anyone with that," Hunter said as he gave Joel a light swat on the ass and left the room.

After showering and dressing, Joel walked down to the kitchen where the boys were making breakfast. As he entered the room all four turned to look at him. Joel hesitated in the doorway, unsure why they were staring at him.

"So Hunter says you're hung," Peter said suddenly and they all began laughing.

"Fuck you guys," Joel said, beginning to blush but smiling back at them.

"I don't think we could handle that," Raphael replied playfully. "Well maybe Peter could."

Peter threw a piece of bread at Raphael, hitting him in the back of the head. Raphael turned and gave him a mock glare.

"You know you could make a lot of money with that thing," Hunter said, taking a bite of toast and winking at him. "Lots more than dishwashing."

Joel hesitated, bothered by the way Hunter had mentioned his job.

"Yeah?" he replied, trying to play along. "Do they pay by the inch?"

"No, by the hour. But the bigger you are the more you can get per hour," Jared replied. "If Peter wasn't a big bottom he'd be getting spare change, but Raphael, they'd have to back the Brinks truck up to his door."

Raphael smiled and Peter gave Jared the finger, making a sour face. Though their tone was still playful, Joel sensed that they weren't entirely kidding. He looked at Hunter who met his gaze steadily.

"I think I'll stick with dishwashing for now," he said after a moment, trying to keep his tone light.

He walked to a cabinet and grabbed a cup.

"Well, let us know if you change your mind," Jared said, leering comically.

Talk returned to its usual topics of hot guys, celebrity gossip and clothes while they ate. After cleaning the kitchen, Raphael, Peter and the twins left for Canal Place to do some shopping while Joel went back to his room.

*****

Unlike what he'd expected, Joel had rarely seen Miss Zelda since moving into her house. She seemed to be on the opposite schedule from the rest of them, going to bed before they got home at night and leaving before they woke up in the morning. He didn't know what she did all day. Sometimes they crossed paths in the late afternoon before Joel left for work. Joel noticed that while Zelda was always warm to him, with the other boys she seemed more reserved. She never asked them how they were doing at work or inquired about their personal lives. Still, he sometimes heard voices coming from Zelda's room at the top of the stairs and assumed she was talking with one of the others.

He'd never been in her room. The door was always closed and he often wondered whether she was actually at home.

He'd seen Lady Chanel only twice. Once she'd stopped by the house to visit Zelda, but Joel had been on his way to work and couldn't spend any time with her. On the other occasion she'd invited him over for the afternoon. They'd spent a few hours in her garden, Joel pulling weeds while she cut flowers. She'd asked him about work and how he liked living at Zelda's, and whether he was making friends. She seemed disappointed that he hadn't spoken with Chance but said she was sure it would happen with time, and she'd encouraged him to make friends outside of the house. He'd enjoyed the afternoon and had vowed to see Chanel more often. But that was a week ago.

Joel thought about the conversation at breakfast. Had they really been serious? He had never asked what they did for work, but they were always stylishly dressed when they got home at night and seemed to have plenty of cash. He had assumed that they worked at nice hotels or restaurants in the Quarter, but now he wasn't so sure.

For some reason the thought that they might be hustlers intrigued him. Maybe it was because he hadn't known them for years, or maybe it was because they weren't transvestites, but he didn't feel the same way about them that he had about Chance. He was curious and decided that he'd ask them when he felt the time was right.

He looked at his watch. It was 2 pm. He had three hours before he had to go to work. He opened the drawer of the nightstand next to his bed and took out a small glass pipe Hunter had given him. Time to get stoned and take a nap, he thought, as he packed the bowl.

Chapter 14

Michel was looking forward to a quiet evening as he drove home. The tedium of the day had exhausted him. Like most of the detectives he knew, he'd become something of an adrenaline junkie. During an active investigation he could go for days without sleep. The rest of the time he felt as though he were hibernating. He felt lethargic, and tired quickly. We better get a break soon or I'm going to be in a coma, he thought. Still, he felt better than he had a few weeks ago. He felt more focused and had stopped his visits to Lafitte's except for an occasional drink after work. The sense of possibilities that he'd felt after his night with Joel had stayed with him, though he had yet to figure out exactly what he wanted or how to go about making it happen.

The vibration of his cell phone broke his reverie.

"Doucette," he answered.

"Meet me at the LaMothe House," Sassy's voice replied.

"Sassy, I told you I'm not that kind of girl."

"Very funny, Mr. Smart Ass," Sassy replied. "Looks like we have another body."

"I'm almost there," Michel said quickly, then hung up.

As he turned left onto Esplanade from Decatur, Michel could already see flashing blue lights a few blocks in the distance.

The LaMothe House had been built as a family estate by a sugar plantation owner in 1839. The pink stucco facade of the building had been augmented by four white Corinthian columns in 1860, giving it a somewhat incongruous though distinctive look. No longer one of the crown jewels of Esplanade, the building—which had been converted to a guest house in the 1980s—still possessed a tired elegance.

Sassy and Al Ribodeau were waiting for him on the curb as he pulled up in front of the building.

"What do we have?" he asked.

"Black male, 44 years old. Name of Darnell Coolidge. This one's local. Lives in Bywater," Ribodeau said. "Based on the pictures in his wallet it looks like he is or was married. Has a couple of kids. The desk clerk found him. Tied to the bed, stabbed and slit like Brennan. I'd guess he's been dead about twenty hours."

"And they just found him?" Michel asked.

"He had a 'Do Not Disturb' sign on the door," Ribodeau replied, "but the clerk got a call from the people who just checked into the room next door complaining that something smelled funky, so he started sniffing around, so to speak, and found the body."

Michel nodded and looked at Sassy.

"You been in yet?"

"No, just got here myself."

"Shall we?" he asked, gesturing for her to go first.

As they entered the building Michel knew immediately they were unlikely to get any information from the clerk on duty the night before. A narrow hallway lead to an alcove that opened onto a large courtyard. Most of the guest rooms were in two wings that extended back from the main building, forming a u-shape around the courtyard. The rooms were directly accessible only from the courtyard. There was no front desk. Darnell Coolidge's room was at the end of the right wing on the first floor.

Coolidge's naked body was bound by the hands and ankles to the four-poster bed that dominated the room. A small pool of blood had dried in the curve of his lower back. Michel noted that he was well muscled. As with Brennan, most of the blood was concentrated on the pillows and upper half of the bed. Michel could clearly see the wound in Coolidge's throat: a deep, pink-edged gash that exposed two cartilage rings on his larynx.

Michel looked at Ribodeau curiously.

"Lecher's not here yet?"

"We just got the call fifteen minutes ago," Ribodeau replied. "He's on his way."

"All right. Well let's not fuck up his crime scene. Let's wait outside."

They walked back into the courtyard. The area was paved with large flagstones and surrounded by dense flowering bushes. Several sets of wrought iron tables and chairs were arranged around a rectangular stone water garden whose jagged contours had been softened by a thick blanket of moss. A well-patinated brass frog perched at the far end, spitting a steady stream of brownish water that struck the surface below with a gentle burble. Beyond the wings of the building the space opened up into a wide concrete patio with a pool in the center. Michel headed toward it.

The patio was surrounded by a seven-foot pink stucco wall with more flowering bushes and plants along the left and right sides. The far wall was obscured by a small forest of low palms and hibiscus. Lounge chairs and cocktail tables were arranged neatly around the pool. Looking to his right, Michel saw a small stone patio with tables and chairs outside the side French doors of Coolidge's room.

"Make sure you check to see if those are locked," he said to Ribodeau.

Sassy had walked to the far end of the pool and stood looking into the dense vegetation.

"Check this out," she called, motioning for them to join her.

"That look like a table to you?" she asked, pointing to something shrouded by the foliage along the back wall.

"Could be," Michel said, getting onto his hands and knees and peering under the tangle of branches.

He could see what looked like two wrought iron table legs.

"Looks like it. Let's send a few guys in there. See if they can lift any footprints or find any forensic evidence. Check with the management and see if they put it there for any reason," he said to Ribodeau.

He straightened up and dusted off his hands, scanning the arrangement of tables and chairs around the pool. The two chairs closest to them were missing a table between them. As Ribodeau went to organize his team, Michel and Sassy returned to Coolidge's room. When they entered, Stan Lecher was already well into his examination of the body.

"You didn't fuck up my crime scene did you?" he asked without looking up.

Michel and Sassy exchanged amused looks. Lecher seemed to see and hear everything.

"Good to see you, too, Stan," Sassy replied.

Lecher looked up and gave her a small smile.

"Find anything out back?" he asked, returning to his examination.

"Looks like a table by the back wall. The killer might have gone over the top," Michel replied.

"Makes sense. Those were unlocked," Lecher said, indicating the French doors with a nod of his head. "Probably didn't want to chance going out the front, even without a desk clerk. From the blood on the wall over there, I'd say Mr. Coolidge gushed. No way the perp walked out without some blood on him."

Again Michel was amazed by how much Lecher noticed and how quickly he processed information.

He turned and saw specks of dried blood on the baseboard of the wall to their right, then looked down at the dark red oriental rug covering the floor. There seemed to be darker spots on it, leading from the bed to the blood on the wall.

"So he cut the artery on the right this time?" he asked.

Lecher looked at him and Michel thought he detected a hint of surprise in the look.

"Yeah, cut them both." Lecher said, pointing at Coolidge's throat, "but I don't think it was on purpose. There's a clean cut from the left to the center of the throat, then it gets kind of ragged from there to the right. I'd guess our friend here was struggling hard. May have turned his head to the left, pulling the blade to the other artery. When he turned back we would have gotten that."

He indicated the trail of blood to the wall.

"Mr. Coolidge put up quite a fight," he continued, pointing at the blood stained towels tied to the body's wrists. "The ligatures have cut right into his skin."

"Anal penetration?" Sassy asked.

"Yup," Lecher replied. "I'm going to go out on a limb here and say this was done by the same guy who killed Father Brennan."

Michel and Sassy smiled at his small joke.

"One more thing," Lecher said.

He handed Michel a clear plastic bag.

"What is it?" Michel asked, holding the bag toward the fading sunlight coming through the open door.

"Hair. Long and blond. Looks synthetic."

Michel and Sassy exchanged confused looks.

"You saying the killer was wearing a wig?" she asked.

"Someone in the room was," Lecher replied. "It was stuck in the blood on his back so it's unlikely that it came from anyone he had contact with before he got here. I'd say either it's from the killer or Mr. Coolidge was one big, ugly drag queen."

Chapter 15

At 5 am Michel finally got out of bed and went to the kitchen to make coffee. His body was exhausted but his mind was alert and excited. He'd already been awake for four hours, since Stan Lecher had called to tell him they'd matched the hair found in Darnell Coolidge's room to one recovered at the first crime scene. Michel was sure that he'd detected embarrassment in Lecher's voice as Lecher explained that his team had assumed the first hair had belonged to a previous guest at the Creole House and hadn't even realized it was synthetic until they'd checked it against the second hair. I guess he's human after all, Michel had thought, suppressing the desire to exploit Lecher's discomfort by asking more questions. Both hairs had come from a platinum blond nylon wig.

Since then Michel had lain awake, sorting the pieces in his mind, searching for that elusive perspective that would allow him to see how the three murders fit together. He'd been sure that the first two killings were related and had believed that the motive for both was tied to the victims' positions in the clergy. But Darnell Coolidge had thrown an unexpected twist into his thinking.

Coolidge had no obvious religious affiliations. He was an insurance adjustor. He'd moved to an address in Bywater, a few miles outside the Quarter, eight months earlier. He was married and had two daughters. So far there'd been no answer at the house. Michel didn't know if Coolidge and his wife were separated.

Michel was certain that the link between the murders would eventually reveal itself, but there was still no physical evidence tying the second killing to the others. He'd decided to go back to Caleb Reynolds' room at the Royal Inn. Although he knew Lecher's office was extremely thorough, he hoped he might be able to find something they'd missed now that he knew to look for wig hair.

He showered and dressed while the coffee brewed, then forced himself to eat breakfast and read the paper, impatiently biding his time. He didn't relish the idea of dealing with a tired, paranoid night clerk at the end of a shift who was afraid of losing his or her job for doing the wrong thing. At ten of seven he left the house and made the short drive to Royal Street, arriving just as the manager appeared for work.

The room was still sealed as part of the investigation. The inn's owners had decided to close off the entire first floor, posting a sign reading "Undergoing Renovations. Please enter courtyard from second floor." in the doorway leading from the lobby. Reservations during the summer months were low anyway and they wanted to avoid the concerns that the yellow police tape across Caleb Reynolds' door would certainly raise among the guests.

Michel let himself into the room and turned on the lights. The heavy curtains were drawn. He pulled on a pair of white latex gloves and began slowly examining the bed, working his way across the bloodstained mattress in 1-foot-square sections. The bedding and pillows had been taken to the coroner's lab two weeks before. Then he performed the same methodical search of the tops of the night stand and two dressers. He was about to begin searching the floor when he heard muffled high-pitched laughter coming from behind the curtain that ran along one wall of the room. He pulled the curtain open.

Outside in an enclosed courtyard he could see two young children wearing bright yellow water wings splashing around in a pool. A woman lay on a nearby chaise lounge chair reading a book. He pulled on the handle of the sliding door and it opened. I wonder if anyone checked to see if that was locked, he thought, as he stepped outside.

Although it wasn't yet 8 am, the temperature was already well into the 80s. He took off his jacket and hung it on the back of a chair as he made his way by the pool toward the wall that ran across the back of the courtyard. The woman looked up at him for a moment then went back to her reading, apparently deciding that a man with a gun holstered around his shoulder represented no imminent threat to her children.

At the far end of the patio that ringed the pool was a dense shade garden about fifteen feet deep, running to the base of the wall. A thick, twisted magnolia tree rose in the center, its heavy branches extending over the wall. Michel stopped and studied the ground around the tree. A small area of mulch on the far side looked as though it had recently been disturbed. He walked to the area and extended his arms up. The nearest branch was just beyond his reach.

He walked back to the pool and grabbed a sturdy-looking wrought iron chair. The woman looked up again and eyed him cautiously. He smiled reflexively at her as he carried the chair back under the tree. The roots of the tree gnarled the ground for several feet in all directions around the trunk. Digging his foot into the thick mulch, he began searching for level ground in the disturbed area.

He heard the woman calling her children and looked up to see her pulling them out the pool as they whined in protest. As she dried them and dragged them back toward their room she continued to watch Michel. With my natural gift for putting people at ease I really should have gone into the hospitality industry, he thought wryly.

He finally found a level spot and positioned the chair, pushing it deep into the mulch. I'm going to catch holy hell for this, he thought, as he reached up and grabbed the branch directly above him. He pulled himself up, swinging his legs forward and wrapping them around the branch. He reached up with one hand and grabbed another branch, finally pulling himself up into a sitting position on the first branch.

He studied the branches around him. They were old and scarred and the bark was brittle. He looked at the sections where he'd gripped the two branches and could see that the outer bark had pulled away in places, exposing the bare wood beneath.

Great, he thought, now I've fucked up the crime scene. He knew he should climb down and call in a forensics team, but he wanted to satisfy his own curiosity first. He looked at the branches around him. A patch of bark about six inches long had been scraped away on the large branch to his left that reached over the wall. He looked a few feet farther up the branch and saw another scraped patch. He looked at the branch above and saw more exposed areas of wood, closer together.

You fucker, he thought, you walked right over that wall, didn't you? He could picture the killer, holding the upper branch as he inched his feet along the lower one. But you had to get down on the other side somehow, he thought.

He looked at the top of the wall. Like many older walls in the Quarter, the top had been imbedded with colorful shards of broken glass, an archaic method of discouraging intruders. Twisted into the glass directly below the branch he saw what he was looking for: a tangle of blond hair.

"Detective Doucette?"

Startled, Michel looked down to see the hotel manager standing below him a few feet away.

"Oh, hey," he said sheepishly.

"One of the guests said there was a man out here with a gun," the manager said.

"Yeah, that would be me. Sorry about that. I was going to tell you about her. She seemed a little concerned."

"To say the least," the manager replied somewhat sharply.

"Why don't you bill her room for the night to the

department? Tell her I was trying to rescue a lost cat or something."

"I'll do that," the manager replied. "Is there anything I can help you with?"

"Yeah, did you find a chair out here before?" Michel asked, pointing down at the wrought iron chair.

"I'm not sure. I'll check with the maintenance crew."

"Great," Michel replied. "Oh, and one other thing. Can you get me a ladder so I can get down?"

*****

After getting Michel down, the hotel manager called the head of maintenance at home and found that he had moved a chair from under the tree a few days after Caleb Reynolds' murder. The forensics team arrived ten minutes later. Michel met them on St. Philip, outside the alley that ran behind the wall of the Royal Inn. He was thankful that Lecher wasn't with them. He wanted to delay the reprimand he knew would be coming for potentially contaminating the crime scene.

He stood on the sidewalk smoking while the forensics team combed the area behind him. Something was beginning to bother him about the scenario. He saw Sassy's car turn onto St. Philip and walked to the edge of the curb to meet her.

"Been doing a little climbing this morning, partner?" she asked, looking at the dirt and flakes of bark on Michel's pants and shirt.

"Yeah, you know how us kids love trees," he replied, giving her a goofy grin.

They walked to the head of the alley.

"So the perp went over the wall?" Sassy asked.

"I think so. The branches above it are scraped up and it looks like some hair stuck in the glass up there," Michel replied, then gave her a troubled look.

"But you're not sure?" she asked with surprise.

"It's not that," he replied, pointing into the alley. "How far would you say the drop is from the branch to the ground?"

"About twelve feet," Sassy replied.

"Right. You'd probably bust an ankle doing that."

"Yeah, but if the guy's trying to get away he's going to chance it."

"Maybe," Michel replied.

Sassy tried to figure out where Michel was headed.

"So what are you saying?" she asked finally.

"What if he knew he was going out that way? There are plenty of old barrels and crates in the alley that he could have stacked up to climb onto."

"Then the victim wasn't random," Sassy said, picking up on his thinking.

"Exactly," Michel said. "If he made his escape route in advance, the only way it's random is if he climbed in the same way and just killed the first person he saw. That doesn't make sense with this guy. He wants intimate interaction with his victims."

"So he picked Reynolds and set this whole thing up," Sassy said, finishing Michel's thought process.

"Yeah, I think so."

"Which means he's very deliberate and premeditated," Sassy continued. "We know he probably went over the wall at Lamothe House. What about Creole House? Is there a safe way out?"

"There is if he knew Bouchard wasn't going to be there."

Sassy considered the possibility.

"I know this is going to sound crazy," she said, "and it goes against anything I've ever learned about serial killers, but is it possible he's picking his victims based on where they're staying rather than who they are? That he's staking out places that he knows he can get out of easily?"

"I don't know, Sas," Michel replied, shaking his head. "I just can't figure out what links the three victims together. One and two were members of the clergy; two and three were married; one and three had sex with the killer. We can't even find one thing that applies to all of them."

"Except that they're dead," Sassy replied.

Michel nodded and lit another cigarette.

Chapter 16

Michel and Sassy sat in a cafe on Jackson Square. They'd spent the morning shuffling papers while waiting for the lab results on the hair found at the Royal Inn. When they still hadn't heard anything by noon, Sassy had suggested they take a walk and get some lunch. She could tell that Michel's mind was elsewhere.

"So what's going on in there?" she asked after a few minutes of silence.

"Nothing," he replied without looking at her.

"Look, if you want me to play the game, I'll play the game. Or we can just cut to the chase. You've obviously got something on your mind. What is it?"

Michel studied her for a moment before speaking.

"I know I'm stating the obvious here, but it looks like our killer's a transvestite, right?" he asked.

"Yeah," Sassy replied, shrugging. "Why else would he be wearing a wig? And it would explain why Reynolds took him back to his room. He probably thought it was a real woman."

"And there's only so many places you're going to find a transvestite around here," Michel continued. "Unless they called a personal ad, they had to meet the guy somewhere. "

"You think Reynolds was in a gay bar?" Sassy asked.

"He was staying within three blocks of four of them. Maybe it was an accident," Michel replied with a shrug.

"Okay, so let's assume the killer's picking his victims in one or more gay bars. I'm still not getting what's bothering you."

"We're not getting any new leads. The mayor's got us hamstrung because he won't let us release the victims' names and pictures to the papers," Michel said.

The frustration in his voice was clear.

"Hey, dead tourists are bad for business," Sassy replied sarcastically.

Michel gave her a small smile.

"So then we're going to have to send someone into the bars," he said. "It's the only way we're going to find out where they were and who they were with."

Sassy nodded at him.

"But if we send in uniforms or a stranger starts hanging out for more than a few days it's going to attract attention," Michel continued. "This is a small town and people will notice. The killer's going to know something's up and he's going to disappear."

"So what do you suggest?"

"I'm not a stranger," Michel said flatly.

Sassy studied him for a moment.

"True," she said slowly, "but the captain's going to want to know who we're sending in and why. This is too big a case for us to just say we've got it covered. He's going to want to know every detail."

"I know," Michel said.

"And you're willing to do that?" Sassy asked.

"Yeah," Michel replied, nodding slightly.

Sassy gave him a hard look.

"Look, Michel, you and I know that your sexuality has nothing to do with your ability as a cop, and you're a damn good cop. But the boys upstairs aren't going to see it that way. They're not comfortable with anyone who's not just like them. You could severely fuck up your career by coming out."

"I understand that, Sas," Michel replied, "but I guess it's something I feel I need to do to be happy with myself."

Sassy gave him a mock scowl.

104

"Oh Lord, don't go getting all touchy-feely on me here. You know I hate the touchy-feely."

Michel smiled appreciatively at her.

"I know that since my mother died I've been a little nuts...at least until this whole thing started," he said, his tone more serious now. "But it wasn't for the reasons you probably think. It wasn't grief. I loved my mother, and I miss her every day, but it was more like I was lost."

"Lost how?"

Michel closed his eyes and took a deep breath. He opened his eyes and gave her a rueful smile.

"Sorry, but this is going to get real touchy-feely now."

Sassy gave him a nod of reluctant acceptance and gestured for him to continue.

"My whole life I've felt like I had to be perfect. The perfect little boy. The perfect student. The perfect cop. But mostly the perfect son. I was afraid to do anything that might disappoint my mother."

"Everyone lives with that fear," Sassy said carefully.

"I know, but it's different when you know that the disappointment is going to be in who you are rather than what you do. It would be like if your parents were disappointed in you for being black."

Sassy gave a sharp laugh.

"I think my daddy would have been real disappointed if I were anything else. He would have gone after that milk man with a shotgun."

Michel rolled his eyes at her.

"I'm sorry," she said, frowning comically. "I told you I'm not good at this stuff. Just trying to keep the mood light. Go on. I'll shut up."

"Thank you," Michel replied sarcastically. "But when my mother died that pressure to be perfect went away. On some level it freed me."

"I guess we're all freed in some way when our parents die,"

Sassy said thoughtfully, "whether it's from responsibility for caring for them as they get older or from pretending we're something that we're not."

"Yeah," Michel said, nodding, "but I didn't know how to handle it. I'd identified myself with that image I'd presented for her sake for so long that I was kind of paralyzed. It's like I was stuck between my past and future."

"That all makes sense," Sassy said. "And now?"

"And now I feel like it's my choice who I am and what I do. I can go into the bars without having to lie and say I was on an investigation or worrying that one of my mother's friends is going to see me on the balcony of the Bourbon Pub. And I can fall in love and share my life with someone."

"Joel," Sassy said, nodding in comprehension.

"Yeah," Michel said, nodding back at her. "That's why what happened bothered me so much. For the first time I could see the choices I had. I was actually free to have a relationship, free to have some sort of life outside the job. Regardless of whether Joel and I would have gone anywhere, he helped me see the possibilities to change my life."

"But what about the job?" Sassy asked.

"The job is always going to be part of who I am. You're right, I'm a damn good cop and that's something I want to be. But I don't want it be my whole life. I want to be that cop who lives with his boyfriend and their little dog in the cute house with the white picket fence, who reads chick lit novels and makes a mean étouffée and always catches the bad guy."

"Who the fuck *are* you?" Sassy said, shaking her head and laughing. "You don't even have a white picket fence."

"Yet!" Michel said, beginning to laugh with her. "The fence comes with the boyfriend and the dog. It's a package deal. I saw an ad in 'Out' magazine."

They both began laughing hard, barely able to breathe as their eyes filled with tears. The diners around them began looking at them and laughing in response.

After a minute Michel calmed himself down, suppressing the giggles that threatened to erupt again. He wiped his eyes with his napkin.

"Seriously, Sassy," he said, provoking another burst of laughter from his partner.

He gave her a look of mock annoyance and finally she was able to bring herself under control.

"I'm sorry," she said, patting the back of his right hand as she dried her eyes.

"Seriously, I think it's important to the case, and it's important to me, so I'm willing to live with the consequences.

"Hey, whatever you need to do," Sassy said, "You know I've got your back."

*****

After lunch they walked back to the station. Michel felt good, energized, as though he'd emerged from under a heavy weight. Although he was still apprehensive about the conversation he faced with the captain, he felt good about the decision.

The lab report from the Royal Inn was waiting for them, along with the coroner's report on Darnell Coolidge and a note from the captain asking to see them immediately.

Capt. Carl DeRoche had been Chief of Detectives for the 8th district for fifteen years, though he was only in his mid-50s. He had been the youngest commander appointed in the history of the department and had a reputation as a thorough and tenacious investigator and a fair, though demanding, boss.

"Good a time as any," Michel said, giving Sassy a mock grimace as he knocked on the door to DeRoche's office.

DeRoche looked up from his desk and waved them in. As Michel closed the door behind them DeRoche gave him a curious look.

"So what's going on?" DeRoche asked.

"We just got the lab report from this morning and the coroner's report on Coolidge," Sassy said, opening the folder for the lab report as she handed the other to Michel.

She scanned the report quickly.

"It's a match on the hair," she said quickly.

"Nice work, Michel," DeRoche said. "But next time you might want to call the forensics guys before you go climbing any trees."

Michel accepted the mild rebuke with a nod.

"Anything else, Sassy?"

"They took some castings from the ground in the alley. Looks like there had been a barrel under the branch at some point. There were a few in the alley that they dusted for prints but didn't come up with anything. They also pulled shoe prints from a pair of high heels. Big ones and lots of them. Looks like the killer spent some time in the alley before or after."

"So now we've got a wig and high heels," DeRoche said frowning. "That pretty much seals the deal that the guy's a cross-dresser."

"That's our assumption," Sassy replied.

DeRoche nodded.

"What about the report on Coolidge?"

Michel opened the folder and read the top page.

"Same as Brennan," he summarized. "Anal penetration. The knife matches."

He turned to the second page. A Polaroid picture had been paperclipped to the page with a handwritten note from Lecher across the bottom: "Did you notice the matches on the night stand?" Michel looked at the photo. It was a pack of matches from MRB. Good old Lecher, he thought with a smile.

"What is it?" Sassy asked.

"Coolidge was at MRB," he said, handing her the Polaroid.

"So now we know where to start looking," she said.

"You want to put an undercover in there?" DeRoche asked.

"Until we figure out how he's picking his victims it doesn't make sense to put in a decoy to try to draw him out," Michel said. "We want to put in someone to stake out the place and ask a few discreet questions."

He could hear the blood pounding in his ears.

"But it's got to be someone familiar who won't attract a lot of attention."

"Okay. Who?" DeRoche asked.

Time seemed to slow down. Michel could feel his mouth forming the word but minutes seemed to pass before he heard the sound of his voice.

"Me."

DeRoche looked from Michel to Sassy and shrugged.

"Okay, so long as it doesn't interfere with the rest of your investigation," he said.

Michel stifled the urge to laugh. He looked at Sassy who was staring at DeRoche with an expression of confusion. DeRoche looked back at her and turned his palms upward.

"What?" he asked.

"That's all you have to say?" she replied.

"Why?" he asked. "You think I didn't know Michel's gay? Give me some credit. I'm a detective and this is a small city. I know what all my officers are doing in their spare time."

He gave Michel a mischievous smile.

"You should hear the places your partner's been hanging out."

Michel laughed and watched as Sassy's expression changed from surprise to offense to amusement.

"Thanks a lot, Captain," she said, smirking.

"Any time," he said. "Just be careful, Michel. I'm sure some people already know you're a cop. If they see you around too much or asking a lot of questions they're going to figure out you're investigating. That could put you in danger."

Michel nodded and stood.

"Thanks, Captain," he said.

He extended his hand across the desk toward DeRoche.

DeRoche looked at him curiously for a moment, then gripped Michel's hand.

"You're welcome," he said.

Chapter 17

"We located Mrs. Coolidge," Michel said as Sassy walked into the squad room carrying two coffees and a bag of beignets from Cafe du Monde that she'd picked up to get them through the afternoon. "One of the neighbors told a uniform she was in Detroit."

"Did you talk to her?" Sassy asked.

"Yeah. That was a lot of fun. She'd taken the kids to visit family for two weeks."

"So she and her husband weren't separated?"

"No," Michel replied.

"What did you tell her?"

"Just what I had to. I didn't give her the details. She'll find out soon enough and I figured it was hard enough on her already."

"I'll bet," Sassy said, rubbing her eyes. "Sometimes this job really sucks."

"Yeah," Michel replied. "Something else. The manager at the Lamothe called and said Coolidge stayed there twice before. Once in early November for a week and again in March for two nights."

"But he didn't move to Bywater until December."

"I figure the first time he was looking at houses," Michel said.

"And the second time?"

"I ran a check with the airlines. Mrs. Coolidge and the kids were in Detroit the week of March 7th. Coolidge rented the room on the 10th and 11th."

"What makes a man do that?" Sassy asked, shaking her head sadly.

"I don't know, Sas," Michel replied. "I don't doubt he loved his wife and kids, but maybe it wasn't enough. Maybe he needed something else, too."

"Needed or wanted?" Sassy asked, fixing Michel with a hard stare. "Everybody wants something else, but we make choices and commitments. He could have brought AIDS or syphilis or God-knows-what into that house. He made choices that put his family at risk and those choices got him killed. I feel sorry for his wife and family, but maybe they're better off without him," she finished harshly.

Michel knew that Sassy had been married once and that the marriage had ended badly, though she'd never told him the details. He wondered now if Sassy was speaking for herself or Mrs. Coolidge. He decided to let the subject drop.

"I'm going to go to MRB tonight," he said after a minute.

He could see Sassy working hard to push her anger back into the little compartment where she kept it locked away.

"I'm sorry," she said, looking up at him with a remorseful smile.

"Don't sweat it," he replied.

*****

Michel arrived at MRB at 8 pm. The place was nearly empty. Two small groups of men stood chatting near the entrance to the patio while two other men sat at the far end of the bar. Michel hadn't been in MRB in over a year and noted how little the place had changed during that time. Tattered posters for long-past events were still taped to the walls by the entrance.

He walked up to the bar. A tall red-headed bartender was facing the other way, taking inventory of the bottles that lined the shelves along the wall. Michel cleared his throat and the man turned around. It was Kenny Gaughin, a friend of Michel's from high school. Kenny had moved to New York after graduation and Michel hadn't seen him since.

"Hey, Michel, how's it going?" Kenny asked, a broad smile on his face.

He reached across the bar and shook Michel's hand. Michel noticed that Kenny looked a lot older than his years, with deep creases around his mouth and at the corners of his eyes.

"Hey, Kenny. Doing okay, thanks. How about you? When did you get back to town?"

"About two months ago," Kenny replied. "I decided I'd had enough of the big city and my dad's been having some trouble with his heart so I thought I'd come back and help my folks out. By the way, I was really sorry to hear about your mom."

"Thanks," Michel said softly.

They looked at one another for a moment, each searching for something to say. Living in a small city, Michel had gotten used to these encounters, running into old friends with whom he'd lost touch, but they never seemed to get any less awkward. Sometimes he wished he'd left New Orleans as well.

"So what can I get you?" Kenny asked, breaking the silence.

"Jack on the rocks."

"You got it."

Kenny filled a glass with ice then moved down the bar to get the bottle. Michel was grateful for the momentary reprieve from having to make conversation.

"You still a cop?" Kenny asked as he returned and placed the glass in front of Michel. "I heard you were a detective."

"Where'd you hear that?" Michel asked as he watched Kenny pour the amber liquid.

Kenny shrugged. "Small town."

"I guess so," Michel said, raising the glass in a cheer and downing half of it. "Yeah, I'm still a cop."

"I heard about the murder at the Lamothe the other night," Kenny said, shaking his head. "Too bad. He was a nice guy."

"You knew him?" Michel asked, trying to sound casual.

He wanted to ask how Kenny knew who had been killed but decided it would seem conspicuous.

"Darnell? Yeah. Came in here about once a week. Maybe a little more. Always around 5:30. He'd have one drink and leave."

"Did you see him here the other night?"

"No, I wasn't working. You want me to ask the other guys?" Kenny asked enthusiastically.

"No, that's okay," Michel replied, trying to maintain his casual tone. "You ever see him talking to anyone?"

"Yeah, he knew a lot of the guys."

"But you never saw him with anyone special?"

Michel realized he was beginning to sound too much like a cop. He wanted to get as much information as possible, but he also wanted to be cautious. Although they'd been friends, Michel knew that Kenny liked to traffic in information. In high school it had been his way of making himself feel more important, by sharing the secrets he knew.

"You mean a boyfriend?" Kenny asked.

"Or a trick," Michel replied, deciding to push a little further.

"No. I always had the sense he had to get home. I figured maybe he was on the down low. Maybe had a wife at home."

"Why do you say that?"

"He was real discreet," Kenny replied. "Didn't say too much about what he did or where he lived, and he was always out of here by 6:30 sharp. So are you working the case?"

Michel hesitated.

"No, not really," he lied. "Just thought I'd help out. Ask around the bars. Nothing official."

Kenny nodded and gave Michel a sly smile.

"I get you. I won't mention it to anyone," he said

"Thanks," Michel said.

He wanted to get out of the bar. He knew that he'd pushed

114

too far. He finished his drink and stood up to leave, then reconsidered.

"One other thing, Kenny."

He pulled out the snapshot of Caleb Reynolds that his wife had sent to the department.

"You ever see this guy?"

Kenny studied the photo for a minute.

"Yeah, he was in about 2 weeks ago. I noticed him because it was slow and he was pretty hot. Not in great shape, but just kind of natural, you know what I mean?"

"I know what you mean," Michel replied.

Michel studied Kenny for a moment and decided to change tactics.

"He's the guy who got killed at the Royal Inn," he said matter-of-factly.

"Holy shit," Kenny said, a look of awe on his face.

"Did you see him talking with anyone?" Michel asked, his tone suddenly clipped and serious.

"Yeah, he and Cally seemed to hit it off like a house of fire," Kenny replied slowly, seemingly confused by the sudden shift in Michel's demeanor.

"Who's Cally?"

"Guy who comes in here semi-regular. Maybe a few times a month. Nice guy," Kenny answered quickly.

"Do you know his last name or where he lives?"

Sweat had begun to appear on Kenny's upper lip and his eyes darted nervously around the bar as though he were afraid to be overheard. Michel sensed that Kenny had had some less-than-favorable dealings with the police in New York and decided to exploit it.

"Why? You think he had something to do with killing the guy?" Kenny asked, his voice low and quiet.

Michel fixed Kenny with a hard stare but kept his face impassive. He wanted Kenny to know that it wasn't all right to ask questions.

"No," Michel replied finally. "But he might be able to tell us something. Maybe Reynolds said something to him about where he was going that night."

"No, I don't know anything about the guy except his first name," Kenny said, shaking his head vigorously.

"What does he look like?"

"Tall black guy. Slim. Short white hair."

"How old?"

"I don't know," Kenny replied, his voice breaking slightly. "40? 50? 60? Tough to tell. You know what they say, 'black don't crack'."

Michel didn't smile at the joke.

"Listen, could you do me a favor?" he said, shifting his tone to sound more congenial. "Next time he's in, give me a call."

He slid a business card discreetly across the bar. As Kenny reached for it, Michel clamped his hand over Kenny's.

"And Kenny," he said, his tone suddenly hard-edged again, "this conversation stays between us."

He raised his eyebrows as though awaiting a response to a question.

"You got it, chief," Kenny said, quickly pulling his hand back as Michel released it.

Michel smiled broadly at him.

"Not chief yet," he said smoothly, "but I'm working on it."

He laid a $20 bill on the bar, rapped it twice with his knuckles and left. As soon as he was outside he hit the speed dial on his cell phone. Sassy answered on the first ring.

"What do you want?"

"Boy, that charm school really paid off for you," Michel replied. "Anyway, looks like Coolidge was a regular at MRB. Came in a few times a month. Always for an hour around dinner."

"And his wife thought he was working late."

Michel hoped that Sassy wouldn't become angry again.

"I don't know if he was with anyone the other night yet," he said quickly, "but I'll keep asking around."

"So what aren't you telling me?" Sassy asked.

Michel smiled at Sassy's ability to read him.

"Guess who else was at MRB?"

"Reynolds?" she asked with surprise.

"Yup. And he was with a friend."

Chapter 18

After he finished his call with Sassy, Michel began walking to the Bourbon Pub. It was a little after 9 pm. He didn't expect to find any information there but hoped that Joel might show up. He knew that if Joel was still in the city it would just be a matter of time before they'd run into one another again. He hoped that tonight would be that time.

The side doors of the pub were open and Michel could hear Cher singing from half a block away. He smiled to himself, remembering the vision he'd had of Cher sipping cocktails with the cockroaches at the bar. That, too, is just a matter of time, Miss Cher, he thought as he approached.

The pub was already crowded. Michel surveyed the room and decided that most of the men looked like they'd stopped by for a pre-dinner drink and stayed. He pushed past the small groups who had staked their claims by the doors and walked around to the far side of the bar where the crowd was thinner. He ordered a Jack Daniels and settled into an open space along the wall.

Most of the crowd looked familiar. He felt as though he'd seen them standing in the same places, drinking the same drinks, and having the same conversations each time he'd been there. God don't let me become that predictable, he thought.

Suddenly he was sure he was being watched. He shifted his position and scanned the crowd, searching in ten-foot-wide swaths starting to his right. Several men he knew casually waved to him and he nodded back quickly before continuing his search. Finally his eyes reached a row of stools against the wall to his left and there sat Chance, watching him.

Michel pushed himself off the wall and walked over.

"Mind if I join you?" he asked.

"Suit yourself," Chance replied without emotion.

Michel sat on the stool to Chance's left and lit a cigarette.

"You know, if I'd had a gun I could have shot you six times by the time you finally saw me," Chance said without looking at Michel. "Guess you're not such a hot shit cop."

Michel felt himself blush. He hadn't realized he'd been so obvious.

"Guess my Spidey sense isn't working too well tonight," he joked.

Chance continued staring straight ahead without changing expressions. They fell into silence while they sipped their drinks.

"So how's Joel?" Chance asked after a moment.

"I was kind of hoping you could tell me," Michel replied with surprise.

Chance slowly turned to look at him. Michel could see a mix of anger and hurt in his eyes. For a second he thought he also saw a touch of concern.

"How would I fucking know?" Chance asked, his eyes becoming hard again. "I haven't seen him since you told him I was a hustler."

Michel felt as though he'd had the wind knocked out of him. A sudden rush of panic swept over him and he had to fight the urge to grab Chance and force him to tell him everything he knew about where Joel might have gone. Instead he stared into the middle distance of the room, concentrating on his breathing. I need to salvage this conversation to find out anything, he thought.

He turned back to Chance.

"I'm sorry," he said. "I know it's a lame excuse, but I wasn't trying to hurt you. I just didn't realize what I was doing."

Chance studied him.

"You're right. That is lame," he said.

Michel was silent. He'd been prepared for Chance to accept his apology or tell him to fuck off, but the blunt statement threw him. He didn't know how to respond.

"Relax," Chance said after a moment, swatting Michel on the side of the leg. "I was just fucking with you."

"What?" Michel asked.

"You're so serious. No wonder Joel liked you," Chance replied, rolling his eyes.

"You're not pissed at me?"

"I was, but I'm over it. It was that heartfelt apology," Chance said, smirking. "If I was still pissed at you I would have thrown a drink in your face and caused a big drama."

Michel fought the urge to laugh. He was starting to like Chance.

"So you haven't seen Joel either?" Chance asked seriously.

"No, not since I dropped him off that morning. What happened with you guys?"

Chance sighed dramatically.

"He told me he didn't want to be around me hustling and I threw a hissy and kicked him out. It was a big fucking scene."

"And you have no idea where he went?" Michel asked.

"Uh uh," Chance replied, shaking his head. "But you should ask those two."

He gestured with his head across the room. Michel turned and saw Lady Chanel and Miss Zelda sitting by a window off Bourbon Street.

"You haven't talked to them?" he asked.

"I fucking hate Zelda. I wouldn't talk to that cunt if you paid me. And there's not a lot I won't do if you pay me," Chance replied, giving Michel a playful smile. "I figured Lady Chanel would be all over my shit for it. She really likes Joel."

Michel looked back at Lady Chanel and Miss Zelda. The idea of finally meeting them made him both nervous and excited. He discreetly pulled a card from his wallet and tapped Chance on the leg with it.

"If you hear anything about Joel give me a call?"

"No problem," Chance replied.

*****

Michel walked to the bar and ordered another drink. He thought about buying a drink for Chance, too, but when he looked back Chance was gone. He began navigating through the crowd. He considered going outside and approaching the table from the sidewalk but decided against it. It seemed inappropriate. Although he knew they were men, he felt a natural inclination to treat Lady Chanel and Miss Zelda with a certain amount of deference. He continued to move through the crowd.

"Ladies," he said, bowing his head slightly as he reached their table.

"Detective Doucette," Lady Chanel said, extending her hand.

Michel was momentarily taken aback, surprised that Lady Chanel knew his name. He recovered and took her hand, holding it lightly in his upturned palm. He nodded toward Zelda who nodded back in acknowledgment.

"Detective," she said.

"Please, call me Michel."

"It's a pleasure to meet you, Michel," Lady Chanel said. "I've heard so much about you."

Michel paused, curious what she'd heard and from whom. Something in her tone seemed to imply that it had been someone other than Joel. He suppressed the impulse to ask her.

"And I, you," he said awkwardly instead.

"To what do we owe the pleasure of this visit?" Zelda asked.

Her smile suggested that she viewed his presence as anything but a pleasure. Michel remembered what Chance had said about her and decided that the boy had a gift for character analysis.

"I'm sorry to interrupt you," he said, "but I'm trying to find Joel."

He looked at Lady Chanel but Zelda spoke first.

"We heard he was working at a restaurant somewhere in the Quarter," she said, "but we don't know where. There are so many."

She shrugged her shoulders and smiled weakly.

"Do you have any idea where he's living?" Michel asked, looking again at Lady Chanel.

Again Zelda spoke.

"I wish we did. We're worried about him."

Michel looked back at her quickly.

"Any particular reason?" he asked.

"This can be a very dangerous city," she replied. "You know that, detective. And Joel is a very vulnerable boy."

Although there was nothing overtly offensive about what she'd said, Michel felt a sudden strong dislike for Zelda. He sensed that she'd intended her words as an accusation against him. He looked at Lady Chanel.

"And you haven't heard anything?" he asked.

"I'm afraid not," she replied quickly.

She held Michel's gaze but he sensed it was an act of will.

"Well, I'm sorry to have taken your time," he said finally.

He pulled two cards from his wallet and placed one in front of each of them on the table.

"If you should hear from him I'd appreciate it if you gave me a call," he said.

"Of course," Lady Chanel replied.

"Thank you. And it was nice to finally meet you both."

As he walked toward the door Michel fought to keep his anger and hurt in check. He was certain that Lady Chanel and Zelda had lied to him. Apparently Joel doesn't want me to find him, he thought, as he stepped onto the sidewalk.

*****

"Why didn't you tell him the truth?" Lady Chanel asked in a harsh whisper.

"It's not our business to tell," Zelda replied. "If Joel wants to see Detective Doucette he knows where to find him. If you like I'll give Joel his card."

Lady Chanel shook her head dismissively.

"But what's he going to think when he finds out Joel's been living in your house the whole time?"

"And how would he find that out?" Zelda replied, fixing Chanel with a hard stare.

"It's a small city," Chanel replied, looking away. "They're bound to run into one another eventually."

"Then we'll just tell him we were trying to protect the boy," Zelda said.

Chapter 19

Joel finished his shift a little after eleven. The restaurant had been slow all night and he'd spent most of his time cleaning out the walk-in refrigerator. The hours had seemed to drag by and he was anxious to leave, partly because he wanted to get home, but also because he wanted to get away from the restaurant. Being there had begun to depress him. He stayed only for the obligatory drink before making an excuse about having a dentist appointment early the next morning and heading back to the Marigny.

When he walked into the house it was quiet and he thought that he was alone. He made himself a screwdriver in the kitchen then walked into the living room to wait. Hunter was on the couch, his body bent forward as he snorted a line of white powder off the glass coffee table.

"Hey, J.," Hunter said as he sat back, rubbing the back of his index finger under his nose. "How was your night? Make a lot of money?"

Joel thought he heard a tone of mockery in the question and felt a twinge of embarrassment.

"I did okay," he replied quickly. "How about you?"

"I got a real nice tip," Hunter said, indicating the powder on the table. "Want some?"

"What is it?"

"Tina."

Joel looked at Hunter blankly.

"Boy, you really are from the sticks aren't you?" Hunter said, shaking his head but smiling warmly at Joel. "Crystal meth. It's good shit. Makes you feel like you own the world. Just can't do too much of it or it makes your dick limp."

He motioned for Joel to sit next to him.

"You've gotta lighten up," he said, putting his right arm around Joel's shoulder.

In his left hand he held out a 3-inch long silver tube.

"I don't know," Joel said, shaking his head. "I've never snorted anything."

"It's okay," Hunter said.

It sounded as though he were absolving Joel for a sin.

"I'll look after you. After all, we're friends, aren't we?"

Joel hesitated. He wanted to believe that Hunter and the others were his friends. He wanted to share in the bond between them. Finally he took the silver tube and leaned forward, inhaling a thin line of the powder into his right nostril. As he sat back against the couch he waited, his heart thudding with both fear and anticipation. Hunter sat forward on the couch and looked at him.

"What do you think?"

Joel was about to reply that he couldn't feel anything when the first wave of the high washed over him. For a moment he felt dizzy, disoriented. Then the high seemed to resolve itself and he felt suddenly euphoric. Unlike what he had experienced smoking pot and hash, the high from the crystal meth was immediate and powerful. The colors and textures in the room became vivid. His mind felt focused and sharp. He felt strong.

He looked at Hunter and smiled. Hunter smiled back and leaned in, kissing Joel softly. Joel kissed him back. He closed his eyes and concentrated on the sensation of Hunter's lips against his own. Every nerve ending in his body felt more alive, more sensitive, than he'd ever felt before. He could feel each tiny ridge of Hunter's teeth with his tongue. He could feel each pore in Hunter's tongue. He didn't feel aroused. Their kisses didn't feel sexual. They were just sharing an experience.

When they stopped kissing Joel opened his eyes. He didn't know how much time had passed, but Jared, Peter and Raphael were sitting with them now. He didn't feel surprised or embarrassed. He smiled at them. Raphael who was sitting next to him placed a hand on Joel's leg and gave him a kiss.

"Cool, huh?" he asked.

"Very cool," Joel replied.

Jared, Peter and Raphael took turns snorting the powder while Hunter and Joel went to the kitchen to make drinks. Before they walked back into the living room Joel hugged Hunter and kissed him again. He'd never felt so good or fearless before. When they returned he and Hunter each snorted another line while Raphael turned on the CD player.

A synthesized bassline and pulsing beat suddenly filled the room. Small blasts of melody began filtering through the percussion. Peter jumped up onto the couch, closed his eyes, and began slowly gyrating his hips in rhythm with the beat. His shoulders dipped and rose, undulating in opposite time with one another. His left hand rose and began to gracefully paint the air in front of him. Joel was mesmerized. He'd never seen anything so beautiful.

He felt himself being pulled to his feet and turned to see Raphael holding his hand. Raphael smiled at him and slowly extended his other hand, cupping it behind Joel's neck. Raphael began swaying from side to side. Joel began to move in time with him. He felt the rhythm trying to force its way inside him through Raphael's arm and he surrendered himself willingly.

He turned his head and saw Hunter and Jared standing on the couch on opposite sides of Peter. Their bodies seemed to flow around his, their sinuous movements seeming random yet perfectly synchronized. Joel closed his eyes. He felt his body joining in perfect harmony with Raphael's.

They danced for hours, stopping only to snort more crystal meth or sip their drinks. They danced in pairs and in groups, sometimes all of them coming together. Joel allowed himself to become lost in the rapture. He could feel himself becoming connected to each of the other boys. For the first time he felt like he was truly one of them, and he felt happier than he'd ever felt in his life.

Finally around 3 am the music stopped and they all fell exhausted onto the couches. They were slick with sweat. The twins had stripped to matching white boxer briefs, and they were all shirtless. Raphael and Peter sat on one couch, their legs intertwined on the coffee table in front of them. Joel and Jared sat a few feet from one another on the other couch. Hunter lay across them, his head resting in Joel's lap and his eyes closed while he absently ran his left hand through Joel's hair.

After a few minutes of silence Hunter opened his eyes and looked up at Joel.

"So'd you have fun?" he asked.

Joel nodded and smiled in reply.

"I told you I'd take care of you. Now you're one of us."

Joel looked around the room. The others were smiling tiredly at him.

"Can I ask you a question?" he asked, looking back at Hunter.

"Sure."

"Don't take this the wrong way, but are you guys hustlers?"

Hunter let out a harsh laugh and shook his head.

"Hustlers are low lifes who sell their asses on the streets," he said. "We're professional escorts. We get paid to keep people company."

"Sometimes we fuck them, sometimes we just go places with them," Raphael added matter-of-factly.

"Tonight I was some guy's date at an art gallery opening," Hunter said. "Those are the best gigs. You get to drink champagne, eat good food, meet nice people, and all you have to do is be cute and charming and make them look good in front of their friends. I got $500 and the 'tina' for two hours."

"Are you serious?" Joel asked.

"Fuck yeah. The guy didn't even want to blow me."

Joel looked at the others. There was nothing in their even gazes or the tone of Hunter's voice to suggest they were kidding.

"How do you find your tricks?" he asked.

"Clients," Hunter corrected. "They find us. We just get the call telling us what they're looking for, where to go and when."

"From who?"

The others exchanged uncomfortable looks.

"Sorry, can't tell you that yet," Hunter said.

Joel considered his next question carefully, wondering whether it would start him on a path from which he couldn't turn back. You'll always have free choice, he thought. You can always change your mind.

"Could I be an escort?" he asked suddenly.

He heard the words as if from a distance and time seemed to slow down as he waited for a response that he knew might change his life. Hunter stroked the side of his face and smiled warmly up at him.

"If it was up to us, babe, you'd already be one, but it's not," he said. "So just be patient."

Joel felt a combination of relief and anxiety. He felt that he'd been given a reprieve from a choice he wasn't really ready to make. At the same time he felt that he would never truly be a part of the group until he was what they were. Tonight he'd felt connected to them for the first time and the thought of losing that connection was unbearable. He'd felt whole and alive with them. He wanted to feel that always.

Hunter pulled himself up into Joel's lap and wrapped his arms around his neck. He kissed Joel softly.

"Don't worry," he said. "You're one of us now."

For a moment Joel wondered whether Hunter could read his mind or if he'd spoken his thoughts out loud. Hunter smiled at him.

"Come on, let's get some sleep," he said.

Hunter stood up and took Joel's hand, leading him toward the stairs as the others fell in behind them. That night Joel slept with the twins, one on each side of him, their naked bodies wrapped tightly around his own. He felt contented. But as he drifted into sleep a question came to him: if it's not up to them, then who?

Chapter 20

Michel was sitting at his desk arranging paper clips into patterns on a blank sheet of paper when Sassy arrived.

"What's up, partner?" she asked, looking at her watch curiously. "I can't remember the last time you got your ass in here before me."

Michel looked up and gave her a thin smile.

"Couldn't sleep."

"Trying to figure out what Reynolds was doing at MRB?"

"No, that would actually be productive," Michel replied. "Personal stuff. All right if we take a walk?"

Sassy gave him a worried look. She couldn't recall the last time he'd made a direct overture to talk about anything personal.

"I just need a little help putting something into perspective," Michel said, reading the concern on her face.

They walked the few blocks to Cafe Du Monde in silence and took a table in an empty corner of the patio.

"So what's going on?" Sassy asked after they'd gotten their coffees.

"I went to the Bourbon Pub last night after I spoke to you. I was hoping to find Joel."

"And?"

"I ran into his friend, Chance."

"Coco?"

"Yeah. He told me he hasn't seen Joel since the day I dropped him off at their apartment. Joel told him he wanted to move out and they got into a big fight. Says he has no idea where Joel went."

"And you believe him?" Sassy asked.

"Yeah," Michel replied. "He thought I'd know where Joel was. He was sincere. I could see he was really worried."

"So do you think Joel is still in town?"

Michel nodded.

"Afterward I talked to Lady Chanel and Miss Zelda. They said the same thing but I think they were lying."

"Wait a second," Sassy said, her voice suddenly harsh. "You're investigating three murders committed by a drag queen and you talk to two drag queens about some boy you took home one night? You don't see a conflict of interest in that?"

Michel felt a sudden mix of rage and shame.

"What the fuck are you talking about?" he replied.

"Michel, they're potential suspects and you're getting them involved in your personal life."

"They're not potential suspects," Michel said sharply.

Sassy looked around the cafe to see if anyone was looking at them.

"Why not?" she asked, her voice quieter and more even. "You always talk about having to see things from the right perspective. I think you're not seeing the forest for the trees. They've been in front of you for so long that you aren't even noticing them."

Michel felt embarrassed. He knew she was right. Although he didn't believe in his heart that either of them could be the killer, he'd ignored the possibility.

"I'm sorry," he said softly. "You're right. I made a mistake."

He looked at Sassy but she seemed lost in thought.

"Maybe, maybe not," she said.

"What?"

"If one or both of them is involved, maybe it's not such a bad thing if they think you're in the bars just looking for Joel. You fucked up, but it may work to your advantage."

"I planned it that way," Michel said with a sly smile.

"My ass," Sassy replied, shaking her head. "At least it gives you an excuse to talk to them. Maybe you can draw them out a bit."

"Maybe with Chanel," Michel said. "I got the feeling she wanted to talk to me, but Zelda wouldn't let her."

"Wouldn't let her?" Sassy asked with surprise. "Every time I've seen them together I've gotten the sense that Chanel is the queen of that prom."

"I know," Michel said, "but Zelda was taking the lead. I had the feeling that if she'd been alone Chanel would have talked to me."

"Then maybe you'll have to get her alone," Sassy said.

They sat in silence.

"Now what about your boy?" Sassy asked after a minute.

Michel paused, considering what he wanted to say.

"To be honest, I'm not really sure," he said. "It really scared me when Chance told me he hadn't seen Joel. And I know Chanel and Zelda were lying when they said they didn't know where he was."

"Why would they lie?" Sassy asked.

"Because he asked them to," Michel replied resignedly. "Because he doesn't want me to find him."

Sassy regarded Michel carefully.

"Look, maybe you're right," she said, "but I think that you're putting too much onto Joel."

"In what way?" Michel asked, giving Sassy a curious look.

"You hardly know him," she replied, trying to keep any judgment out of her voice. "You don't know if you really even like him. You like the image of him that you created after one night."

"And one morning," Michel added with a small smile.

"Whatever. The point is you hardly know one another. Maybe you are meant for each other. Maybe you'd be the greatest couple since Pam and Tommy," she said.

Michel shot her a mordant look.

"But maybe you wouldn't," she continued. "I think you're putting too much responsibility for your own happiness onto a relationship that hasn't existed."

Michel gave her a questioning look.

"Michel, in many ways you are probably the most mature man I've ever met—not that that's saying much—but when it comes to love you're like a thirteen-year-old girl. You've never really been in a relationship. Everything you know is from movies and those Harlequin romances I know you read."

She gave him a warm smile.

"And Joel's just a kid," she said. "Everything at that age is a big drama. Look what happened when you told him about Coco. He overreacted. He doesn't think about consequences or tomorrow. It's all about what he feels in that moment. He's probably confused as hell about you or he's moved on to the next big thing in his life."

Michel looked at her for a moment.

"What you're saying makes sense," he said, "but I'm not sure exactly what I feel toward him either."

"What do you mean?" Sassy asked.

"Don't get me wrong," Michel replied, "the initial attraction was definitely sexual, and maybe I fantasized for a moment about a relationship, but there's more to it than that. Joel helped me understand the possibilities in my life. I'm grateful to him for that and I feel I owe it to him to look out for him. I see the kids out in the bars. This city will eat you up if you let it. Once upon a time Speck Bouchard might have been just like Joel. I just need to make sure he's doing okay."

"You are one complicated homo," Sassy said, shaking her head. "All this time I thought you just had a hard-on for the kid."

Michel smiled at her.

"Maybe," he said. "But I need to see him and talk to him."

Sassy nodded.

"Okay, but don't push, don't hunt, don't be a stalker. Some day you'll run into him again."

Michel nodded with reluctant acceptance.

"And you can't allow it to interfere with doing your job," Sassy said.

Chapter 21

Joel could feel Michel's hand moving slowly across his chest and down his stomach. He felt Michel's warm lips kissing the back of his neck. This was what he'd wanted. He could feel Michel's body pressing tightly against his back as his hand moved lower.

Joel opened his eyes. In the dim light he could see Jared sleeping beside him. With a start he tried to roll away but the hand around his hip held him tight.

"Shhh, don't wake Jared," he heard Hunter whisper in his ear. "Just relax."

Joel lay still, confused by what was happening. He hadn't wanted to do this, but now as he felt Hunter's hand delicately stroking him and felt Hunter's body pressing against him, he was becoming aroused.

"I don't think we should do this," he whispered.

"You said you wanted to be one of us," Hunter whispered back. "I need to sample the goods before I can recommend you."

He kissed Joel's neck again, more passionately.

Hunter's words chilled Joel. Although his tone had been joking, it had sounded so calculated, like a business transaction. At the same time, the excitement was beginning to overwhelm him. He liked the idea of submitting to Hunter.

He felt Hunter's hand close around his penis and his resistance dissolved. He wanted this as badly as anything he'd ever wanted in his life. He sighed and pushed back against Hunter.

"If that's what you want," Hunter whispered, laughing softly.

*****

Joel didn't know how long he'd been asleep. The twins were sleeping quietly on either side of him. He could see the sun shining brightly around the edges of the window shades. He got up quietly and went to the bathroom. After he showered, he dressed quickly and left the house before anyone else had come out of their rooms. He began walking toward the Quarter.

He was confused by what had happened. Part of him felt exhilarated. It had been an amazing experience. He'd allowed himself to be completely open about his desires for the first time with another man. He hadn't felt any embarrassment, even when Jared had woken up and watched them.

But afterward he'd begun to feel anxious. Last night had been perfect. He'd felt like one of the boys, their equal. Would they view him as something less than an equal now? He didn't want to lose the feeling of being connected. He wondered how far he'd be willing to go to keep it.

He turned right onto Royal, still lost in thought. He wished he could talk to someone. He thought briefly of going to Lady Chanel's house, but knew he could never tell her what had happened. He didn't want her to think of him that way. He realized suddenly how much he missed Chance. He could have told Chance and Chance would have understood without making any judgments.

At the next corner he stopped to light a cigarette, his eyes coming to rest on the street sign: Frenchman Street. Michel's street. Michel would know what he should do. Michel could have made everything different. None of this would have happened and he could feel secure and happy if Michel had loved him. But maybe Michel was right, he thought. Maybe he knew me better than I know myself.

He turned around and began walking back to the house.

*****

The four boys were in the kitchen performing their breakfast ritual when he walked in. Joel felt a sour sickness in his stomach and his mouth felt dry as he waited for a reaction from the others. Peter was standing just inside the doorway to the left. He smiled and gave Joel an affectionate kiss on the cheek.

"Where've you been?" Hunter asked.

"I just went for a walk. I needed to get cigarettes," Joel replied slowly.

He looked expectantly around the room. No one was looking at him any differently.

"So did you have fun with the twins?" Raphael asked, arching his eyebrows comically.

"A lady never tells," Hunter replied with mock coldness.

He looked at Joel and gave him a warm smile. Joel could feel the tension in his body suddenly ease. He smiled at the others and walked to the cabinet next to Jared to grab a coffee cup.

"Hungry?" Jared asked.

Joel caught the impish look in his eye.

"Starving," he replied, smiling furtively. "I haven't had a thing in me all morning."

Everything is fine, Joel thought as he poured his coffee. I still belong.

Chapter 22

Michel lay on the kitchen floor, his upper body wedged uncomfortably under the sink. After dinner he'd decided to replace his garbage disposal and now, three hours later, he was slick with sweat and nearing the point of surrender. When his cell phone began vibrating on the counter across the room he was grateful. Maybe someone will be dead and I can quit for the night, he mused.

"Doucette," he answered.

He heard loud music and voices.

"Hello?" he asked loudly.

"Michel? It's Kenny," a muffled voice replied. "Sorry, I can hardly hear you."

"Kenny, what's up?" Michel asked.

"Cally just walked in. Thought you'd want to know."

"Great, I'll be right over."

"What?" Kenny asked.

"I said I'm on my way," Michel yelled into the phone.

"Okay," Kenny replied, then the line went dead.

*****

Ten minutes later Michel parked his car illegally on Royal Street and walked to MRB. It was nearly eleven and the room was packed. He waved to a few men he recognized as he pushed his way to the bar. Kenny was at the far end pulling beer bottles from a cooler but saw him and nodded discreetly. Michel waited, scanning the crowd for anyone who fit the description of Cally that Kenny had given him.

"What can I get you?" Kenny asked behind him.

"Jack on the rocks," Michel said, turning around.

As Kenny placed the drink on the bar Michel gave him a questioning look. Kenny looked over Michel's left shoulder and gave a slight nod. Michel put twenty dollars on the bar and began moving into the center of the room.

He moved slowly, sipping his drink and trying to appear casual as he studied the crowd. A group of five men were standing tightly bunched together to his right and as Michel walked past them he found an opening in the crowd. He looked to his right and saw a tall black man with short gray hair standing fifteen feet away. Cally, he thought.

Suddenly the man looked in his direction and for a second they locked eyes. Michel was sure that he saw a glimmer of recognition cross the man's face. Then the gap between them closed and Michel lost sight of the man. He turned quickly and pushed his way backward to another opening in the crowd. When he looked again the man was gone.

Michel looked to the bar and saw Kenny standing where he had left him. Kenny nodded quickly toward the door and as Michel turned he saw the man looking back at him from the doorway.

Michel lowered his right shoulder and began forcing his way past people. He heard cries of protest and shattering glass at his feet but kept moving forward. When he reached the door the man was gone and Michel rushed into the street. He looked quickly in both directions, carefully studying the shadows, but no one was there.

He walked slowly back to his car, stopping to peer into the alley behind the Royal Inn. He recognized me, he thought, and he was scared. He tried to form a clear picture of Cally's face in his mind. There was something familiar about him. He imagined Cally in a blond wig and nodded: Lady Chanel.

Chapter 23

Fuck this shit, Joel thought as an acrid cloud of steam rose into his face, causing him to close his eyes for a moment. He began unloading dishes, stacking them loudly on the stainless steel shelves that separated the cooking line from the rest of the kitchen.

"Hey, take it easy," one of the line chefs yelled to him. "You break one and you're paying for it."

"Fuck you," Joel said under his breath.

As the day had gone on he'd been feeling increasingly sullen and irritable. He knew that part of it was just tiredness. His body felt weary from the drinking, drugs and dancing the night before and from his experience with Hunter that morning. But he knew that the larger part of it was embarrassment. He felt that Hunter and the others looked down on his job. He'd begun to view himself through their eyes and he resented working in the sweltering heat for minimum wage. He was also frustrated. Now that he had experienced a connection with the others it made him angry to have to wait for someone unknown to allow him to be one of them.

As he pulled a hot plate from the rack it slipped from his fingers, dropping to the floor and fracturing loudly. Applause broke out around the kitchen and Joel could feel his anger building.

"I guess somebody's working for free tonight," a voice said.

The cooks and wait staff began laughing.

"Go fuck yourselves," Joel said loudly.

The laughter stopped and an uncomfortable silence filled the room as the executive chef walked toward Joel.

"What did you say?" he asked.

"I said go fuck yourselves," Joel said, not looking at him.

"You need to watch your mouth," the chef said, folding his arms across his chest. "And that's coming out of your paycheck."

"Yeah?" Joel said.

He reached for another plate and held it out in front of him as he locked eyes with the chef. He let go of the plate and it shattered on the floor.

"Put that one on my tab, too," he said, smiling calmly.

The chef took a step toward him.

"Are you out of your mind?" he asked, looking at Joel with disbelief. "Do you want to get fired?"

"Don't bother," Joel said, shrugging his shoulders. "I quit."

He walked silently to the back door of the kitchen and walked out.

*****

When he got home the others weren't there yet. Joel walked into the kitchen and made himself a screwdriver. He sat at the kitchen table and lit a cigarette.

"You're home early," Zelda said from the doorway.

Joel turned with a start.

"Oh hi," he said uneasily.

"The restaurant close already?" Zelda asked.

Joel hesitated, unsure whether to tell the truth.

"No," he said finally. "I quit."

Zelda looked at him appraisingly for a moment.

"Well you know there are no free rooms here," she said.

"I know," Joel replied, looking down at the table. "I think I already have something else lined up."

"Do you? And what might that be?" Zelda asked.

141

Joel wanted to be away from her. It made him suddenly angry that she felt entitled to ask him questions about his life.

"Don't worry about it," he said sharply. "You'll get your rent. All right?"

He'd spoken more harshly than he'd intended and waited nervously for Zelda to respond. She stared at him without expression.

"See that I do," she said finally, her tone hard and vaguely threatening.

She turned away and walked slowly from the room. Joel could hear her mounting the stairs toward her room. He let out a deep breath and downed half of his drink. He didn't want to wait downstairs for the others in case Zelda came back. He went to his room and lay down to wait. Five minutes later he was asleep.

*****

Joel heard soft knocking and sat up, looking around the room in confusion.

"Yeah?" he asked, his voice thick and uneven.

The door opened partway and Hunter's head peaked around the side.

"Hey," he said. "We're going to bed but I just wanted to make sure you're okay. We missed you tonight."

"What?" Joel asked. "What time is it?"

"A little after 4," Hunter replied. "We didn't know if you were sick or just didn't feel like playing tonight. Can I come in?"

Joel nodded and reached for the glass on his night stand. The ice had melted, leaving an inch of water on the top of the vodka and orange juice. He took a sip.

"You okay?" Hunter asked.

"Yeah," Joel replied, nodding his head and trying to clear his throat. "I just came up here to wait for you guys and I guess I fell asleep."

"You must have been pretty beat," Hunter said.

"Yeah, I guess so," Joel replied.

He rubbed his eyes and yawned.

"That sucks. I wanted to party with you guys. I had something I wanted to tell you."

"What?" Hunter asked excitedly.

"I quit my job."

Hunter frowned slightly.

"I'm not sure you should have done that," he said.

"Why?" Joel asked, giving him a worried look.

Hunter sighed.

"The guy we work for doesn't think you're ready yet," he said.

"What does that mean?" Joel asked.

Hunter shrugged.

"I'm sorry."

Joel stared down at the bed. He felt suddenly alone and struggled to hold back tears.

"Don't worry," Hunter said, climbing onto the bed beside him and wrapping his arms around Joel. "It'll happen. Just not now."

Joel began to cry and Hunter kissed his cheek softly. He pulled Joel back on the bed and began to stroke the side of his face, wiping away the tears that ran toward his ears.

"I promise," Hunter said and kissed Joel's cheek again.

They lay together as Joel continued to sob and Hunter tried to soothe him. Just before sunrise they fell asleep.

Chapter 24

"So you think Chanel is our killer?" Sassy asked.

Michel shrugged.

"I'm not even positive it was her. I only caught two quick glimpses of her."

"So why don't we bring her in and take her wig off?"

"If we bring her in everyone in the Quarter is going to know about it in ten minutes," Michel replied. "If it's not her then the real killer's going to know we've figured out he's a transvestite and he's going to make a run."

"So what do we do? Stake out her place?"

Although she was the senior officer, Sassy was sensitive to Michel's personal connection to the case and had decided to lay back and let him direct the investigation for the time being.

Michel shook his head.

"There's no way we can do it discreetly. It's a tight neighborhood. They'll notice any strangers."

"So then what?" Sassy asked, sighing with exasperation.

"Find out who owns the house. I assume the deed doesn't say Lady Chanel. And then check into her past. See if there's anything that suggests she's capable of killing: sexual abuse as a child, arrests for violence or sex crimes. "

"You don't think it's her, do you?" Sassy asked.

"No," Michel replied. "It just doesn't make sense. She doesn't fit the profile."

"But the profile is only good until someone comes along who doesn't fit it," Sassy said.

"I know," Michel said, "but whoever's doing this has some big issues with their sexuality. Chanel may be a transvestite but she doesn't seem conflicted. And transvestites don't have a predisposition to violence. They're already acting on their psychosexual impulses, not repressing them."

Sassy nodded.

"Okay," she said, "so we stay the course for now and run a background check."

Chapter 25

Joel had spent the day by himself. When he'd woken up around ten that morning Hunter was sleeping beside him. They were both still dressed in their clothes from the night before. Joel had grabbed some clean clothes and gone into the bathroom to shower and get dressed. He'd gone to Cafe du Monde for breakfast, then wandered Canal Place for an hour until the movie theater opened. He'd passed the afternoon in the darkness watching two movies, then started back to the house a little after 3:30 pm.

He felt an odd sense of resignation. Nothing was working out as he'd hoped, yet instead of being upset he felt a melancholy acceptance. He remembered what Hunter had said the night before as they lay in bed. He'd wanted to believe it then, but now it felt like a false promise or a lie to comfort him. His life was on hold and beyond his control.

He felt ambivalent about seeing the boys. It seemed as though it had been days since he'd been with them and he missed them, but at the same time the thought of seeing them made him anxious. He knew he wasn't really one of them and wondered if their feelings toward him would eventually change.

The first floor of the house was empty and Joel was grateful to be alone. He mixed a screwdriver and walked quietly up to his room. Hunter was laying on his bed. He'd showered and changed into camouflage shorts and a white tank top. Joel couldn't remember ever having seen him dressed so casually. It made him look younger.

146

"Hey," Hunter said. "I've been waiting for you. Where'd you go?"

"I was at the movies," Joel said flatly.

"Why didn't you wake me? I would have gone with you."

Joel noticed that Hunter seemed unusually animated.

"I don't know," he replied. "I guess I just wanted to be alone for a while."

Hunter gave him a concerned look.

"Are you okay?"

Joel looked at him for a moment, then nodded.

"Yeah, I'm fine now. Where's everyone else?"

"Shopping or something," Hunter replied with a shrug.

"How come you didn't go with them?"

"Because I was worried about you," Hunter replied in a tone that suggested the answer should have been obvious. "I woke up and you were gone. I didn't know if something had happened to you."

Joel was touched by Hunter's concern and felt his mood lift slightly.

"Guess what?" Hunter asked excitedly.

Joel shrugged in response.

"I'm not working tonight," Hunter said. "What do you say we go out? Zelda and Lady Chanel are going to the Bourbon Pub. You want to go with them?"

He raised his eyebrows expectantly.

Joel hesitated a moment. He wondered if Chance would be there and worried about seeing him again. He also thought of Michel.

"It'll be fun. You'll be with me," Hunter said as though reading his thoughts.

"Okay," Joel said after a few seconds.

The idea of seeing Lady Chanel and spending time with Hunter appealed to him and he found himself getting excited at the prospect.

"Cool," Hunter said with a broad smile. "And if the old

ladies get to be too much of a drag we can ditch them and go someplace else."

Joel walked to the bed and kneeled on the edge. He leaned forward and kissed Hunter.

"Thank you," he said.

"For what?" Hunter asked, giving him a quizzical look.

Joel smiled.

"For being my friend."

Chapter 26

"What are you reading?" Sassy asked wearily.

It was almost quitting time and she'd spent the last three hours fruitlessly searching the archives at the Registrar of Deeds' office, looking for information on the owner of Lady Chanel's house. When she'd called earlier that day an irritable clerk had informed her that the electronic database went back only to 1980 and that no one was available to do a manual search.

"The life and times of Calvin Haden," Michel said, not looking up.

"Who is Calvin Haden?" Sassy asked.

"That would be one Lady Chanel," Michel replied, looking up at her and grinning with satisfaction.

"How the fuck did you find that out?" Sassy asked, shaking her head in disbelief.

"They have this new thing called the Internet," Michel said sweetly. "I checked out the tax bills on the house."

"And you let me haul my ass down into a dusty old basement to go looking through a bunch of nasty, dirty books?"

"I figured you needed the exercise," Michel replied, giving her a faux innocent look. "Seriously, it didn't occur to me until a half hour ago. I tried calling your cell but I couldn't get through so I called the Registrar's office and they said you'd already left. Sorry."

"I'm going to see if you really tried to call me," Sassy said, arching an eyebrow at him. "You know that, don't you?"

Michel gave her a warm smile.

"So what did you find out?" Sassy asked.

"Well, he bought the house in 1966 for $12,000."

"What else?" Sassy asked impatiently.

"Calvin Haden, born June 20, 1944, in Jackson, Mississippi."

"That makes her sixty. Damn she looks good for an old broad."

Michel nodded.

"But this is when it gets interesting," he said, lifting the file to read it. "Calvin Haden, aka Cally Haden. Arrested August 14, 1958. Convicted of prostitution September 12, 1958. Sentenced to six months in the Lafayette Institute for Juvenile Offenders."

"He was arrested in New Orleans?" Sassy asked with surprise, recognizing the name of the former detention facility.

Michel nodded.

"He was only fourteen," Sassy said, shaking her head. "There had to have been something bad going on at home to get him out on the streets that early. Any info on the parents? Reports of sexual abuse?"

"Nothing in here," Michel replied, "but I contacted the police in Jackson. They didn't seem too hopeful of finding any records going back that far."

Sassy nodded.

"Then he was arrested again on April 6, 1959, less than a month after he got out of juvie," Michel continued, summarizing the file, "for the murder of a Malcolm Whittier, age 45."

Sassy let out a low whistle.

"According to the case notes, Whittier was a banker from a prominent family who apparently had a taste for young black boys. He was under investigation for diddling the sons of some of the people he had working for him. A few of them went to the police but nothing ever came of it."

"There's a surprise," Sassy said bitterly. "I'm sure back then the cops figured it was his right to fuck the children of the 'niggers' he had working for him."

Michel gave her an empathetic look.

"I don't think so," he said. "The detective investigating the case thought Whittier was paying the families off not to prosecute. The investigation was still active when he was killed."

"And what about Cally?" Sassy asked.

"They let him go. He had an alibi. Another suspected prostitute said Cally was with her all night."

"And they bought that?" Sassy asked with a dubious look.

"I think they wanted to buy it," Michel replied. "I don't think anyone considered Whittier's murder much of a loss and I'm sure the DA was being pressured by Whittier's family to keep the details from going public."

"Then what happened?" Sassy asked.

"Cally disappeared for seven years. No records on him again until he bought the house, and no criminal record since. My guess is that by the time he came back Cally Haden had transformed into Lady Chanel, literally."

"What do you mean literally?" Sassy asked. "Sex change?"

Michel shook his head and began writing out capital letters on a single line on a piece of paper. Below it he wrote another line.

CALLY HADEN
LADY CHANEL

"An anagram," Sassy said.

Michel nodded.

"So I'd say we have a suspect now, wouldn't you?" Sassy asked. "Possible victim of sexual abuse. Suspect in a murder."

Michel nodded reluctantly.

"So let's bring her in," Sassy said.

"Not yet," Michel said.

"Why not?" Sassy asked with exasperation.

"Because everything we have is circumstantial. We'd never be able to make it stick. Hell, we wouldn't even be able to get a search warrant for her place to look for the knife with what we've got."

"She was seen with one of the victims the night he was killed," Sassy said. "What more do you need?"

"I don't know, Sassy," Michel said, shrugging helplessly. "Something that will convince me she might have done it, because I'm still not believing it."

Sassy studied him for a moment.

"Michel, you can't let your personal feelings cloud your judgment. I know she was some kind of icon to you growing up, but all the evidence we have right now is pointing at her, circumstantial or not."

"I know that," Michel said, "but it just doesn't feel right to me. I'm sorry, but that's all I can say. And if I'm right and we bring her in, then we lose the one thing we have going for us right now. The killer still doesn't know we know he's a transvestite. Can you just trust me on this for a day or two?"

Sassy gave him a doubtful look.

"Look," Michel said, "if it'll make you feel any better we can put someone at MRB tonight to keep an eye out for her, just in case."

"And what do we do in the meantime to convince you we should bring her in?"

Michel considered for a minute.

"It's Thursday. It's a big night at the Bourbon Pub. Chances are she'll be there."

"So?"

"So maybe I'll be there, too, and have a little chat with her."

"About?" Sassy asked.

"Darnell Coolidge," Michel said with a wicked grin.

"Darnell Coolidge? Are you crazy?"

Sassy gave him a bewildered look.

"You're afraid of letting the killer know we know he's a transvestite, but now you want to walk right up and tell Chanel we think she's the killer?"

"I don't want to scare off the killer we don't know," Michel replied carefully, "but if Chanel is the killer, why not let her know we're onto her? If she tries to run then we'll know you're right. And if she's scared there's a better chance she'll make a mistake, right?"

"You are really pushing it this time," Sassy said, shaking her head. "You're asking me to put a lot of trust in your instincts."

"I know," Michel replied, "and if I'm wrong we're fucked."

"Very fucked," Sassy said with a baleful look.

Chapter 27

Lady Chanel arrived at Zelda's at 9:30 pm. Joel was waiting anxiously for her in the living room and jumped up from the couch when he heard her walk in the back door. He met her in the doorway with a warm hug.

"Hello, my dear," she said, kissing him on each cheek. "It's wonderful to see you. You've been very naughty not visiting your auntie."

Joel gave her an embarrassed smile.

"I'm sorry."

"Not to worry," Chanel said. "Yesterday happened yesterday. No need to dwell on it."

Joel thought he detected a tone of admonishment and wondered if Lady Chanel's comment was meant to convey a greater significance. He thought of Chance.

"In any case, tonight you're going out with your old aunties," Chanel said with an affectionate smile.

As they walked into the living room they heard footsteps coming quickly down the stairs. Hunter appeared in the doorway, dressed in his camouflage shorts and a black tank top.

"Hey," he said to Lady Chanel.

He walked over and kissed her on the cheek.

"Hello, Hunter," Lady Chanel replied, accepting his kiss stiffly.

Joel noticed her apparent awkwardness and the cool tone of her voice and wondered if she disliked Hunter.

While they waited for Zelda to join them, Lady Chanel and

Joel settled on one couch and Hunter went to the kitchen to mix a pitcher of Cosmopolitans. As Hunter walked back into the living room carrying a tray with the pitcher and four martini glasses, Zelda appeared in the other doorway. Her face seemed slack and her clothes were slightly dishevelled, as though she'd just woken up and hurried to get dressed. Joel thought he saw her swaying for a moment.

"Hello, all," Zelda said, nodding with what seemed intended as a regal gesture.

Instead it looked to Joel as though she'd suddenly fallen asleep and then woken just as quickly, her head lolling forward then snapping back up. He looked at Lady Chanel but she continued to watch Zelda. Her expression was blank but Joel thought he saw a flicker of concern in her eyes.

"Good evening, Miss Zelda," Chanel said with a tight smile. "Won't you join us for a cocktail to start our evening?"

"Thank you," Zelda said.

She walked to the seat closest to Chanel on the other couch and sat down. Her body movements seemed exaggerated, as though she were making an effort to be graceful.

Hunter placed the tray on the cocktail table between the two couches and filled the four glasses. He handed the first two to Lady Chanel and Zelda, then the third to Joel before he took one and raised it. He was still standing.

"Here's to friends," he said with a warm smile.

The others raised their glasses and echoed his toast before sipping their drinks.

Hunter walked to the stereo and placed a CD in the disc changer before taking a seat next to Zelda.

"An excellent choice," Lady Chanel said as the voice of Nina Simone floated into the room.

While they drank their Cosmopolitans, Joel gave Lady Chanel a sketchy recap of what he'd been up to since he'd last seen her.

"And your job?" Chanel asked after a few minutes.

From her tone it was clear that Zelda had already told her that he'd quit.

"I quit," Joel replied, bracing himself a reprimand.

"Well, I'm sure Miss Zelda has already told you no one lives here for free," Chanel said matter-of-factly.

"I still have some money from my grandparents," Joel said quickly, "plus Hunter is helping me find a job."

As soon as the words were out of his mouth he regretted them. He wondered how much Lady Chanel and Zelda knew about what Hunter and the others did for a living. He watched Chanel carefully for a reaction but didn't see any.

"I see," is all she said.

After they'd finished their drinks they left the house and walked to the Bourbon Pub. Joel was surprised how quickly Lady Chanel and Zelda were able to walk in their high heels. He noticed that Zelda seemed to have revived a bit but that Chanel was slightly subdued, only speaking when addressed directly.

The pub was almost full when they arrived. Three older men were seated at Chanel's and Zelda's usual table. When they saw the group walk in they quickly stood up and waited while Chanel and the others made their way to the table.

"We kept your seats warm for you," one of the men said.

"Thank you, dear," Chanel said, kissing him on the cheek.

Joel smiled in admiration at the respect she was accorded and wondered if he would ever be treated the same way.

Lady Chanel and Zelda settled in at the table while Joel and Hunter went to get drinks. They were on their way back to the table when Joel saw Lady Chanel lift her eyebrows at him and tilt her head slightly to her left. Joel looked in the direction she'd indicated. He could see Michel pushing his way through the crowd toward the table. He stopped abruptly.

"What the fuck?" Hunter said, bumping into Joel's back.

Joel could feel cold liquid running down the back of his shirt. He turned toward Hunter.

"We need to get out of here," he said.

"Why?" Hunter asked. "What the fuck is wrong?"

"There's someone here I don't want to see."

Hunter looked over Joel's shoulder and saw Michel holding Lady Chanel's hand.

"Who's that?" he asked.

"I'll tell you later, but I really want to get out of here," Joel said, looking at Hunter with urgency.

Hunter gave him a confused look.

"Okay," he said finally, "but should I go tell Chanel and Zelda we're leaving?"

"They'll know," Joel said.

He pushed past Hunter and started making his way through the crowd, moving diagonally away from the table to the far corner of the room.

*****

"Detective Doucette," Lady Chanel said, extending her hand. "Twice in one week. What a pleasant surprise."

"Thank you," Michel said, taking her hand briefly. "I was hoping I'd find you here again."

He let the words hang for a moment before continuing.

"I wonder if I could speak to you alone for a few minutes?"

He kept his eyes on Chanel but could see Zelda suddenly sit upright out of the corner of his eye.

"Is that necessary?" Chanel asked, giving him a wary look. "Miss Zelda and I have no secrets."

"It's personal," Michel said.

He held Lady Chanel's gaze for a moment, then looked at Zelda.

"If you don't mind, Miss Zelda?"

Zelda knew it wasn't really a question and nodded absently. Michel could see that she was taken off-guard.

"Very well," Lady Chanel said. "Shall we step outside?"

Michel was struck by the phrase, as though Chanel were challenging him to a fight, and wondered if her choice of words had been intentional. He smiled at her.

"That won't be necessary," he said. "I was thinking we could go upstairs. It's just quieter up there."

They left Zelda at the table and made their way upstairs to the back bar in Parade. There were only a few people engrossed in quiet conversations in the room. No one bothered to looked up as they walked to the far side of the bar and sat on the corner stools. Michel ordered a Jack on the rocks for himself and a Cosmopolitan for Lady Chanel. While they waited for their drinks Michel lit a cigarette.

"So what can I do for you, Detective Doucette," Lady Chanel asked after the bartender had walked away.

"Please, Michel," he corrected.

"Michel," Lady Chanel repeated with a nod. "So what can I do for you, Michel?"

Michel hesitated for a moment.

"The other night when I was here," he said finally, "I got the sense that you weren't being entirely honest with me about Joel."

Lady Chanel looked down at her drink.

"Michel, you're putting me in a very awkward position. I really wish you wouldn't ask me about Joel."

Michel frowned slightly.

"Is he okay?" he asked.

"Yes," Lady Chanel said with a sigh. "He's fine."

"Where is he?"

Chanel paused before looking up to meet Michel's eyes.

"I'm sorry, but I can't tell you that," she said.

Michel nodded.

"Does he not want to see me?"

Lady Chanel thought about the way Joel had reacted when he'd seen Michel downstairs. She wondered whether she should tell him.

"I don't know," she said, shrugging slightly. "We haven't talked about you."

Michel felt a stab of hurt. He'd been prepared to hear that Joel didn't want to see him, but the idea that Joel hadn't even mentioned him was far worse. He struggled to keep his expression blank.

"But then I haven't seen him very much," Lady Chanel added quickly.

Michel knew that she'd read the hurt in his eyes.

"That's okay," he said, giving her a small smile.

"I'll tell him you were asking after him the next time I see him," Lady Chanel said gently. "He's very young, Michel. I think he's confused right now about what he wants."

She seemed about to continue but stopped. Michel smiled at her. He knew that she was trying to be kind to him by making excuses for Joel. He regretted that he'd actually come to question her about the murders and felt a pang of guilt. He tried to imagine what inner darkness could have allowed her to kill Malcolm Whittier when she was a boy.

"Is there anything else?" Chanel asked after a moment. "Miss Zelda doesn't like to be left alone for very long."

"Just one more thing," Michel said. "Do you know a Darnell Coolidge?"

He watched her face carefully for a reaction. She seemed to be considering the question thoughtfully.

"It sounds familiar," she said finally, "but I can't place it. Who is he?"

"He's the man who was killed at the LaMothe House a few days ago," Michel said.

Again he waited for a reaction but saw nothing unusual.

"Perhaps I read it in the paper then," Chanel replied.

"No," Michel replied, shaking his head. "We didn't release his name to the press."

Lady Chanel gave him a look that was both quizzical and concerned.

"Why would you ask me if I know him?"

"Apparently he frequented some drag bars in town," Michel said casually. "I thought maybe you might have run into him."

Lady Chanel gave him a hard look.

"Detective, I don't frequent drag bars," she said with a hint of indignation. "Not all men who live as women hang out in drag bars, anymore than all men who are gay hang out in gay bars."

Michel felt himself sit back involuntarily.

"I'm sorry," he said quickly. "I didn't mean to imply you did. I just thought..."

He trailed off without completing the thought.

Lady Chanel had looked away from him and was staring across the bar. Michel followed her gaze but saw no one there. He turned back and studied the profile of her face. She was perfectly still, seemingly lost in thought. Suddenly Michel thought he detected a slight tremor go through her body. He started to reach his hand toward her shoulder when she turned back to face him. Her eyes were glazed but Michel thought he detected an emotion in them as well: fear.

"Are you okay?" he asked.

Lady Chanel shook her head and her eyes cleared. Whatever Michel had seen was gone.

"I'm fine," she said evenly. "I'm sorry. Sometimes I just drift off into my own world. That's what happens when you turn forty."

Michel smiled at her joke but continued to study her face carefully. She seemed perfectly composed.

"I'm sorry I couldn't be more help," she said as she stood up and carefully picked up her drink.

"Well, you have my card if you think of anything," Michel said.

"Yes," Chanel said with a smile. "And I will tell Joel you were asking after him.

"Thank you," Michel said.

He watched her as she walked gracefully out of the room, then motioned to the bartender for another drink. Okay, what the hell just happened?, he thought as he reached for his wallet.

Chapter 28

Joel and Hunter walked back to the house in silence. When they'd gotten outside the pub Hunter had suggested they go someplace else, but Joel had said he wanted to go home, then had resisted Hunter's attempts to talk to him. By the time they got to the house Joel had finished the two Cosmopolitans he'd been carrying when they saw Michel. As they walked into the kitchen he went to the cabinet and filled one of the plastic cups with ice and vodka.

"So you want to tell me what's going on now?" Hunter asked with a worried look. "Who was that guy?"

"Michel," Joel said.

He began to tell Hunter about meeting Michel and the night and morning they'd spent together, but stopped short of telling him about their final conversation.

"He sounds like a cool guy," Hunter said when he finished. "So why didn't you want to see him?"

Joel considered how to answer. He'd been excited when he saw Michel. He'd wanted to grab him and kiss him and tell him how much he'd missed him. But then he'd remembered he was with Hunter and it had stopped him. He didn't want to admit it, but he'd been embarrassed. He'd wondered if Michel would know who Hunter was and what he did. He thought that if Michel saw him with another hustler it would justify Michel's initial suspicions about him.

"Don't be offended by this," Joel said finally, "but it was because of you."

Hunter gave him a curious look. "Did you think he'd think we were boyfriends or something?"

"No, it's because you're an escort," Joel said quietly.

"Oh," Hunter said, his face suddenly clouded with hurt.

Joel walked over and wrapped his arms around Hunter.

"It's not because I'm embarrassed by you," he lied, "it's just that the reason I never saw Michel again is because he thought I was a hustler."

Hunter looked into Joel's eyes.

"Why did he think that?" he asked.

"Because when he first saw me I was with Chance and Taylor and Louis," Joel said, letting go of Hunter, "and he knew they were hustlers."

"How?"

"He's a cop," Joel said.

Hunter studied Joel's face for a minute then shook his head.

"Does he know where you live now?"

Joel sensed anxiety in Hunter's voice.

"No," he said. "That's why I wanted to leave. I don't want him to know where I am."

"Because he'll think you're a hustler if you're here, or because you're trying to protect us?" Hunter asked.

His tone held a hint of challenge that unnerved Joel. Joel stared at him blankly for a moment, unsure how to respond. He wanted to say he'd been protecting the others, but he knew that his reasons had been selfish.

"I guess because I didn't want him to think I was a hustler," he said finally.

Hunter stared at him appraisingly for a minute and Joel could feel his stomach tightening. Then Hunter seemed to relax.

"I understand," he said, smiling. "I know you don't think we're shit because we're escorts."

Joel shook his head.

"Not at all."

"And you know you don't have to become an escort for me to like you?" Hunter asked. "You know that, don't you?"

Joel shrugged. It bothered him that Hunter had only spoken for himself.

"What about the others?" he asked.

"I don't know," Hunter said, "but it doesn't matter. We'll still be friends. I don't think they'll care either, but they can be assholes sometimes so who knows?"

Joel felt anxious at the thought of being rejected by the others.

"But I want to be an escort," he said suddenly.

Hunter gave Joel an uncertain look.

"It's not what you think it is," he said. "I know it seems really glamorous and we always have lots of money and drugs, but the work itself is different. Even when we don't have to have sex with someone we still have to pretend we like him. Some of these guys are the most boring assholes in the world and we have to make them feel like we're interested in every word they say. Sometimes I think I should get a fucking Academy Award."

Joel laughed and Hunter smiled at him for a moment. Then his face grew serious.

"When we have to have sex with them it's worse," he said, shaking his head sadly. "No matter how fat or ugly or smelly they are, we still have to get it up and act like we think they're friggin' Brad Pitt. You just have to keep in your mind that you're doing it to get what you want."

He paused and looked at Joel. Joel tried to imagine himself having sex with someone who repulsed him. He'd had sex only a few dozen times in his life and most of those times had been with Chance. He wondered if he could fake being attracted to someone.

"Look, Joel," Hunter said, "I don't want you doing anything you don't want to do. If you're not comfortable with it, then forget it. Don't worry about Jared and Peter and Raphael. I'll still be here for you, no matter what."

Joel didn't know what to say. What Hunter had said scared him. At the same time he wondered who Hunter would choose if the others turned against him, and the thought of being alone made him feel sick. He was suddenly very tired.

"I'm going to bed," he said.

"Can I come with you?" Hunter asked.

He gave Joel a pleading look.

"Okay," Joel said.

He draped his arms over Hunter's shoulders and kissed him. "I'd like that."

Chapter 29

Michel placed a large iced cappuccino on the edge of Sassy's desk and draped his jacket over the back of the chair next to it. He pulled the chair out so it was perpendicular to Sassy's chair and sat down, stretching his legs toward his partner. Sassy eyed the plastic cup suspiciously.

"What's that for?" she asked.

"I figured if I got you jacked up on caffeine you might tell me where you were when I called you at eleven-thirty last night."

He arched his eyebrows and grinned mischievously. Sassy gave him a half-lidded scowl and reached for the cup.

"I do have a personal life, you know," she said.

"I'm beginning to think the captain was right about what you do during your off-hours," Michel said with a smirk. "One of these days I might have to follow you."

"And one of these days I might have to break your kneecaps," Sassy replied.

She took a long sip and sighed happily.

"So what was so important?"

"I talked with Chanel last night."

"About Coolidge?" Sassy asked with a hint of surprise.

Michel nodded.

"Among other things, but I'll fill you in on the other things over lunch."

"So?"

"When I mentioned Coolidge's name it didn't seem to mean

anything to her," Michel said. "She said it sounded familiar, but she wasn't sure why."

"And you believed her?"

"Yeah. I mean if she were trying to hide anything why would she even admit his name was familiar?"

Sassy nodded.

"True. So then what?"

"Then I think something clicked," Michel said.

"What do you mean?" Sassy asked, giving him a puzzled look.

Michel tried to think of a way to adequately describe Chanel's reaction.

"I was in the middle of saying something when she suddenly zoned out. Just staring off into space. Then it was like something hit her. She kind of shuddered."

"Literally?" Sassy asked.

"Yeah," Michel said, nodding his head. "At first I thought maybe she'd had some sort of mild seizure or a stroke. When she looked back at me she seemed dazed, like she'd just woken up from a trance."

"What do you think happened?" Sassy asked.

"I think she figured out how she knew Coolidge's name," Michel said. "For just a second I swear she looked scared."

"Did you ask her?"

"No." Michel shook his head. "It was only for a second, and then it was like nothing had happened. She was back to her usual self."

Sassy considered what Michel had said.

"So does that make you feel more or less confident that she's a suspect?"

"I don't know," Michel replied, "I still can't see her killing, but she knows something. It certainly tells me we need to bring her in for questioning."

Suddenly there was a muted beep from near Michel's right hip. He twisted on the chair and pulled his cell phone from his jacket pocket. The message on the tiny screen read NEW VOICEMAIL.

"You really ought to keep that thing on ring," Sassy said.

"Have I ever missed one of your calls?" Michel asked as he hit the voicemail button. "Besides, you're the only one who ever calls me on it and I'm with you."

He put the phone to his right ear and listened. A combination of surprise and curiosity registered on his face.

"Who was it?" Sassy asked as he hung up.

"Lady Chanel," Michel replied, giving her a confused look. "She wants to meet me tonight at ten at the Quarter Scene. Said she has something she needs to show me and it needs to be discreet."

"Why don't we just pick her up now?" Sassy asked.

"No," Michel replied, shaking his head. "Let's let her come to us. But let's have some back-up there just in case."

Chapter 30

When Joel woke up he was alone. He looked at the alarm clock: 1:20 pm. He groaned and stood up. He was naked. His body ached from his exertions with Hunter the night before. He shuffled to the bathroom and stepped into the shower. The warm water felt good as it eased the soreness in his muscles and he stood under the heavy spray for ten minutes until it started to turn cool.

As he turned off the water he could hear muted voices coming from somewhere in the house. He dried himself quickly and wrapped the towel around his waist, then stepped into the hall. He could hear the voices more clearly now. They were coming from above and they sounded angry. He peeked his head into the twins' rooms, then wrapped the towel more tightly and walked to the foot of the stairs. He began to quietly ascend.

When he reached the third floor he looked in Raphael's and Peter's rooms. No one was there. Then he stepped into the bathroom next to the stairs to Zelda's room and pressed his ear to the wall. He could hear the voices more clearly.

"It's got to end, Zelda."

It was Lady Chanel. Her voice was strained and had lost its usual softness.

"It's too late for that," Zelda replied with a bitter laugh.

The voices were silent for a moment and Joel could hear footsteps moving away from him. When the voices began again he couldn't tell who was speaking any more.

169

"I won't let you."

"You can't stop me."

Joel heard footsteps moving toward the stairs and stepped behind the door. The sound continued down through the wall behind him. The door in the hallway opened and then the footsteps began moving quickly down the stairs to the second floor. He waited for the sound to fade away. He was about to step out from behind the door when he heard more footsteps coming down the stairs from Zelda's room.

The footsteps stopped in the hallway and Joel could hear angry breathing. He leaned forward carefully and looked through the crack where the door was hinged. He could see Zelda. She stood with her back to him, her shoulders rising and falling visibly in time with her breathing. Finally she began walking slowly down the stairs. Joel waited. After a minute he heard a door slam below and stepped out from behind the bathroom door. He moved quickly down the stairs and locked himself in his room.

Ten minutes later after he'd dressed he walked down to the kitchen. The house was quiet. He poured a cup of cold coffee and sat at the table, trying to make sense of what he'd heard. He'd never heard Lady Chanel that angry before and it scared him.

The back door banged loudly behind him and Joel jumped in his chair. He turned and saw Zelda standing inside the doorway holding a brown paper bag. She eyed him suspiciously.

"Where were you?" she asked.

"What do you mean?" Joel replied, stammering slightly. "I was here."

Zelda narrowed her eyes at him.

"Where? I didn't see you."

Joel tried to think of a plausible lie. He knew that his bedroom door had been open while he was hiding in the bathroom and Zelda might have looked inside as she walked past.

"I went out on the front porch for a while. Why?" he asked, struggling to keep his tone nonchalant.

Zelda hesitated, studying him carefully.

"I guess I didn't see you when I went out," she said finally, her voice tired and thick.

She walked to the table and put the bag down in front of Joel, then took a tall glass out of the cupboard and filled it with ice. She walked to the table and pulled a plastic half-gallon bottle of vodka from the bag. Joel looked up at her. She looked back at him but it seemed as though she was no longer seeing him.

"I'll be in my room if anyone needs me," she said flatly.

She grabbed the bottle and walked out of the room. Joel could hear her slow, heavy footsteps as she made her way up the stairs. He exhaled deeply.

I don't know what the fuck is going on, he thought, but I'm getting out of here. He put his cup in the sink and left the house.

Chapter 31

Joel stood on the balcony of the Good Friends Bar. He looked down at the dark V that stained the front of his gray t-shirt and pulled out the bottom, trying to unstick the damp fabric from his skin. He'd been looking for Hunter and the others all afternoon. He'd stopped by the restaurants he knew they frequented and had gone to Canal Place and the Riverwalk mall in hopes of finding them. He wanted to talk to Hunter, tell him what he'd overheard. He wondered if they were back at the house. Although he'd slept for nearly twelve hours he felt exhausted.

It seemed like years since he'd stood in that same spot with Chance on the day of the murder at the Creole House—on the day he'd met Michel. He remembered how full of hope and possibilities he'd felt then. He looked at his watch: 6:50 pm. Time for another drink, he thought as he finished the rest of his beer.

"Hey, stranger," a voice said behind him.

He turned and saw Chance standing in the doorway. Joel felt his heart begin to race and struggled to catch his breath. He wanted to throw his arms around Chance and kiss him, but he waited, uncertain of what Chance would do. Then Chance smiled.

"Oh my God," Joel said, walking to Chance and locking his arms around him. "I've missed you so much."

"I've missed you, too," Chance said, hugging him back tightly. "I was worried about you."

172

They held one another for a long time, each contented to let the embrace continue.

"Want to get a drink, or just stay like this?" Chance asked finally.

Joel kissed him on the cheek.

"Let's get a drink."

They walked inside and ordered two screwdrivers, then walked back onto the balcony. They were the only people there.

"I'm really sorry about what happened," Joel said as they reached the railing.

"Me, too," Chance replied remorsefully. "I kind of lost it."

"It's okay," Joel said softly. "I understand."

"I wanted to find you, but I thought maybe you'd left the city," Chance said. "I ran into Michel at the Bourbon a few nights ago. He was looking for you, too. He seems pretty cool."

Joel gave Chance a puzzled look.

"Lady Chanel didn't tell you?"

"I haven't talked to her. I figured she'd be pissed at me. What?" Chance asked.

"I've been living at Zelda's."

Chance's expression became suddenly dark.

"What the fuck are you doing there?" he asked sharply.

"I needed a place to stay," Joel said, confused by the shift in Chance's demeanor.

"And Chanel let you?" Chance asked.

Joel hesitated, thinking back to the way Lady Chanel had reacted when Zelda offered him the room.

"Yeah," he replied. "Why? What's the matter?"

"Just get the fuck away from her, all right?"

"Why?" Joel asked again more forcibly, shrugging his shoulders in exasperation.

Chance seemed to wrestle to control his emotions for a moment, then the anger swelled again.

"Because she's a fucking pimp," he shouted. "Zelda and her little sluts. And she's going to try to turn you into one, too."

Joel could feel his face flush.

"You don't know what you're talking about," he said, shaking his head vehemently.

"No? How do you think I got started?" Chance asked more quietly. "Me, and Taylor and Louis. We all lived there. She gets her boys to treat you nice and get you fucked up and tell you how much money they have, and pretty soon you start thinking it's not such a bad idea."

Joel thought about the nights he'd spent partying with the boys and hesitated, suddenly uncertain. Then he thought of what Hunter had said to him the night before—"you don't have to become an escort for me to like you"—and felt angry.

"They're my friends," he said, his eyes flashing at Chance.

"Your friends?" Chance laughed derisively. "They don't give a shit about you. Hunter turned his own fucking brother into a whore."

Joel gave Chance a hard look. The idea that Hunter had been playing him seemed impossible.

"You're hardly in a position to judge anyone else," he said coldly.

Chance stared back at him, fighting to hold in his anger.

"But at least I keep what I make," he said, his voice barely controlled. "That's why Zelda hates me. I convinced Louis and Taylor we could go out on our own. Better to be my own bitch than someone else's."

Joel recoiled. He stared back at Chance and shook his head slowly.

"Bullshit," he said. "She probably cut you loose because you couldn't earn enough to pay your way."

Chance took a few deep breaths. Tears began to well up in his eyes.

"I'm just trying to protect you," he said in a soft, breaking voice.

Joel gave him a contemptuous look and shook his head.

"Just stay the fuck away from me," he said.

He turned his back and left Chance standing on the balcony.

Chapter 32

The house was dark except for a light in the kitchen. Joel opened the side gate and walked to the back door. His anger had subsided and he felt in control again. He wanted to talk to Zelda. As he walked into the kitchen she was seated at the table with her back to him. She didn't move when he closed the door.

"Hi," he said.

She turned her head slowly and looked at him. Her eyes were distant and hazy.

"Well, if it isn't our little dishwasher," she said derisively. "Or should I say ex-dishwasher?"

She turned away. Joel could see the half empty vodka bottle over her shoulder. He walked hesitantly to the table. An overflowing ashtray rested next to Zelda's right arm. He picked it up and emptied it into the garbage can.

"Thank you," Zelda said absently as he placed it back on the table. "You want a drink?"

Joel filled a glass with ice and sat down. Zelda picked up the bottle and filled his glass.

"Cheers," she said, lifting her own glass.

Joel noticed that her movements were unsteady and her voice was thick and slow. He wondered how often she'd been drunk when he'd seen her lately.

"I want to work for you," he said suddenly.

Zelda stared at her glass, seeming not to have heard him. He opened his mouth to repeat what he'd said.

"What makes you think you can?" she asked slowly.

176

"You invited me to live here," he replied.

Zelda let out a soft chuckle and lifted her head to look at him. Her eyes seemed suddenly clear and focused.

"I was just helping out a friend," she said, drawing out the last word.

"That's not what Chance said," Joel replied, feeling bolder. "He said you bring boys here to work for you."

Zelda chuckled again, this time more deeply.

"Dear Coco needs to learn to keep her mouth shut," she said, a hint of cold menace in her voice.

She picked up her glass and took a long swallow.

"Please," Joel said, haltingly as he struggled to find the right words. "I want to be like the others."

"Do you, now?" Zelda asked, raising her eyebrows. "But you're not like the others."

Joel thought he heard a challenge in her voice.

"I am like them," he said.

Zelda studied him for a moment.

"We'll see," she said finally, shaking her head.

She stood and walked behind Joel, placing her hand on top of his head. She began to stroke his hair softly and Joel suppressed the urge to shudder.

"I had to turn a client away tonight," she said. "Maybe I can still reach him. But he likes it a little rough. Do you think you can handle that? He's a very important client and I wouldn't want to disappoint him."

"I can handle it," Joel said uncertainly.

Zelda didn't respond. She lifted her hand from his head and walked into the living room. Joel could hear her speaking in a low voice. He felt suddenly dizzy, filled with both panic and excitement. The sound of his heart seemed to echo in the room. He took a deep breath and willed the panic away.

"It's all arranged," Zelda said as she walked back into the room. "Meet him at 9:30 at the Bourbon Orleans Hotel. Room 217. His name is Mr. Smith."

Joel nodded. He was beginning to feel calmer.

"Wear something young," Zelda said. "Our Mr. Smith prefers his boys younger. If he asks, tell him you're seventeen. He won't ask for your ID. He'll want to believe you."

"When you get there the room will be dark," she continued. "There'll be a blindfold on the inside of the door knob. Put it on before you turn on the light. Don't forget. Mr. Smith insists on discretion. After that he'll tell you what to do."

Joel nodded again and began to stand, but stopped.

"One thing," he said quietly. "Please don't tell Lady Chanel."

Zelda began laughing, softly at first, then more loudly. There was something pitiful in the sound and Joel felt suddenly uneasy.

"Don't you worry about Lady Chanel," Zelda said.

"What do you mean?" Joel asked nervously.

Zelda hesitated for a moment, seeming unsure how to respond.

"I mean that Chanel won't judge you," she said finally. "She may seem the proper lady now, but it wasn't always that way. She killed a man once."

Joel looked at Zelda with disbelief. Her eyes had become distant again.

"It was a long time ago," she said as if in a dream. "We were both working the streets back then."

"Why didn't she go to jail?" Joel asked skeptically.

"Because I lied," Zelda said, her voice suddenly choked with contempt. "No jury back then was going to let some little nigger hustler off for killing a white man. So I lied and they dropped the charges."

Joel thought back to the argument he'd overheard that morning. He tried to make sense of it with what Zelda had just said.

"Even if she did kill someone," he said, "she's different now."

Zelda shook her head pityingly at him.

"It doesn't matter," she said. "Our past is always with us, and eventually it comes back and we're punished for it."

Joel felt a chill travel up his spine. He remembered the last words he'd heard in Zelda's room: "You can't stop me." Suddenly he thought he understood.

"I won't do this," he said abruptly. "Chanel tried to stop you. She didn't want me to do this."

Zelda stared blankly at him for a moment, then a look of comprehension came across her face. She smiled acidly.

"Someone had his ear to the key hole," she said, wagging her finger slowly at him. "Naughty boy."

Joel shifted uncomfortably.

"I won't do it," he said, trying to sound decisive.

"It's too late for that," Zelda said, shaking her head slowly. "Unless you want to see Lady Chanel hurt you'll do it."

Joel stared at her uneasily, trying to gauge whether she was bluffing. She looked back at him with cold certainty and he knew he had no choice.

"You'd better hurry," she said. "Mr. Smith likes his boys clean."

Joel stood unsteadily. His forehead and upper lip felt suddenly clammy and he could feel his stomach tighten convulsively. He walked slowly out of the room and down the hall to the stairs. He began to climb, gripping the hand rail tightly to maintain his balance. Halfway up a surge of nausea welled in his throat and he began to run. As he lurched through the bathroom he dropped to his knees and began to vomit.

*****

Joel looked at himself in his bedroom mirror. He felt as though he were in a dream. His movements felt slow and heavy. He pulled his shorts lower, exposing his stomach below the black tank top, and checked his watch. It was 9:05 pm.

He turned off his bedroom light and walked across the hall to the twins' room. From the top drawer of the dresser he removed a small, inlaid wooden box. He opened it and took out a razor blade, silver straw and a bag of white crystals. He pulled two crystals from the bag and placed them on the top of the dresser, then began chopping them with razor blade.

Chapter 33

Michel arrived outside the Quarter Scene Restaurant at 9:40 pm. He looked through the plate glass window and surveyed the room. At the nearest table a man and woman picked slowly at their salads. In the far corner three men were chatting desultorily as they shared a plate of crawfish, their drinks untouched on the table. Back-up is in place, he thought. Two other couples were seated in the upper half of the room. He crossed the street and stepped into a shadow.

"Anything?" he asked into his radio.

"Nothing yet," a voice replied.

A plain-clothed officer had been stationed several blocks up Dauphine Street toward the Marigny.

"Okay," Michel said, lighting a cigarette.

*****

Lady Chanel left her house and began walking quickly up Dauphine. The moon was nearly hidden by the dense cloud of humidity that clung to the city, and as she walked she searched the shadows around her. She reached down and nervously patted her shoulder bag.

"Hey there," a voice said behind her.

She turned quickly, trying to appear calm.

"What are you doing here?" she asked.

As the knife punched into her stomach she dropped to her knees and screamed.

*****

Michel checked in on the radio again.

"Still nothing," said the voice.

"Okay," Michel said. "She may be coming from a different direction. I'm going in. If you see her, call me."

He dropped his cigarette into the gutter and crossed the street.

*****

Lady Chanel could hear distant voices and the sound of running footsteps. She opened her eyes and looked across the surface of a dark lake. It seemed to spread as she watched it. She saw a giant knee descending into the lake.

"You're going to be okay," a soft voice said.

She smiled and closed her eyes.

*****

Michel had taken a seat by the window, facing the door. The two other couples had left and now it was just him and the five undercover officers. He could hear his waiter chatting loudly in the kitchen. He looked out the window and checked his watch: 10:30 pm.

"Let's give her ten more minutes," he said to no one in particular.

*****

Joel waited until he heard the door click shut, then pulled off the blindfold. The room was dark but he could see his clothes scattered on the floor. He stood up and slowly walked over and picked up his shorts, his whole body aching as he moved. He reached into the right front pocket and checked that the carefully folded bills were still there, then dropped the shorts back on the floor and walked to the bathroom.

As he flipped on the lights he winced at the harsh brightness. He closed his eyes and waited for them to adjust, gradually opening them a little at a time. Finally, after what seemed like minutes, he was able to open them enough to look at himself in the mirror. He looked like he'd been in an accident. His whole face was red and slightly puffy, and dried blood ran from his right nostril and the right corner of his mouth. He ran his fingers delicately over the swelling on his right cheek as tears began to wet his face.

He turned on the shower and immediately stepped under the cold stream. He didn't want to wait for it to warm up. He just wanted to wash all traces of Mr. Smith off his body. After ten minutes he turned the water off and gingerly dried himself, then walked back into the bedroom and began to dress.

As he exited the hotel onto Bourbon Street five minutes later he could hear loud music farther up the block to his right. He crossed the street and began walking toward the Bourbon Pub.

*****

"Let's call it a night," Michel said at 10:45 pm.

The five undercover officers in the restaurant stood in unison and Michel handed his credit card to the confused waiter.

"They're with me," he said.

Outside he pulled the radio from his pocket.

"We're packing it up here," he said. "You may as well call it a night. But let's have a patrol car in the area. Tell them not to pick her up if they see her. Just give me a call on my cell."

"You want to send a patrol over to her house?" the radio crackled back.

"Sure," Michel replied wearily.

He knew that if Lady Chanel had decided to go into hiding she wouldn't be at her house. He looked up the street one last time and frowned. Maybe she went to the pub, he thought, as he crossed the street.

Chapter 34

Joel sat at the back upstairs bar, a small pile of crumbled bills in front of him. He'd broken one of the $100 bills that Smith had given him and had decided to drink until the money was gone. He'd already finished his second screwdriver and started a third. He felt drained and numb. He didn't want to think about the night and the things he'd allowed Smith to do to him anymore. He wanted to forget it ever happened. He drank half of the screwdriver and lit a cigarette.

Downstairs Michel sipped his Jack Daniels and checked his watch. He'd been standing at the bar for almost an hour, watching for Lady Chanel, waiting for his cell phone to ring. He looked around the room and headed for the stairs.

The main room of Parade was crowded. Michel walked outside and slowly made his way along the balcony overlooking St. Philip, studying the faces of the men who stood in the shadows along the wall. He turned the corner onto the Bourbon Street side. Three boys stood smoking along the rail. They gave him cursory glances and resumed their sullen conversation. He went back inside.

He stood along the wall and carefully surveyed the room. He felt obtrusive and out of place in his suit but tried to appear casual. Finally satisfied that Lady Chanel wasn't there, he pushed his way through the crowd to the dance floor and took up a position in a corner.

While three dozen men undulated in unison to the pulsing rhythm, Michel studied the faces that crowded the edge of the dance floor. They seemed so engaged, so happy. Michel wondered if he'd ever felt as carefree as they looked, and what dark secrets they hid behind their smiles. After a few minutes he sighed and finished his drink. May as well complete the circuit, he thought hopelessly, as he walked through the door that connected the dance area to the back bar. Joel was sitting at the far corner of the bar on the same stool where Lady Chanel had been sitting the night before, his body turned in profile to Michel.

Michel took a sharp breath and stood still. Joel's head was lowered and he was staring at his drink, seemingly lost in thought. He looked somehow smaller and more fragile than Michel had remembered. Michel studied his face. Joel's right cheek looked puffy and red. Michel felt a sudden swell of conflicting emotions. He knew that he should honor Joel's wishes not to see him, but at the same time he felt an overwhelming need to make sure that Joel was all right. Suddenly Joel turned his head and looked at him.

For a moment there was no expression on Joel's face. Michel could hear the beating of his own heart and fought the urge to turn and leave. Then Joel gave him a small smile. Michel thought it was the most heartbreaking smile he'd ever seen. He walked toward Joel and as he reached him Joel fell into his arms and began to cry.

Michel held him tightly. He could feel Joel's body trembling as he tried to breathe through his tears. The crowd around the bar had begun to stare at them.

"Shhhh," Michel soothed softly. "It's going to be all right."

He picked Joel's money up from the bar and lead Joel onto the balcony to the bench where they'd talked that first night. They sat down, Michel's arms still around Joel.

"What's the matter?" Michel asked.

Joel sat up straight and struggled to regain his composure. He wriggled his upper body uncomfortably and Michel let go of him. Joel wiped his eyes and nose with the back of his hand.

"Nothing," he said finally.

He was breathing more steadily and gave Michel an awkward smile.

"Bullshit," Michel said as he gently touched Joel's right cheek with his left hand.

"I don't want to talk about it," Joel said, pulling his face away from Michel's hand. "I'm just really happy to see you."

Michel decided to let the injury drop for the moment.

"Are you?" he asked cautiously.

"Why wouldn't I be?" Joel replied with a searching look.

"I didn't think you wanted to see me after what I told you about Chance."

"No," Joel said. "I saw Chance tonight. He told me you were looking for me."

"So is everything cool with you guys again?"

Joel shook his head and looked down.

"He cares about you, Joel," Michel said. "He's been worried."

Joel didn't respond for a moment. He stared at the ground.

"It's kind of complicated," he said finally. "Can we go someplace else?"

"How about my house?" Michel asked.

Joel nodded and smiled sadly.

*****

Michel turned his head and looked at Joel sleeping beside him. In the dim light he could still see traces of tears on the side of Joel's face. He got up, carefully sliding his arm from under Joel's neck, and walked into the hallway, closing the door quietly behind him. He went to the kitchen and lit a cigarette. He needed to make sense of the things Joel had told him and his own feelings.

He didn't want to blame Joel for the things he'd done, at least not in the end. He understood that Joel had felt he had no choice. He'd been trying to protect Lady Chanel. And he knew that Zelda had manipulated Joel, probably from the beginning. Still, he'd observed too much of human nature to believe that Joel was an innocent victim of his circumstances. Though he'd been forced to go to Mr. Smith, he'd chosen to put himself on that path and he'd travelled it willingly.

He thought about what Sassy had said about Joel: "He doesn't think about consequences or tomorrow. It's all about what he feels in that moment." Was that really an excuse? Did it justify the choices Joel had made? He knew that Joel was smarter than that, better than that. He'd chosen to ignore what he knew was right out of weakness and the need to be accepted.

And what about Chanel? He wanted to believe that Chanel was innocent and that she'd tried to protect Joel, but now he questioned his feelings. Zelda had confirmed to Joel that Chanel had killed Whittier. Why couldn't he accept that she might be the killer now? He remembered being fascinated by her as a boy, the strange, graceful creature who seemed so much larger than the life he knew. Was he trapped holding onto that image?

His thoughts were broken as his cell phone began vibrating on the counter beside him. He looked at the clock: 4:10 am.

"Doucette," he answered.

"Michel, it's me," Sassy said flatly. "Meet me at the Frenchman Inn. We've got another body."

"I'll be there in ten," Michel replied.

He splashed cold water on his face in the kitchen sink and looked at his reflection in the window. I look like shit, he thought. He contemplated changing the shirt he'd been wearing since the previous morning but decided not to chance waking Joel. He wrote a note and placed it on the kitchen counter:

Joel – I had to run out. Hopefully be back before
you wake up. If not, please wait for me. – M.

Before he left he turned off the hall light and quietly opened the door to the bedroom. He could see the silhouette of Joel's body in the moonlight and hear him breathing steadily. He closed the door and walked outside.

Chanel set me up, he thought bitterly.

Chapter 35

Stan Lecher was already busy examining the body when Michel walked into the room.

"You planning to catch this guy soon?" he asked without looking up. "I don't like having my beauty sleep disturbed."

"We're working on it," Michel said, thinking that they wouldn't be here now if he'd picked up Lady Chanel that afternoon.

Sassy was standing by the window. By her expression he knew she'd been thinking the same thing.

"Well, you may have caught a break with this one," Lecher said.

"Our guy's getting sloppy. He didn't tighten the bonds well enough and our John Doe here got an arm free."

Michel looked at the body for the first time. The ankles and left arm were still tied to the bedposts, but the right arm was down by the victim's side.

"No ID on the victim?" Michel asked.

"Not yet," Lecher said.

Michel nodded.

"How long ago?" he asked.

Lecher looked at Sassy.

"Didn't tell him much did you?" he asked.

Michel gave Sassy a questioning look. She seemed to avoid meeting his eyes.

"The call came in 20 minutes ago," she said. "One of the guests heard screaming and called the front desk. The night clerk came up, found the door open. When he saw the victim he called us."

"Did he see anyone else?" Michel asked.

Sassy shook her head.

"But maybe someone else did. Ribodeau's people are questioning all the guests now."

"Bingo," Lecher said suddenly.

He motioned Michel and Sassy to the side of the bed.

"Looks like he got a good hold of the killer," he said, pointing to the fingernails of the victim's right hand.

"Skin?" Sassy asked.

Lecher nodded.

"Now we can run a DNA test," he said. "See if we can narrow down the search a little."

Sassy gave Michel a reproachful look. He looked away toward Lecher.

"Thanks, Stan," he said. "Let us know as soon as you have something."

*****

"I'm sorry," Michel said as soon as he and Sassy had gotten free of the crowd of policemen standing on the curb.

"Sorry isn't going to cut it, Michel," she said, turning to face him. "Try telling it to that guy's family."

"I thought I was doing the right thing," Michel said helplessly.

"I know you did," Sassy replied more softly, "and that makes it worse. You allowed your personal feelings to get in the way of your professional judgment."

Michel nodded.

"She set me up," he said. "She lured me to the Quarter Scene while she went out and picked her next victim."

"You set yourself up," Sassy said harshly, "and I allowed you to do it."

"I'll put out an arrest warrant for her," Michel said.

"I did it before I even called you," Sassy said, shaking her head disappointedly.

She turned and walked away.

Chapter 36

Michel got back to the house as the sun was beginning to rise. He made coffee and sat at the kitchen counter smoking. He knew he should wake Joel and tell him what was happening but he wanted to postpone telling him that Chanel was the killer as long as possible. Suddenly he heard the bedroom door open and turned. Joel stood in the doorway rubbing his eyes.

"What are you doing up so early?" he asked.

"There was another murder," Michel replied. "You want some coffee?"

Joel walked into the room and sat at the counter while Michel poured his coffee.

"I need to talk to you about something," Michel said as he handed Joel the cup.

Joel gave him a worried look.

"We've put out an arrest warrant for Chanel," Michel said softly.

"For what?" Joel asked incredulously.

"For the murders."

Joel stared at him in disbelief.

"It can't be her," he said adamantly.

"I know," Michel said sadly. "I didn't want to believe it either, but when you told me Zelda confirmed that Chanel killed someone I realized I had no choice."

"But Zelda may have been lying to turn me against Chanel," Joel said helplessly. "She was trying to get me to do what she wanted."

Michel shook his head.

"Chanel set me up, Joel," he said. "She told me to meet her at the Quarter Scene last night and while I was there she found another victim. I'm responsible for the murder because I didn't want to accept that she was guilty."

Joel was silent for a moment.

"What will happen to her," he asked finally.

Michel shrugged, unable to tell Joel that she would face the death penalty.

Suddenly the silence was broken by a loud knocking at the front door.

"Stay here," Michel said, giving Joel a worried look.

He walked quietly to the door and looked through the peep hole. No one was there. He felt a sudden rush of apprehension and wished that Joel wasn't in the house. He drew his gun from his shoulder holster and unlatched the safety. He could feel sweat running down his back. Standing to the side he slowly turned the handle then pulled hard. The door flew open. Sassy was standing a few feet to the side on the porch. When she saw him she broke into an amused smile.

"Kind of dramatic, don't you think?" she asked, arching one eyebrow. "Can't you just open the door like regular people?"

Michel sighed in relief and frustration.

"Look, Sas, I can't talk right now," he said.

"Chanel is in the hospital," Sassy said. "She's in a coma."

*****

Sassy sat at the counter across from Joel while Michel poured her coffee. She studied Joel as he anxiously smoked, not making eye contact with her. Nice looking kid aside from the bruises, she thought. Michel could do worse.

"What happened?" Michel asked, sitting next to Joel.

"I got a call about twenty minutes ago from Mike Callahan. He'd just seen the arrest warrant for Chanel. Told me he answered an assault call last night around ten. Chanel was the victim. She'd been stabbed and beaten. Lost a lot of blood."

"Is she going to be okay?" Joel asked, his voice small and tight.

"I don't know," Sassy said softly. "She's in bad shape."

Michel reached over and grabbed Joel's hand.

"Was she conscious?" he asked.

Sassy shook her head.

"But she was probably on her way to meet you," she said. "She was on Dauphine near the corner of Touro."

"Who found her?" Michel asked.

"That's the amazing thing," Sassy said. "A bunch of guys who live in the park near her house heard a scream. They'd seen her walk by a minute before and thought she might be in trouble so they went looking for her. They probably saved her life by scaring off the attacker. It looks like whoever did it meant to kill her."

Michel heard Joel take a wet breath and squeezed his hand more tightly.

"Any description?" he asked, trying not to sound like a cop.

Sassy shook her head.

"It was dark and by the time they reached her she was alone."

"What about the weapon?" Michel asked.

"It looks like it could be the same one used in the murders," Sassy replied.

She looked at Joel to see how he was handling the conversation before continuing.

"But why would the killer..."

She stopped as Michel held up his index finger. She gave him a questioning look but he was staring past her. His body had gone completely still. Sassy took a slow breath and waited. Finally Michel turned to Joel.

"I know this is hard right now," he said, "but can you remember what Zelda said to you about punishment?"

Joel wiped his eyes and tried to remember the exact words.

"The past is always with us and eventually it comes back and we're punished for it," he said. "You think Zelda was punishing Lady Chanel?"

"It wasn't punishment," Michel said, slowly shaking his head. "It was self-preservation. Chanel knew Zelda was the killer and she threatened to stop her."

"Wait a second," Sassy said, shaking her head in confusion. "I think I missed part of the movie."

Michel quickly recounted the argument Joel had overheard and the conversation Joel had had with Zelda the previous night. He left out the circumstances of the conversation.

"Does the word 'partner' mean anything to you?" Sassy asked, giving him an exasperated look. "When were you planning to tell me all this?"

"I just heard it all last night," Michel said. "I would have told you earlier this morning but for some reason I didn't have a chance."

He gave her a reproachful look.

"I'm sorry," Sassy said sincerely.

"You two have a very complicated relationship," Joel said quietly.

Michel gave him an appreciative look.

"You have no idea," he said.

Sassy considered what Michel had told her.

"But what's Zelda's motive?" she asked. "I can understand why she wanted to kill Chanel, but what's the connection between the victims?"

"I don't know," Michel said, shrugging, "but she must have been using Cally to find her victims."

"Who's Cally?" Joel asked.

"Chanel's real name is Cally Haden," Michel said. "Two of the victims were seen talking to Cally the nights they were killed."

"But why would Chanel help her?" Joel asked anxiously.

Michel shrugged again.

"Blackmail?"

"I know there's no statute of limitations for murder, but the Whittier killing was 45 years ago," Sassy said, "and it may have been self-defense. Why wouldn't Chanel take her chances with the police?"

"It seems like she'd decided to last night," Michel replied sadly. "Besides, the hold Zelda had on Chanel may have been stronger than just the Whittier killing. If Chanel was helping Zelda then she was an accomplice and with each killing Zelda's power over her would grow. What if this has been going on for years and we're just finding out about it now? "

"Talk about complicated relationships," Sassy said, glancing at Joel for a second. "I'm warning you now, Michel. You start whacking people and I'm not helping you out. Doesn't matter what shit you think you have on me."

Michel gave her a warm smile.

"Will Chanel go to jail for helping her?" Joel asked, his voice small and choked.

Michel considered how to respond. He wondered whether Chanel would live that long.

"I don't know," he said, squeezing Joel's hand.

Joel seemed to accept the answer but Michel gave him a minute before speaking again.

"I need to take a shower," he said finally. "I'll call a squad car to pick up Zelda and meet you at the station in an hour."

Sassy nodded.

"Can you drop me at the hospital?" Joel asked.

Michel studied him carefully.

"Are you sure?" he asked.

"Yeah," Joel replied, forcing a smile.

"Okay," Michel said reluctantly, "but I want you to come back here after."

He opened a drawer and pulled out a key, handing it to Joel.

"I'll call you as soon as I can," he said.

Chapter 37

The policeman standing in the hallway nodded to Joel as he approached Lady Chanel's room. Michel had called ahead to arrange for Joel to see her.

The room was dark and Joel could hear the steady pumping of the ventilator as he approached the bed. He'd never been in a hospital before. His parents had been killed in the accident. There'd been no visits to the hospital—just a phone call, and then his grandfather had sat him on the porch and told him. He felt anxious as he approached the bed.

The person laying there was a stranger. His eyes were swollen shut and there was a large bandage wrapping his forehead below the short gray hair. Tubes were taped into his nose and mouth. Joel searched the face looking for anything familiar, anything that could tell him this was Lady Chanel. He looked down at the man's right hand. The fingernails still glittered with chipped red polish.

Joel touched the back of Chanel's hand. It felt cool. He wrapped his fingers into the palm and squeezed. There was no response. He began to cry softly.

"I'm sorry," he said.

*****

Sassy and Michel watched Zelda through the observation window of the interrogation room. Her features were bloated and her eyes were bloodshot and puffy. She looked as though she'd been drinking heavily. Although they knew she couldn't see them through the mirrored glass, she seemed to be staring directly at them.

"Try not to smack her," Sassy said only half in jest as Michel headed toward the interrogation room.

"Detective Doucette," Zelda said as he entered the room. "How are you today?"

Michel ignored her and sat down on the opposite side of the table. The room smelled of liquor and stale sweat.

"Where were you last night?" he asked.

"I was at home," Zelda replied.

"Any witnesses to that?"

Zelda's brow knitted together momentarily.

"Well, Joel was with me until just after nine," she said.

Michel gripped the sides of his chair below the table and took a slow breath.

"After that?" he asked, keeping his voice steady.

"The other boys got home around ten," Zelda replied with a shrug.

"And I suppose they'll testify that you were there all night?"

"I imagine so," Zelda replied, "though they certainly don't sleep in my room."

Michel gave her a measured look and smiled. He looked forward to seeing her reaction when he told her they'd recovered DNA evidence from the latest victim. Suddenly the door to the room opened and Sassy gestured to him.

"I'll be right back," he said, giving Sassy a curious look.

Zelda watched silently as Michel left the room.

As she closed the door behind them, Sassy gave Michel a worried look.

"I can handle it," he said reassuringly. "I'm not going to let her piss me off."

"It's not that," Sassy said abruptly. "Lecher just called. He got the lab results on the skin under John Doe's fingernails. The killer is white."

*****

Joel took a cab from the hospital to Chance's apartment. He felt drained and sad. He didn't want to be alone. He wanted to be with a friend. He knew he'd been wrong to judge Chance and turn against him when Chance had tried to protect him. He needed to make things right.

He rang the doorbell and waited.

*****

Chance sat in the window of Petunia's four blocks away, picking at his breakfast. He'd been awake all night and had left the apartment shortly after dawn, ending up at the tiny restaurant an hour later. Everyone was buzzing about the attack on Lady Chanel and he thought sadly about the closeness they'd lost. Lady Chanel had been like a mother to him since he'd come to the Quarter. He couldn't imagine life there without her and made a promise to himself to mend their relationship when she got out of the hospital...if she got out of the hospital. He pushed the thought away.

Everything seemed to be falling apart. He thought again about the night before and felt a fresh flush of anger. How could Joel have turned against him like that? He closed his eyes and breathed deeply. He'd already relived their argument a hundred times that night and didn't want to remember it again. Although he was hurt and angry, he still loved Joel. He still wanted to protect him.

He finished his coffee and made his decision: he would go to Zelda and offer to work for her if she left Joel alone.

*****

"How can that be?" Michel asked incredulously.

Sassy shrugged.

"No," Michel said, shaking his head, "I know Zelda's involved."

"Michel, Lecher found blood from the killer, too," Sassy said. "Unless Zelda was standing in the corner just watching she wasn't there."

Michel let out an exasperated sigh.

"I don't fucking believe this," he said.

Sassy gave him a steadying look.

"We have to cut her loose," she said.

Michel pressed his palms against his eyes for a moment.

"All right," he said irritably, "but I want her alone for a few minutes first. No videotape."

"Wait a second," Sassy said, giving him a worried look. "Don't do anything stupid."

"Don't worry about it," he said curtly.

He stood outside the door for a minute, trying to regain his composure, then stepped inside.

"You're free to go," he said.

For a second he saw an expression of confusion cross Zelda's face. Then she began to stand.

"But you'll be back," Michel said.

Zelda stopped. Michel moved to the other side of the table and leaned toward her. He could feel his temples throbbing.

"I know exactly what you are," he said in a low voice.

Zelda stared at him blankly.

"I know what happened with Joel," he said, "How your boys played him and about his appointment with Mr. Smith last night. I'll make sure you pay for that."

Zelda's gaze faltered for a moment, then she looked at Michel with a cool calm.

"No," she said evenly. "I don't think either of us would want people to know Joel was hustling, would we?"

Michel felt a sudden rage and began to walk around the table toward Zelda. The door opened and Sassy stepped quickly inside.

"Get the fuck out of here," she said to Zelda.

Chapter 38

Michel stood silently staring out the window of the squad room. He knew that Zelda had the upper hand. Regardless of his desire to punish her, he knew he wouldn't put Joel through the humiliation of the trial just to put her in jail for six months. He sighed deeply and turned around. Sassy sat on her desk watching him.

"Now what?" she asked.

"I have no fucking idea," he said, walking toward her. "We're back to square one. We don't have a suspect. We don't have a motive."

"That's not what I meant," Sassy said. "I meant about Zelda."

She gave him a hard look.

"Do you mean am I planning to kill her?" Michel asked with a tired smile.

Sassy just stared at him. Michel shook his head.

"I'm done with her," he said.

Sassy studied him carefully for a moment, then nodded.

"I better call Joel to let him know what's going on," Michel said.

He picked up the phone and dialed his home number. Joel answered on the second ring.

"How was Chanel?" Michel asked.

"She didn't even know I was there," Joel replied, his voice catching.

"She did," Michel said comfortingly. "I'm sure she did."

He could hear Joel begin to cry.

"Joel, I've got to tell you something," Michel said. "We let Zelda go. She's not the killer."

There was silence on the other end of the phone for a moment.

"But what about attacking Chanel?" Joel asked finally.

"No, it wasn't her," Michel replied.

"Was it the killer?" Joel asked.

"I don't know," Michel replied. "I suppose so. I don't know."

He felt helpless. He wanted to give Joel some tangible answers to hold onto but knew he couldn't.

"Listen," he said. "I want you to get some rest. I'll be home in a few hours."

"Okay," Joel said in a small voice.

"And Joel, don't leave the house or answer the door," Michel added. "I don't think there's anything to worry about, but I just want to be safe."

"Okay," Joel said and hung up.

He walked to the bathroom and washed his face, then searched through Michel's dresser for a clean shirt, choosing a dark blue t-shirt with the letters NOPD in yellow on the back.

I've got to make things right, he thought, as he locked the front door behind him.

*****

Back in his apartment Chance undressed and turned on the water in the shower.

Chapter 39

Joel stood on the sidewalk and looked up at Zelda's house. The shades were drawn in all the windows. What had felt like his home only yesterday now seemed strange and cold to him. He knew that the life he'd known there had ended. He walked up the steps and rang the doorbell. Although he'd been living there for almost a month it felt inappropriate to let himself in now. He could hear movement inside, then Hunter appeared at the narrow window to the left of the door. When he saw Joel he broke into a joyful smile.

"Where the hell have you been?" he asked as he opened the door. "I was scared shitless something happened to you."

He reached out and grabbed Joel by the shoulders, pulling him close. Joel limply returned the hug. He was happy to see Hunter, but at the same time it made his heart ache because he knew he'd come to say goodbye. Finally Hunter released him.

"What happened to your cheek?" he asked as he studied Joel's face.

Joel felt a rush of shame and wondered whether to tell the truth.

"Mr. Smith," he said finally.

Hunter gave him a sympathetic look and nodded.

"Come on in," he said sadly.

They walked to the kitchen and Joel sat at the table while Hunter poured coffee for them.

"I need to talk to Zelda," Joel said as Hunter put a cup in front of him and sat down.

Hunter gave him a questioning look.

"She's asleep," he said. "She just got home from the police station a few minutes ago and she was a wreck so I gave her a pill."

Joel looked around the room. It seemed different now. The life was gone from it. He sensed that the whole house was empty. He gave Hunter an awkward smile and took a long swallow of coffee.

"What did you want to talk to her about?" Hunter asked after a moment.

Joel hesitated. He didn't want to hurt Hunter. At the same time he knew this might be the last time they would ever be together as friends and he wanted to be honest with him. Part of him was glad that Zelda was asleep.

"I don't want to work for her anymore," he said. "I came to pick up my things. I can't stay here anymore."

He reached into his pocket and put what was left of the money he'd gotten from Mr. Smith on the table.

"Tell her she can keep all of it," he said.

Hunter gave him a confused look.

"But you earned it," he said.

Joel shook his head and took another sip of coffee.

"I don't want it," he said firmly.

He began to feel lightheaded.

"If you're sure," Hunter said, studying him carefully. "Are you feeling all right? You don't look so good."

"Just tired," Joel replied, though he'd begun to feel dizzy. "Will you do me a favor and tell Zelda? I don't really want to face her."

He took another sip of coffee and tried to concentrate.

"Sure, I'll tell her," Hunter replied smiling, "but there's really no need. You were never working for her anyway."

"What do you mean?" Joel asked.

His tongue felt thick and his voice seemed to be coming from far away. He reached for the coffee cup and knocked it off the edge of the table. It shattered on the floor. He stared at the spot where the cup had been for a moment, then looked at the floor.

"Sorry," he mumbled.

He tried to remember what Hunter had been saying.

"Don't worry about it," Hunter said casually.

He leaned closer to Joel.

"You were working for me, Joel. Everyone was working for me. Zelda was just a figurehead. She had nothing to do with it."

Joel looked up at Hunter with an effort and tried to focus on his words.

"Even Chanel was working for me," Hunter said, raising his eyebrows conspiratorially, "only she didn't know exactly what she was doing for me. She thought she was just scouting tricks who liked drag queens. She was doing an excellent job, too, until your cop boyfriend had to fuck it all up by asking her about Darnell Coolidge. Clever girl that she is, she figured it all out. She even managed to find some information on Jared and me that she was planning to give to Detective Doucette."

Joel tried to speak.

"How did...?" he trailed off, unable to form the words.

"How did I know she was going to the police?" Hunter asked. "You're not the only one who likes to listen to other people's conversations, Joel. And just for the record, the sound quality in Raphael's closet is much better than the bathroom."

Joel felt very tired. He closed his eyes to rest for a moment. His head dropped forward. When he opened his eyes again he looked around the room. It seemed much darker and he wondered how long he'd been asleep. He looked for Hunter. He was standing in the doorway, his face hidden in shadow.

"Just get some rest," Hunter said. "I'll clean up the mess."

*****

Across town, Chance left his apartment and began walking toward the Marigny.

Chapter 40

Joel's head ached. He tried to move but his arms and legs felt paralyzed. He opened his eyes. His right arm extended in front of his face, the wrist tied to a wood post by a nylon stocking. In panic he tried to lift his head. A burst of pain exploded in his forehead and he dropped his head back down with a load groan. It came to rest on a pillow.

He looked over his bare shoulder. The light in the room was dim but he could make out a few details. The ceiling was high and vaulted with exposed beams. There was a dressing table along the far wall next to a dormered window that had been covered with a heavy curtain. The air smelled of old fabric and stale perfume.

Suddenly he felt fingertips running up the back of his right thigh and over his naked buttocks. His body tensed.

"Awake are we?" Hunter asked.

*****

Michel and Sassy sat at their desks in awkward silence. Michel knew that they should be reviewing the case files and planning the next steps in the investigation, but he'd lost his heart for it. He wondered if they should turn the case over to someone else. He was about to broach the subject with Sassy when his phone began ringing.

"Doucette," he answered.

"Detective Doucette, this is Officer Pruitt at the hospital.

Lady Chanel is conscious and wants to talk to you," a voice said. "You better hurry. The doctors aren't sure how long she'll be conscious."

"Be right there," Michel replied.

He hung up the phone and looked at Sassy.

"Come on," he said. "Chanel is awake."

*****

Joel looked up at Hunter.

"I tried to warn you," Hunter said, with a reproachful look. "I gave you every chance to change your mind. But you ignored me."

Joel struggled to clear his head, trying to make sense of what Hunter was saying. He began to remember what Hunter had said in the kitchen.

"What are you talking about?" he asked thickly.

"Joel, Joel," Hunter said, shaking his head sadly. "I told you you didn't have to sell yourself. I told you that I'd still be your friend if you didn't, and I meant it. But you were so desperate for acceptance that you were willing to sell your ass to get it."

"You lead me there," Joel said angrily.

"No," Hunter said with a small laugh. "I just put the temptation in front of you. The world is full of temptation, but we choose whether to embrace it or turn away. You chose to embrace it. And then you tried to change your mind afterward. You're pathetic."

Joel could feel his cheeks flush. He knew that what Hunter said was partly true.

"I realized it was wrong," he offered weakly.

"You didn't realize that until after Mr. Smith beat you up and fucked you?" Hunter asked sarcastically. "I don't think so. You turned your back on your best friend for being a hustler. You didn't suddenly decide it was okay for a day and then change your mind again. No. You always thought it was wrong, but you were willing to ignore that in hopes that we'd accept you as one of us. What's the matter, Joel, still trying to find the love you lost when mommy and daddy died?'"

Joel could feel tears welling up in his eyes and tried to blink them away.

"You know, you're really not cut out for being a hustler," Hunter said. "Frankly you're too nice. You don't have it in you to use people. Fortunately, I don't have that problem."

He sat on the edge of the bed and began to stroke Joel's hair. Joel tried to twist his head to see Hunter's face but it was outside his peripheral vision.

"I thought you were my friend," he said.

Hunter chuckled softly.

"I told you that part of my job is to make people think I like them, that I find them sexually attractive," he said.

Joel felt a twinge of hurt as he thought about the intimate moments he'd spent with Hunter. His fear was turning to anger.

"What gives you the right to judge me for something you do?" he asked sharply.

"You just don't get it, do you, Joel?" Hunter asked, leaning in close so that his face was only inches from Joel's. "Being a hustler isn't the bad thing. I'm a hustler. My brother and my friends are hustlers. The bad thing is that you made a conscious choice to do something you believed in your heart was wrong."

He stood up abruptly and walked out of Joel's range of vision. Joel heard the squeal of metal wheels rolling across the wood floor. Hunter reappeared pulling on the back of a cracked, green leather chair. As the chair came into view, Joel could see Zelda. Her torso and arms were bound to the chair with silver duct tape and she was gagged with a white towel that encircled her head. As Hunter spun the chair toward him, Joel could see that Zelda's eyes were open but listless. Her head lolled loosely as the chair came to rest.

"I believe you two have met," Hunter said with a genial smile.

Joel gave Hunter a hard look.

"Why Zelda?" he asked. "What did she do to you?"

"Do you think this is personal?" Hunter asked, giving Joel a quizzical look. "It's not about what she did to me. It's just about what she is. She's a liar and a hypocrite."

"What are you talking about?" Joel asked derisively.

"It's a very interesting story," Hunter said, striking the air with his index finger. "I think you heard the story about how Chanel killed someone once upon a time, didn't you?"

Joel nodded slowly.

"I figured as much," Hunter said. "Miss Zelda does like to talk after she's had a few cocktails. Don't you Zelda?"

He caressed the side of her face for a moment and Zelda stirred slightly.

"But there are some details she probably left out. You see, Zelda was there when it happened. It seems that Mr. Whittier took both Chanel—or should I say Cally—and Zelda home with him, thinking they were both little boys. But when Zelda took her clothes off he found out she was a little girl and got quite angry."

He paused for emphasis and looked at Joel expectantly. Joel looked away. He could see Zelda beginning to move behind Hunter.

"And then he began to beat Zelda," Hunter continued, seemingly disappointed that he hadn't gotten a reaction from Joel, "and Cally tried to stop him. In the struggle Cally managed to hit Whittier with a fireplace poker and when he fell he cracked his head open and died. One of Whittier's servants heard the commotion and found Cally trying to escape out the window, but Zelda was already gone."

"How do you know that?" Joel asked skeptically.

"She told me," Hunter replied matter-of-factly. "One night a few years ago, just after I'd moved in. We were sitting around having cocktails and as the night went on she began to tell her sad tale. I think she meant it to be helpful to me. You know: be careful what you do, your past can haunt you, blah, blah, blah. And she was right. It was helpful. Just not in the way she intended."

Joel's head was clearing. He suddenly realized what Hunter had said: Zelda was actually a woman. He looked at her and could see that the focus had returned to her eyes. She was glaring at Hunter.

"The Whittier family paid a visit to Cally in jail," Hunter continued enthusiastically, "and offered to pay him to leave town if they could get the charges dropped. They didn't want a public scandal. So Cally called Zelda and offered to split the money if Zelda would say that Cally had been with her all night."

Joel knew in his heart that Hunter was telling the truth. The dependency between Chanel and Zelda suddenly made sense to him.

"So Cally and Zelda left town for a few years. Cally must have saved his money so he could buy that big house when he came back," Hunter continued, "but not Zelda. Do you know what Zelda did with her money?"

Joel shook his head slowly. He felt suddenly anxious, unsure that he wanted to know. Hunter moved behind Zelda and placed his hands on her shoulders. Zelda recoiled at his touch and began moaning against the gag.

"Hush now," Hunter said, patting her head. "Zelda spent the money for surgery."

He reached forward and grabbed the hem of Zelda's dress. She began to struggle violently in the chair.

"And she got this," Hunter said as he pulled the dress up over Zelda's chest.

Joel stared in horror for a moment before closing his eyes. A twisted finger of brown and pink flesh protruded from between Zelda's legs. The remains of her vagina were scarred and gnarled. Hunter let the dress drop and moved closer to Joel. When he heard the footsteps Joel opened his eyes again. He could see tears cascading down Zelda's cheeks into the towel. He looked at Hunter.

"You're sick," he said angrily.

"I'm sick?" Hunter asked as though offended. "First she pretends she's a little boy, then she tries to become a man, then when that doesn't work out she pretends to be a man pretending to be a woman. Now that is sick."

*****

Sassy and Michel rushed down the corridor of the hospital toward Lady Chanel's room. Officer Pruitt met them partway.

"She's breathing on her own and they took the tubes out. She can't speak very well," he said quickly, "but she can write."

Pruitt waited in the hall while Sassy and Michel went into the room. Chanel's eyes and lips were grotesquely swollen and her jaw twisted awkwardly to one side. She didn't move. A note pad lay by her side and a black felt pen rested loosely between the fingers of her right hand. As they approached the bed Michel looked at the pad and saw the word "DOUCETTE" scrawled on it.

"Chanel," he said softly.

She turned her head slightly and opened her right eye. Michel thought she was trying to smile.

"Who did this?" Sassy asked.

Chanel lifted her hand and began writing.

"ZELDA"

Sassy and Michel exchanged confused looks.

"No, Chanel," Michel said. "It wasn't Zelda."

Chanel moaned and tapped the pad agitatedly with the pen. She began writing quickly, her whole body shaking with the exertion.

"SAVE ZELDA"

Michel gave Sassy a panicked look.

"From who, Chanel? From who?" he asked urgently.

Lady Chanel opened her mouth and Michel and Sassy could see her straining to make a sound. Finally a tattered whisper escaped.

"Hunter."

*****

Joel stared at Hunter for a moment then laughed bitterly.

"You condemn Zelda for pretending to be something she isn't? What makes you think you're any different?" he asked. "You dress up as a woman to kill people."

Hunter gave Joel a surprised look, then nodded in comprehension.

"I guess the police are a little further along than I thought," he said. "So is that why they brought Zelda in? She's a suspect?"

Joel didn't reply but Hunter nodded as though he had. He seemed to be lost in thought for a moment, then his eyes settled on Joel again. They were angry.

"I don't dress up out of a need to be something I'm not," he said, spitting out the words. "That's the difference. I pretend to be what they want me to be so that I can punish them."

"Punish them for what?" Joel asked.

Hunter was silent for a moment.

"For their lies," he said finally.

Joel felt suddenly calm. The certainty that he was going to die emboldened him.

"And what the fuck gives you the right to pass judgment on them?" he asked coldly.

"What gives me the right?" Hunter screamed.

He moved toward Joel so quickly that Joel flinched. Hunter's fists were clenched and Joel could see them shaking with rage.

"Having a father who dressed my brother and me up as little girls and fucked us gives me the right," Hunter shouted. "Having a mother who knew what was happening but ignored the screams and the blood in our underwear gives me the right. Having a priest tell us we were lying and turn us back over to our father gives me the right."

Hunter stopped. He was breathing heavily. He closed his eyes. When he opened them they were clear and calm. He knelt down in front of Joel.

"People who are supposed to love you but hurt you deserve to be punished," he said matter-of-factly. "People who are supposed to protect you and don't deserve to die."

For a moment Joel could picture Hunter and Jared as children. He could imagine their pain. He willed the image away. He wouldn't allow himself to feel sympathy for Hunter.

"Everyone I killed deserved it," Hunter said. "They cheated on their wives and children. They presented themselves as moral pillars of the community when they weren't. They lied about who they were and hurt people."

"I think you're a little confused," Joel said, his voice calm and reasonable. "If you want to kill child molesters and priests who allow children to be molested, that's fine with me. But to kill anyone you think is dishonest about who they are is going a little far, don't you think?"

Hunter looked at him curiously for a moment as though considering the logic of his words.

"Well maybe if your father had lived long enough to fuck you you'd understand," Hunter said abruptly.

He stood up.

"That's funny," Joel said coldly, "I thought your father molested both of you, but I don't see Jared here."

The anger flooded back into Hunter's face and he reached behind his back. Joel heard the whisper of a knife being pulled from a sheath. He looked at Zelda. Her eyes were huge with fear.

"Don't fool yourself," Joel said as Hunter walked toward him, the hunting knife extended in his right hand. "Your whole life is a fucking lie. You pretend you're some kind of righteous angel of death but you're just a sick, pathetic fuck."

215

Hunter glared down at Joel. Suddenly a voice called out from deep within the house.

"Zelda?"

Joel immediately recognized the voice. It was Chance.

Before Joel could cry out for help, Hunter took a step closer to the bed and Joel closed his eyes, bracing for the impact of the blade. Instead he felt a hand close on his throat. He opened his eyes. Hunter's left hand was on his throat and his right hand held Joel's boxer shorts.

"Open up," Hunter said.

Joel could feel the hand tighten on his throat and his mouth opened. Hunter began to push the boxer shorts into his mouth and Joel gagged as they hit the back of his throat.

Hunter reached down and picked the knife up from the floor. He walked to Zelda and quickly cut the tape binding her to the chair.

"It's for you," he said flatly as he cut the side of the gag and pulled it from her mouth. "Get rid of him quickly and maybe I'll let you live."

He cut the tape from Zelda's arms and torso and tore it roughly off her. Zelda stood up unsteadily and looked at Joel. Her eyes were frightened but clear.

"We'll be right back," Hunter said, smiling. "Don't go anywhere."

Hunter and Zelda walked out of Joel's line of sight. He could hear them walking down the stairs to the third floor, then the door at the bottom of the stairs close, then more footsteps descending into the house. He began to work his tongue against the shorts.

*****

Michel gave Sassy an alarmed look and dialed his cell phone. The phone rang three times before the answering machine picked up. He waited impatiently, listening to the sound of his own voice, then spoke urgently into the phone.

"Joel, are you there? Pick up. It's Michel."

He waited.

"Joel?" he said more urgently.

He hung up and looked at Sassy.

"We need to get over to Zelda's," he said.

Sassy moved to the door and Michel looked at Chanel.

"Thank you," he said.

He started to turn away but Chanel's hand suddenly gripped his wrist and pulled him closer to her. She began speaking and he leaned closer to hear.

"Your mother," she said, her voice barely audible.

Michel stared at her in confusion.

"What about her?" he asked.

"We were friends," Chanel whispered. "She knew, and she loved you very much."

She let go of him and closed her eyes. Michel looked at her for a moment, fighting to hold back tears, then kissed her on the forehead.

"Let's go," he said finally, following Sassy out the door.

Chapter 41

Chance stood inside the open front door of the house. After a few minutes of knocking he'd tried the doorknob and found it unlocked. He was about to leave when he heard soft footsteps coming down the stairs above. Suddenly Zelda appeared on the landing of the second floor. Chance was startled by her appearance. Her eyes were red and swollen and the skin around her mouth and on her cheeks looked chafed and raw.

"What do you want?" she asked flatly.

"I need to talk to you," Chance replied.

"Come back later," she said.

"It's important," Chance said. "I need to talk to you now."

Zelda hesitated for a moment as though listening to a voice in her head, then started slowly down the stairs.

"All right," she said. "Just for a minute."

Zelda reached the bottom of the stairs and closed the front door, locking it. Chance followed her down the hall to the kitchen.

"Coffee?" she asked.

"Sure," Chance replied nervously.

Zelda turned away and began pouring the coffee while Chance looked around the room. He noticed the broken cup and spilled coffee on the floor.

"What happened?" he asked as she handed him a cup.

Zelda looked at the broken cup and shrugged.

"I guess one of the boys didn't clean up after himself," she said.

Chance felt a chill of apprehension. He remembered what it had been like living in the house. He knew that no one would have risked Zelda's wrath that way. Zelda sat down and indicated the chair opposite her for Chance. He sat down.

"So what do you want?" Zelda asked.

Chance could see her appraising him.

"I want to work for you again," he said.

"Why?" Zelda asked, eyeing him curiously.

Chance heard a floorboard creaking and wondered who else was in the house. He looked at Zelda. She seemed nervous.

"Because I want you to let Joel go," he said, "and I'm willing to trade myself."

Zelda narrowed her eyes at him.

"You'd be willing to do that?" she asked with surprise.

"I'd do anything for him," Chance replied.

Zelda stared at him for a moment. She seemed about to speak when footsteps in the hallway interrupted her. Hunter appeared in the doorway behind her.

"Hey, Chance," he said casually.

"Hey, Hunter," Chance replied. "Long time."

Hunter walked up behind Zelda and placed his left hand on her shoulder. Chance was sure he saw Zelda stiffen at his touch.

"So what brings you here?" Hunter asked, cocking his head and giving Chance a curious look. "Just visiting old friends?"

Chance caught the sarcasm of the question but decided to ignore it.

"I have some business to discuss with Zelda," he said casually.

"Any business you have with Zelda you can discuss with me," Hunter said, fixing him with a hard stare.

Chance was confused by the aggressive tone in Hunter's voice. He looked at Zelda but her expression was carefully composed.

*****

Joel had pushed the shorts far enough forward that he could breathe easily again. He took a few deep breaths and tried to relax his jaw for a moment. With a sudden panic he thought about Chance and wondered what was happening downstairs. He placed his tongue against the shorts and began to push again.

*****

"Since when are you in charge around here?" Chance asked, cocking his head in mocking imitation of Hunter.

Hunter seemed flustered for a moment and worked his mouth without making a sound.

"I'm not," he managed finally. "But anything that has to do with business effects me, too."

"Oh," Chance replied casually.

He'd always found Hunter condescending, and enjoyed seeing his discomfort. He looked back at Zelda sympathetically.

"I know this is a really bad time," he said, "and I'm really sorry, but this is important."

Zelda stared at him for a moment, wondering if he might actually understand what was happening.

"What do you mean?" she asked carefully.

"I mean because of Chanel being attacked," Chance replied with a curious look.

"I really wish you hadn't told her that," Hunter said as he slipped his hand behind his back and pulled the knife free of its sheath.

*****

Joel gave one last push with his tongue. The sodden boxer shorts dropped onto the mattress beside him. He was slick with sweat but his mouth was dry and his throat hurt. He worked up some spit, wetting his tongue and lips with it, then swallowed.

He took a deep breath.

*****

Hunter stepped out from behind Zelda and began to move quickly toward Chance with the knife held low by his side. Suddenly a scream filled the house.

*****

Michel turned the car hard onto Esplanade while Sassy finished her call to the dispatcher.

"We're not even sure he went to Zelda's" she said evenly.

"I am," Michel replied.

*****

When he heard the scream, Hunter froze for a moment. Suddenly Zelda rose from her chair and grabbed him by the back of his collar. She pulled hard and Hunter staggered back, choking.

"You motherfucker," Zelda screamed as she twisted the collar of the shirt tighter. "You goddamn motherfucker!"

Suddenly Hunter spun toward her, slashing the knife across the right side of her neck. Zelda fell backward, losing her grip on Hunter's collar, and a brilliant line of crimson cut across the wall as she fell.

Hunter began to turn toward Chance but Chance was already running at him. Chance's forearm struck Hunter's shoulder hard and drove him into the counter behind him. Hunter's head slammed against the cupboard and the knife slipped from his hand. He pushed himself off the counter and grabbed the front of Chance's shirt, pulling Chance close to his chest, then twisted, throwing Chance sideways against the stove. Chance cried out as his right hip slammed against the metal edge, and he fell forward across the top of the stove. Hunter moved quickly, grabbing the knife from the floor and raised it over Chance's back. Suddenly Chance pushed himself up and spun around. The caste iron frying pan in his right hand struck Hunter across the temple and Hunter dropped to the floor.

Chance stood there for a moment, breathing hard, as a pool of blood began to spread beneath Hunter's head. He could feel a shooting pain in his hip and took a tentative step. He picked up Hunter's knife and walked slowly to Zelda. She lay just inside the doorway to the hall. Her skin was ashen and her eyes were nearly closed. The floor around her was wet and nearly black with blood.

Chance took out his cell phone and dialed 911, requesting police and an ambulance, then grabbed a towel off the counter and wrapped it around Zelda's neck.

"Where's Joel?" he asked gently.

Zelda's eyes fluttered open for moment.

"My room," she whispered in a strangled voice.

Then she closed her eyes and her body seemed to go slack.

Chance stood up slowly and started down the hall to the stairs.

*****

Joel heard the door at the bottom of the stairs creak slowly open. He tried to pull himself forward but his feet were held tightly in place. He could hear quiet footsteps moving up. He took a deep breath and tensed his body.

"Joel," a voice whispered.

Joel lifted his head painfully and strained to look over his shoulder. Zelda stood by the wall that enclosed the staircase in the center of the room. Her features were slack and lifeless. She didn't move. Joel shook his head in disbelief. Another figure caught his eye farther to the left and he shifted his gaze. It was

Zelda again. He struggled to focus his eyes. In the darkness beyond the figure he could see a dozen more Zeldas. They all stared at him with blank eyes. Some wore tattered wigs. Others were bald. Their lips were smeared a dark red that gave them the appearance of open wounds. Joel recognized some of the clothes they were wearing and realized they were mannequins.

A sudden movement caught his eye. Chance's head peered over the top of the stairs with a worried look.

"Is anyone else here?" he whispered.

"No," Joel replied loudly.

Chance moved up the stairs quickly, his body lumbering painfully from side to side. He walked to the bed and began cutting the nylon stockings from Joel's wrists.

"What happened?" Joel asked anxiously.

"I hit the bitch with a frying pan," Chance said with a small dry laugh. "Teach him to fuck with this faggot."

"What about Zelda?"

Chance frowned and shook his head. Joel bit his lower lip and took a deep breath.

"Are you okay?" he asked as Chance freed his ankles.

"Yeah," Chance said as he sat on the bed with a tired sigh. "I just hurt my hip."

Joel rolled over and hugged Chance tightly.

"Thank you," he said.

He kissed the side of Chance's neck.

"Any time," Chance said, hugging him back. "But we better get the fuck out of here. I don't know if I killed him."

Joel let go of Chance and stood unsteadily. He could still feel the effects of the drug Hunter had put in his coffee. Chance held his arm while he pulled on his shorts.

"Good enough," he said.

They began walking toward the stairs, leaning against one another for support.

"Let me go first," Chance said. "I think I'm in better shape than you are. I'll help you down."

He took two steps down to the turn in the stairwell and reached up toward Joel. Suddenly he seemed to lose his balance. A look of shock came onto his face and he fell backward into the wall with a loud gasp. Joel grabbed for him as he began to slide sideways. As Chance slid Joel could see blood smeared on the wall behind him. Then Chance was gone and Joel heard a low laugh from the stairs.

He turned and stumbled toward the Zelda mannequins.

*****

Michel pulled to the curb and slammed on the brakes. He and Sassy drew their guns and ran to the front door. They looked through the side windows. No one was moving. Michel stepped back and kicked in the door.

*****

Joel heard the loud crash downstairs and wondered if he could get to the stairs. He knew that Hunter was hiding nearby, waiting for him. He couldn't hear him moving. He looked to his left. Rows of mannequins stretched into a dark corner of the room. He knelt down quietly and looked across the floor. Long swathes of fabric obscured his view. A few feet away a mannequin head stared at him with its dull eyes. He carefully picked it up and began moving between mannequins toward the far corner of the room.

*****

Sassy looked in the dining room to the left of the door while Michel stepped into the living room to the right. He silently signalled her down the hall toward the kitchen and began walking quietly across the living room. As he reached the far door he stepped quickly into the kitchen, his gun in front of him. Sassy stepped through the door from the hall and almost tripped over Zelda. She reached down and placed her hand against Zelda's neck, then shook her head at Michel. Michel pointed at the pool of blood in the center of the floor and the drops that lead toward Sassy. Sassy looked over her shoulder and nodded toward the stairs.

*****

Joel tried to control his breathing as he slowly stood. Two naked mannequins were pressed against the wall behind him. From the darkness he could see the rest of the room more clearly. He saw a movement along the wall by the stairs. Hunter had his back turned to him. Joel quietly lifted the mannequin head with both hands and threw it hard. It struck a mannequin on the far side of the room, knocking it forward into two others. They tumbled to the floor with a loud thud.

*****

Michel and Sassy had just finished checking the rooms on the second floor when they heard the noise above. They moved quickly down the hall and began to climb the stairs to the third floor.

*****

Hunter's head jerked at the sound of the falling mannequins. He began moving back along the wall, away from the door. Joel watched as Hunter turned the corner and walked away from him. He crouched down and started to walk quietly toward the stairs.

*****

Michel knelt beside Chance and checked his pulse. It was faint. In the distance he could hear sirens. He gave Sassy a questioning look. She gestured toward the stairwell to Zelda's bedroom with her gun.

"I'll go first," she mouthed and began to ascend.

Joel had moved to within ten feet of the door. He thought that he was close enough to make a run for it. His legs felt steadier now. Maybe he could reach whoever was downstairs before Hunter caught him. He closed his eyes and listened. He heard the faint creak of a floor board near the stairs. He ducked down and slowly backed toward the corner again.

Sassy stepped through the doorway and quickly looked around. The room was empty. She could see the shredded nylon stockings laying by the posts of the bed and a t-shirt on the floor beside it. She stepped forward and spun to her left. Her heart jumped and her finger tightened on the trigger of her gun. She stopped. Rows of mannequins stared listlessly at her. She took a deep breath and stepped back toward the door, motioning Michel up.

Michel stepped into the room and looked around. Sassy held up a warning hand and nodded to his left. He turned slowly and saw the mannequins. He gave Sassy a questioning look. She shrugged and pointed toward the bed. Michel recognized his t-shirt on the floor and felt his pulse quicken.

Sassy gestured to Michel's right and began to move along the wall in that direction. Michel watched her as she disappeared around the corner. He stepped into the crowd of mannequins to his left.

Joel could hear the faint rustle of fabric and soft footsteps. He held his breath. They were moving toward the end wall, a few yards in front of him. He began to move slowly the other way.

Sassy stood still, her eyes searching the lifeless faces in front of her. There was an opening ten feet to her right and she moved toward it. Looking down in the dim light she could see a tangle of dark limbs and clothing on the floor. She heard a scraping sound over her right shoulder and turned, studying the mannequins in the shadows by the back wall. She cocked her gun.

Hunter lifted the blue silk robe he'd draped over himself and pushed himself up from the floor. He ran at Sassy from behind. As she spun toward him he plunged the knife below her rib cage and drove it up toward her lungs. Sassy's gun fired. The sound of the discharge was deafening and Hunter winced in pain. The gun dropped to the floor and Hunter stared into Sassy's eyes as they began to grow dim. He pulled out the knife and Sassy fell backwards. The mannequins behind her began to tumble sideways like dominoes and as they fell Hunter saw Joel crouching along the back wall. He began to move toward him.

Suddenly the two mannequins to his right parted and Michel burst from between them, his right shoulder driving hard into Hunter's ribs. The knife fell from Hunter's hand as he hit the floor with Michel on top of him. Michel began to push himself up but Hunter rolled into his body, swinging his elbow. It struck Michel in the right temple and he was knocked to the side.

He scrambled dizzily to his feet and brought his gun up but Hunter was already moving toward him. Michel saw a blur and felt exploding pain in his wrist. His gun skittered across the floor into a crowd of mannequins. For a second he thought he saw Joel crawling after it. Then Hunter swung the mannequin arm again.

Chapter 42

It was quiet. Joel was deep within the rows of mannequins on the far side of the stairs. He couldn't see Hunter or Michel. He sat on the floor cradling Michel's gun.

"Come out, come out, wherever you are," Hunter called, "or I'll just kill your boyfriend now.

Joel stood up and began walking toward the open part of the room.

"Where are you, Joel?" Hunter called sweetly.

Joel walked slowly past the bed, staying in the center of the room. He could see mannequins strewn on the floor ahead, and as he passed the edge of the stairwell he saw Hunter and Michel standing fifteen feet away in the middle of the tumbled wooden bodies. Sassy lay on the floor a few feet behind them. Hunter had a blond wig from one of the mannequins resting loosely on his head.

Michel was bleeding from his forehead and Joel could see that he was having trouble standing. Hunter held him up with his left arm around Michel's chest and his right around his neck. He held the knife against the left side of Michel's throat.

"There you are," Hunter said reproachfully.

Joel lifted the gun and took a few steps forward. Hunter gave him a look of mild surprise.

"I don't think you're going to do that," he said, shaking his head.

"Why not?" Joel asked coolly.

"Because you might kill your precious Michel by mistake."

228

Joel shrugged.

"So what?" he said, trying to sound calm. "You're going to kill him anyway. I'd rather do it myself than let you do it. That way I can make sure you die, too."

Hunter began to laugh.

"Do you really think I don't know you by now, Joel?" he asked. "I know you're still clinging to that last bit of hope that somehow you can save him and live happily ever after. You won't pull the trigger because you could never live knowing you killed him. It would be like killing yourself."

Joel lowered the gun and Hunter gave him a satisfied smile. Out of the corner of his eye, Joel saw Sassy's right arm move.

"You're right," he said simply. "I couldn't live with that."

He brought the gun up to his temple.

"I couldn't live knowing it was my fault he died at all."

Michel began to struggle and cried out. He could feel the blade of the knife lightly pierce his neck. Joel looked steadily into his eyes and smiled. Michel froze. For a split second he saw Joel's eyes dart to the floor behind him. Then he heard a click and understood.

Joel could see everything unfolding in front of him as if it were in slow motion. He saw Michel drop his head and the look of shock on Hunter's face. He saw Hunter turning as the gun went off, and his head exploding. He saw the knife slicing into Michel's neck as Hunter began to fall. He saw the blood-and-brain-spattered remains of Hunter's wig landing at his feet. He saw Sassy lying on the floor holding her gun.

Then his vision became dim and he felt himself falling.

Epilogue

Joel placed five red roses on the gleaming bronze casket and turned away. He didn't want to see the body lowered into the ground. He walked past the long line of mourners and out of the cemetery to a taxi waiting by the curb.

He'd called Chance at the hospital that morning and Chance had asked him to place an extra flower on Lady Chanel's coffin for him. Lady Chanel had died three days earlier without regaining consciousness again.

It had been a week since Hunter had been killed. The police and paramedics had arrived at the house a few minutes after Sassy shot him. They'd been able to save Chance, though he'd suffered some nerve damage when Hunter stabbed him. When he got out of the hospital he planned to go back to Natchez to live with Joel's grandparents while he recuperated. He'd told Joel that he'd move back to New Orleans someday, but Joel wondered whether it was true. Chance had had his adventure there. He knew that no matter what happened, though, Chance would be all right. He had a natural gift for survival.

Joel's grandfather had asked him to move back home, too, but Joel knew he couldn't. Despite all the mistakes he'd made, he felt that New Orleans still held possibilities for him and he wanted to experience them.

He also felt he owed it to Zelda to stay and take care of her after she was released from the hospital that Saturday. She'd inherited Lady Chanel's house and planned to live there and sell her own house. She'd said she never wanted to go back to the old house again, so Joel had gone to collect her things. When he checked their rooms, he'd found that all of Jared's, Peter's and Raphael's things were gone. They hadn't been seen since the night before Hunter was killed.

The taxi pulled up in front of Michel's house. Joel paid the driver, walked up the path to the front door and let himself in.

"Dad, I'm home," he called.

He could hear Michel's voice in the kitchen and walked into the room as Michel hung up the phone.

"Please don't call me that," Michel said, his voice still weak and raspy from the wound to his throat. "I'm not *that* much older than you."

The side of his neck was bandaged and he had a cast on his right hand. Joel had drawn brightly colored flowers on it while Michel had been napping the day before.

"Who was that?" Joel asked.

"Sassy," Michel replied. "She's getting out today. I invited her over for dinner this Saturday."

"I hope you two don't expect me to be feeding you and emptying your bed pans," Joel cracked. "It's getting to be like a fucking hospital ward around here."

Michel smiled warmly at him.

"How was the funeral?" he asked seriously.

He'd wanted to go but Joel had asked to go alone.

"It was okay," Joel said, his voice breaking slightly. "I placed roses for you and Sassy."

"Thank you," Michel said. "Sassy will be glad to hear that."

He walked to Joel and hugged him. Joel began to cry.

"I know," Michel said, "I'm going to miss her, too."

Michel could feel Joel nodding against his shoulder. After a minute Joel lifted his head and stepped back. He wiped his eyes with the back of his hand.

"I'm okay," he said.

"A squad car dropped this off a little while ago," Michel said gently, picking up a manila folder from the counter.

He handed it to Joel.

"What is it?" Joel asked, taking the folder tentatively.

"It's the information Chanel collected on Hunter and Jared," he said. "She must have been bringing it to me when he attacked her. They found it under Hunter's mattress."

Joel eyed the folder for a minute, then handed it back to Michel without opening it.

"What does it say?" he asked.

"Their real names were Drew and Joshua Clement," Michel said. "They grew up just outside of Louisville. Their father was a well-known attorney and their mother was a housewife."

"Their parents aren't alive?" Joel asked.

Michel shook his head.

"They were killed five years ago. They were found in bed with their throats cut. The boys were the prime suspects but they were gone by the time the bodies were found. They were also wanted for the murder of a priest on the same night."

Joel nodded.

"Do you think Hunter was telling the truth about what their father did to them?" he asked.

"I don't know," Michel said.

"Even if it was true, why would he kill other people?" Joel asked. "It doesn't make sense."

"Everyone reacts to trauma differently," Michel said shrugging. "Some people just shut down emotionally. Others internalize it and it develops into a psychosis. Some people are even able to use it as a motivator for positive change."

Joel wondered briefly whether Michel had intended the last part for him or himself.

"Do you think they'll ever find the others?" he asked.

"I imagine they'll turn up sometime," Michel said, "but it doesn't really matter. There's no evidence they had anything to do with it. Maybe Jared helped kill his parents, but I doubt it."

Joel stared at him for a moment, seeming to weigh something in his mind before speaking.

"I was thinking about things," he said finally, "I'm going to move to Lady Chanel's house Saturday when Zelda gets out of the hospital."

"Are you sure that's what you want?" Michel asked, studying him carefully. "You can stay here as long as you want."

Joel nodded. "I think it's best for both of us for now," he said. "Things between us are kind of complicated and I don't think either of us knows what he really wants. I think we need some time."

He gave Michel a hopeful smile.

"Who knows what will happen?"

"Who knows?" Michel repeated.

*****

Michel and Sassy sat on the front porch of Michel's house sipping white wine. The oppressive heat of the last few months had finally broken and Sassy wore a light cotton sweater she'd borrowed from Michel. They watched the stars begin to appear in the clear blue-black sky.

"So how's Joel doing?" Sassy asked.

"I think he's going to be okay," Michel replied. "He's a lot stronger than he thinks. He could have called it quits and gone back home, but he's ready to give it another shot."

Sassy was quiet for a minute.

"And what about you?" she asked finally.

"I'm fine," Michel replied. "My throat still hurts a little, but not too bad."

"That's not what I meant," Sassy said, fixing him with her eyes.

Michel gave her a crooked smile and let out a small resigned chuckle.

"I know. The jury's still out there," he said.

"Why? What's the problem?" Sassy asked.

Michel shrugged.

"We didn't solve it, Sassy. Chanel solved it for us. If she hadn't woken up we'd probably still be looking."

Sassy nodded her head.

"I know, Michel, but we're not always going to be perfect. Sometimes we need luck."

"But it was my fault," Michel said quietly. "I let my personal feelings get in the way. If we'd brought Chanel in for questioning when you wanted she might have been able to tell us it was Hunter then. The last killing wouldn't have happened. Chanel would still be alive. My instincts were wrong and people died because of me."

"No," Sassy said. "People died because Hunter killed them. You were right that it wasn't Chanel. And your instincts found the wig hair at the Royal Inn. Without that we might not even know Hunter was dressing in drag yet."

Michel shook his head dismissively.

"Maybe Chanel would still be alive," Sassy said, "but maybe she wouldn't. And maybe Hunter would still be on the streets and ten more people would be dead by now. You can't fixate on what could have or should have happened. Use it to make you a better cop, but don't beat yourself up over it. I hate to tell you this, but you're only human."

Michel gave her a small smile then sighed.

"I don't know if I can do it anymore," he said.

He looked into the gathering darkness. Sassy studied him for a moment, then placed her right hand over his left.

"I understand what you're feeling," she said slowly. "I've never told you about this. It's something I've tried to forget myself."

She paused for a moment before continuing.

"My rookie year I went through something similar. I allowed what was happening in my personal life to get in the way of an investigation and it cost a young girl her life."

She thought for a moment about the personal losses it had cost her and fought the impulse to touch her stomach. Still she could feel the familiar contours of the small round scar there in her mind.

"For a long time after that I doubted whether I could do the job," she continued. "It tore me up. I was paralyzed because I was afraid to let my emotions enter into my work. But eventually I realized that it was my emotions that allowed me to do the job well. It was the fact that I cared, that I took it very personally, that made me a good cop. I learned to sort out the emotions that helped from the ones that got in the way."

"But you were a rookie when it happened," Michel replied. "I'm not. I have no excuses."

Sassy leaned forward and cocked her head at him.

"Michel," she said gently, "you're not a rookie on the job, but you're a rookie in a lot of other ways."

Michel turned his head toward her and gave her a curious look.

"Since your mother died, since you met Joel, you've been experiencing a lot that's emotionally new for you," Sassy said. "You've always been confident with your emotions in your work, but in your personal life you're still trying to figure out how to handle them. You're a rookie. Don't let the confusion you're feeling personally make you doubt your ability to do the job. Yes, everything happened to get all tangled together in this case, but I know you. You're going to sort it out and it's going to make you a better cop."

Michel gave her a dubious look but attempted a smile.

"It happened," Sassy said more forcefully. "You need to decide whether you can live with it or not. If you can't, if you're always going to second-guess yourself, then quit. I trust your instincts, Michel. I trust you with my life. But you're the one who has to have the trust. Otherwise you're not going to be able to do the job."

She squeezed his hand tightly and gave him a pleading look.

"Just do me a favor," she said. "Don't make any decisions right now. Let it sit in that big brain of yours for a while."

Michel stared at her for a moment, then nodded.

"I will, Sas. I promise."

*****

Joel picked up the bed tray and placed it on the floor by the bedroom door. He noticed that Zelda had hardly eaten anything.

"Thank you," Zelda said.

Joel smiled uncomfortably at her.

"Can we talk?" he asked quietly.

Although he'd been to visit her at the hospital every day, he'd avoided talking to Zelda about what had happened, partly to give her a chance to heal and partly out of anxiety. Zelda patted the bed next to her and Joel sat down.

"What do you want to know?" Zelda asked gently.

Joel hesitated for a moment before responding.

"Did you know what Hunter was doing?" he asked finally.

Zelda shook her head.

"Why were you helping him?" Joel asked helplessly.

Zelda studied him carefully.

"It's complicated," she said with a weary sigh. "The things that Hunter told you were true: about Chanel killing Whittier, about his family paying us off...about my operation. They were things that should have stayed buried in the past, but they didn't and it was my fault because I told Hunter about them. He used them to get what he wanted from me."

"But Chanel killed Whittier to save you," Joel said. "The police would have believed that. Especially after so many years."

Zelda shook her head sadly.

"You may be too young to understand this, but I wasn't worried about Chanel going to jail. I was worried about preserving her dignity."

"You're right, I don't understand," Joel said.

"It's different now," Zelda said, "but thirty years ago it was very hard to be different here. Chanel and I weren't accepted. We moved to the Marigny because it was the only place we could go. The drug addicts and criminals weren't as discriminating about their neighbors. They didn't accept us, but they left us alone."

Joel nodded.

"But Chanel wasn't satisfied living on the outside," Zelda continued. "She'd fought too hard to accept herself to let anyone else keep her out. So she kept fighting, and gradually people began to accept her. They even began to love her. Through the force of her own will she became respected and that respect was the most important thing in her life. Does that make sense to you?"

Joel tried to imagine himself in the same situation.

"Yeah," he said, "I understand."

"When Hunter threatened to expose her past I knew it would break her heart," Zelda said. "I couldn't risk her losing what she'd fought so hard for, so I agreed to help him by pretending to be the boss. He said it would make it easier to deal with the other boys if they thought I was in charge. That's the way it continued for three years and Chanel never knew. Then about a month ago Hunter went to Chanel directly and told her what he knew. He told her she had to help him, too, or he'd start telling people about her. She didn't want to do it but I convinced her it was necessary. He forced her to go to the bars as Cally to find tricks for him."

Tears began to well in Zelda's eyes.

"I think he got pleasure from it because he knew it was humiliating for her."

Joel took Zelda's hand.

"You were just trying to protect her," he said.

"I know," Zelda said, wiping her eyes with her other hand, "but I did it for myself, too. Chanel was all I had. I know that people never really liked me. They seemed to sense there was something wrong with me. On my own I'd be an outcast, but with her I was accepted, too. I didn't want to lose that. Even when Chanel realized what was happening and told me she was going to tell Detective Doucette I tried to stop her because I was afraid of losing what I had. I knew that everything in our past would come out."

"So is that what I heard you arguing about?" Joel asked.

Zelda nodded, then began to cry quietly.

"It's okay," Joel said. "I understand."

He could feel tears forming in his own eyes.

Zelda pulled herself together with an effort and squeezed Joel's hand tighter.

"I know you do," she said, "and I need you to know something. I never intended for you to get involved with Hunter. I thought that if you were away from Chance you'd have a better chance of making it on your own, of avoiding the mistakes he made. That's why I invited you to live in the house. I thought I could protect you. Hunter and I had an agreement, but he didn't keep it, and when I realized what was happening I was willing to let it continue to protect Chanel. I'm sorry."

Joel wiped a tear from his right eye and tried to smile.

"Why do you hate Chance so much?" he asked.

"I don't hate him," Zelda said sadly. "I was disappointed in him. He's smart enough to do whatever he wants with his life but he chose to hustle. When he left the house I thought he'd change but he didn't. Then when you showed up I was afraid he'd get you involved, too."

Joel thought for a moment before he responded.

"Are you disappointed in me, too?" he asked.

Zelda frowned slightly and nodded.

"I don't blame you," she said. "I know how manipulative Hunter could be, but I was disappointed."

Joel tried to hold back his tears.

"What about Chanel?" he asked in a small voice. "Was she disappointed in me, too?"

Tears began to roll down his face.

Zelda pulled him close, holding his head to her shoulder.

"No, she was never disappointed in you," she said softly. "She never knew."

Joel lay against her for a few minutes, enjoying the comfort of her arms around him, until his tears began to dry.

"Thank you," he said.

"Not at all," Zelda said, patting the back of his head. "Life can be very hard sometimes, but we can learn from our mistakes. I didn't. I let the past control me. You don't have to. Use it to become stronger. Make Chanel proud of you. Make yourself proud."

Also Available
from

ECHOES

A Michel Doucette &
Sassy Jones Novel

DAVID LENNON

Chapter 1

She could hear soft crying. She lifted her head from the cool hard floor and looked around in the darkness. Far off she could see a small circle of light. As she watched, the light began to grow larger and brighter, taking on the shape of an open doorway. For a moment she was sure someone was standing in the doorway, but she couldn't make out their features. There was just a heavy shadow, and then it was gone.

She could see a young girl on the far side of the door. The girl was seated on the floor against a wooden post with her arms stretched above her head. Her wrists were held in place by a thick rope that encircled the post, and a dirty white cloth was tied around her mouth. The girl had long blond hair that hung limply around her face and onto her shoulders. She was dressed in just panties and a t-shirt with thin straps over the shoulders. At some point they might have been pale pink, but now they were a dingy gray. Even at a distance she could see the girl looking at her, imploring her with her eyes to help her.

She tried to push herself up to her feet. Pain exploded in her abdomen and she gasped, rolling onto her back. She put her right hand onto the small mound of her stomach and felt warm dampness. She lifted her hand and brought it close to her face. Even in the darkness she could make out the blackness of the blood on her fingertips. She felt her throat tighten and began to fight for air as a convulsive sob escaped her lips. In the distance she heard a phone begin to ring.

Alexandra "Sassy" Jones sat up in bed with a start and looked down at her right hand. Although she'd had the same nightmare every night for almost 25 years she always awoke wondering if it was real. Even in her confusion her right hand began to move reflexively for the cell phone on her nightstand. She could still feel the phantom sensation of the small round hole in her stomach that her fingers had traced thousands of times. She cleared her throat and brought the phone quickly to her ear.

"Yes?" she said calmly.

"Sassy, it's me."

It was the voice of her former partner, Michel Doucette.

"Michel," she said. "Are you okay? What time is it? "

She felt suddenly apprehensive. Michel had been on a leave-of-absence from the New Orleans Police Department for the past six months and she'd grown unaccustomed to hearing his voice on the phone in the middle of the night.

"It's Carl," Michel said.

For a moment Sassy was confused. Why had her ex-partner said that he was her ex-husband? She tried to make sense of the words and wondered if she was still dreaming, somehow bringing together the two most important men in her life.

"This is Carl?" she asked tentatively.

"No, Sassy. It's Michel." Michel said.

"But you said..."

Michel cut her off abruptly.

"I'm sorry," he said. "Carl's dead."

Suddenly the pieces of the conversation fell into place and Sassy came fully awake.

"How?" she asked slowly.

Her words seemed to come from a distance and echo in her head.

"It looks like a suicide," Michel responded gently.

Sassy was silent for a moment. It had been a year since she'd spoken to Carl and 5 years since she'd last seen him, yet he'd been a part of her life every day for the past 25 years.

"Are you still there?" Michel asked.

"Yeah," Sassy responded slowly. "It was our anniversary."

"What?" Michel asked, confused.

"Yesterday," Sassy said, "It would have been our 25th anniversary."

Michel paused before responding, suddenly understanding what Sassy meant: Carl had killed himself because it was their anniversary.

"I'm coming over," he said finally.

"Okay," Sassy replied blankly.

She placed the phone back on the nightstand and turned on the small lamp next to it. She stared at the wall in front of her for a moment, then willed herself to get up and get dressed.

Chapter 2

When Sassy opened the door Michel was surprised by her appearance. For the first time since he'd met her five years earlier, he'd expected her to look something less than her best, but instead the solid woman in the doorway looked as though she were ready to go to dinner or the office. She was dressed in chocolate brown slacks and a short matching jacket that were the same tone as her skin, though two shades deeper. Under the jacket she wore a deep plum silk shirt with a wide spread color, and a delicate gold necklace draped her throat. Her short dark hair with its few silver threads was neatly brushed and her subtle make-up was perfectly applied. As always the effect was both simple and stunning, and Michel wondered not for the first time if Sassy ever just rolled out of bed and slummed it in sweat pants and an old t-shirt.

As Michel walked in Sassy hugged him warmly and gave him a kiss on the cheek. Although their partnership had long ago developed into friendship, it was an unusual gesture of affection and Michel sensed that Sassy's composed appearance was deceiving.

"It's good to see you," she said softly.

While Sassy poured them coffee, Michel walked into the living room and settled onto the plush burnt orange sofa that separated the seating area from the dining room. He'd always felt that Sassy's home was a perfect reflection of her as a person. The room was warm and welcoming, yet devoid of clutter or excess. The rich cocoa walls were tastefully accented by smaller black and white photos with simple black metal frames, and larger, more colorful paintings—all depicting either the Crescent City or African-American culture. The white built-in shelves along one wall were lined by well-thumbed books on a range of subjects from psychology to religion to history to music and art. Here and there were small sculptures or artifacts that Sassy had collected during her travels in Africa and Western Europe. In addition to the sofa, there were two deep-seating chairs covered in pale sage twill. The centerpiece of the room was a coffee table consisting of a large, square glass top that rested between four thick burled olive bases. The overall effect was simple, yet rich with detail that told you everything you needed to know about the home's occupant.

Michel noticed a small silver ashtray on the coffee table directly in front of him and smiled. Not only had Sassy thought to put the ashtray out, but she'd correctly anticipated exactly where he would sit.

"How did you find out about Carl?" Sassy said as she walked into the room carrying two large white ceramic mugs.

She placed one in front of Michel and settled next to him on the couch. Michel knew without asking that she'd put three sugars and more than a little cream into his coffee.

"Al Ribodeau called me," he said, as he lifted the mug and took a small sip. "He took the call and thought it would be better if you found out about it from me."

"How did he know Carl was my ex-husband?" Sassy asked, giving him a genuinely puzzled look. "You're the only one in the department who knows I was even married."

"He saw your pictures."

"Pictures?" Sassy asked, the look of puzzlement growing.

"Carl had a wall of photos of you," Michel said carefully. "Al said it looked almost like a shrine."

Sassy took a deep breath and let the image sink it. She'd closed her heart to Carl long ago but suddenly felt fresh sympathy for him. She imagined him sitting alone in a room staring at the reminders of their life together.

"When was the last time you spoke to him?" Michel asked, bringing her back suddenly.

"366 days ago."

She could see the surprise on Michel's face at the precision of her answer.

"Carl called me every year on our anniversary. Usually around 10 pm after he'd got a few drinks in him."

"And last night?"

"I unplugged my phone," Sassy said matter-of-factly. "I didn't feel like talking to him this year. He didn't have my cell number."

"And you think that may be why he killed himself? Because you didn't talk to him?" Michel ventured.

Sassy shrugged.

"I don't know the man anymore...didn't know him anymore."

Michel took her hand, watching her face carefully to make sure it was all right.

"You're not blaming yourself, are you?"

Sassy met his eyes and gave a sad smile.

"I don't know yet," she said. "I haven't had time to process it. I know logically it's not my fault. I don't have any illusions that I have that kind of power. Carl was angry at me, but I don't think he would have killed himself over me. Not after 25 years."

"What makes you think he was still angry with you?" Michel asked.

He noticed Sassy slowly withdrawing her hand from his as she looked away, focusing on a spot directly in front of her.

"The calls," she said with a weary sigh. "When Carl called, he'd tell me what a cunt I was and how I'd ruined his life by leaving him."

Michel was shocked by both the bluntness of the response and the fact that Sassy had allowed the calls to continue for so long. It seemed out of character.

"Why didn't you change your number?" he asked.

"I don't know," Sassy said, looking back at him. "I guess I figured he needed to vent and it was harmless enough. Maybe I was worried that if he didn't have that opportunity he'd do something more drastic."

"Like kill himself?" Michel asked.

Sassy didn't respond but Michel could read the answer in her expression. He waited a moment before continuing.

"Sassy, I'll understand if you don't want to talk about it right now, but what happened between you and Carl?"

Something about the words "right now" caught Sassy's attention and she looked at Michel more intently, trying to read his expression.

"Are you asking me as a friend or a cop?" she asked.

Michel dropped his gaze for a beat and then looked back at her.

"Both," he said.

"What aren't you telling me?" Sassy asked, a look of anxiety clouding her face.

"I think we should go to the station," Michel said. "There's something you need to see."

CPSIA information can be obtained
at www.ICGtesting.com
Printed in the USA
LVHW092154100220
646520LV00001B/86